Georges Buffon

Buffon's Natural History

containing a theory of the earth, a general history of man, of the brute creation,

and of vegetables, minerals - Vol. 2

Georges Buffon

Buffon's Natural History
containing a theory of the earth, a general history of man, of the brute creation, and of vegetables, minerals - Vol. 2

ISBN/EAN: 9783337377564

Printed in Europe, USA, Canada, Australia, Japan

Cover: Foto ©Andreas Hilbeck / pixelio.de

More available books at **www.hansebooks.com**

Barr's Buffon.

Buffon's Natural History.

CONTAINING

A THEORY OF THE EARTH,

A GENERAL
HISTORY OF MAN,

OF THE BRUTE CREATION, AND OF
VEGETABLES, MINERALS,

&c. &c.

FROM THE FRENCH.

WITH NOTES BY THE TRANSLATOR.

IN TEN VOLUMES.

VOL. II.

London:

PRINTED FOR THE PROPRIETOR,

AND SOLD BY H. D. SYMONDS, PATERNOSTER-ROW.

1797.

CONTENTS

OF

THE SECOND VOLUME.

———

Proof of the Theory of the Earth.

Article

History of Animals.

BUFFON's

NATURAL HISTORY.

PROOF OF THE THEORY OF THE EARTH.

ARTICLE XI.

OF SEAS AND LAKES.

THE ocean surrounds the earth on all sides, and penetrates into the interior parts of different countries, often by large openings, and frequently by small straits; it forms mediterranean seas, some of which participate of its motions of flux and reflux, and others seem to have nothing in common with it except the continuity of water. We shall follow the ocean through all its extent and windings, enu-

　　　　　B　　　　　merating

merating at the same time all the mediterranean seas, and endeavour to distinguish them from those which should be only called bays, or gulphs, and lakes.

The sea which washes the western coasts of France forms a gulph etween Spain and Britain; this gulph, which mariners call the Bay · of Biscay, is very open, and the point which projects farthest inland is between Bayonne and St. Sebastian; another great projection is between Rochelle and Rochefort: this gulph begins at Cape Ortegal, and ends at Brest, where a strait commences between the south point of Britain and Cape Lizard. This strait, which at first is very large, forms a small gulph in Normandy, the most projecting point of which is at Auranche; it continues pretty broad until it comes to the channel at the foot of Calais, where it is very narrow; afterwards it grows broader on a sudden, and ends between the Texel and the coast of England at Norwich; at the Texel it forms a small mediterranean sea, called *Zuyder-zee,* and many other great canals, which are not very deep.

After that the ocean forms a great gulph called the German Ocean; it begins at the northern

northern point of Scotland, runs along the eastern coast of Scotland and England as far as Norwich, from thence to the Texel, along the coasts of Holland and Germany, Jutland, Norway, and above Bergen. This gulph might be taken for a mediterranean sea, because the Orkney islands partly shut up its opening, and seem to be directed as if they were a continuation of the mountains of Norway. It forms a large strait, which begins at the southern point of Norway, and continues very broad to the Island of Zetland, where it narrows all at once, and forms between the coasts of Sweden, the islands of Denmark and Jutland, four small straits; after which it widens to a small gulph, the most projecting point of which is at Lubec: from thence it continues pretty broad to the southern extremity of Sweden, when it grows broader and broader, and forms the Baltic Sea, which is a mediterranean, extending from south to north near 300 leagues, comprehending the gulph of Bothnia, which is in fact only a continuation of it. This sea has two more gulphs, that of Livonia, whose most projecting point is near Mittau and Riga, and that of Finland, which is an arm of the Baltic, extending between Livonia and Finland to Pe-

B 2   tersburgh,

tersburgh, and communicating with the lake Ladoga, and even with the lake Onega, which communicates by the river Onega to the White Sea. All this extent of water, which forms the Baltic Sea, the gulphs of Bothnia, Finland, and Livonia, must be looked upon as one great lake, supported by a great number of rivers which it receives, as the Oder, the Vistula, the Niemen, the Droine, in Germany and Poland; other rivers in Livonia and Finland; others still greater, which come from Lapland, Tornea, the Calis, Lula, Pithea, Uma, and many others that come from Sweden. These rivers, which are very large, are more than 40, including the rivers they receive, which cannot fail of producing a quantity of water sufficient to support the Baltic. Besides, this sea has no flux nor reflux, although it is very narrow and very salt. If we consider also the bearing of the country, and the number of lakes and morasses in Finland and Sweden, we shall be inclined to look on it not as a sea, but as a great lake formed by the abundance of waters from the adjacent lands, and which has forced a passage near Denmark into the ocean, where in fact, according to the account of mariners, they still continue to flow.

From

From the beginning of the gulph which forms
the German Sea, and which terminates above
Bergen, the ocean follows the coasts of
Norway, Swedish Lapland, North Lapland,
and Muscovy Lapland, at the eastern part of
which it forms a large strait, which borders
a mediterranean called the White Sea, which
may be likewise regarded as a great lake;
for it receives 12 or 13 rivers, all very considerable, and which are more than sufficient
to support it; its water is but a little salt.
Besides, in many parts it is very near communicating with the Baltic Sea; it has even
a real one with the gulph of Finland, for,
by ascending the river Onega, we come to
a lake of the same name; from this lake
Onega there are two rivers of communication
with the lake Ladoga; this last communicates by a large arm with the gulph of Finland; and there are many parts in Swedish
Lapland, the waters of which run almost indifferently either into the White Sea, or the
gulphs of Bothnia and Finland; and all
this country being full of lakes and morasses,
the Baltic and White Seas seem to be the re-
ceptacles of its waters, and which afterwards
discharge

discharge themselves into the Frozen and German Sea.

Quitting the White Sea, and coasting the island of Candenos and the northern coasts of Russia, the ocean forms a small arm in the land at the mouth of the river Petzora. This arm, which is about 40 leagues long, by 8 or 10 broad, is rather a mass of water formed by the river than a gulph of the sea, and also has but little saltness. The land there forms a projecting cape, terminated by the small islands of Maurice and of Orange; and between this promontory and the lands which border the Strait of Waigat to the south, there is a small gulph about 30 leagues depth inland. This gulph belongs to the ocean, and is not formed by the land waters. We afterwards meet with Waigat's Strait, which is nearly under the 70th degree of north latitude. This strait is not more than 8 or 10 leagues long, and communicates with the sea which waters the northern coasts of Siberia. As this strait is shut up by the ice the greatest part of the year, it is very difficult to get into the sea beyond it. The passage has been attempted in vain by a great number of navigators, and those who fortunately passed it have left us no exact charts

of

of that sea, which they have termed the Pacific Ocean. All that appears by the most recent charts, and by Senex's globe of 1739, is, that this sea might be entirely mediterranean, and not communicating with the great sea of Tartary, for it appears to be enclosed and bounded on the south by the country of the Samoides, which is at present well known, and which extends from the Straits of Waigat to the river Jenisca; on the east it is bounded by Jelmorland, on the west by Nova Zembla; and although we are not acquainted with the extent of this sea to the north and north-east, yet as there does not appear any interruption of the lands, there is great probability of its being only a mediterranean, and bounded by land on that side: what indeed proves this is, that by leaving Waigat's Strait you may coast Nova-Zembla all along its western and northern coasts as far as Cape Desire; that after having past this cape, keeping along the coast to the east of Nova Zembla, you arrive at a small gulph, which is about the 75th degree, and where some Hollanders passed a dreadful winter in 1596; that beyond this gulph the country of Jelmorland was discovered in 1664, which is only a few leagues distant from Nova Zembla,

so

so that the only land which has not yet been discovered is a small spot near this little gulph; and this part is perhaps not thirty leagues long; so that if the Pacific Sea communicated with the ocean it must be at this little gulph, which is the only way by which they can join; and as this small gulph is in the 75th degree, even if the communication should exist, we must always keep five degrees towards the north to gain the great sea. It is evident, therefore, that if we would acquire the northern route to China, it would be much better to pass by the north of Nova Zembla, at the 77th or 78th degree, where the sea is more open, and has less ice, than to attempt the road through the icy strait of Waigat, with the uncertainty of getting out of this sea, which there is so much reason to believe mediterranean.

By following, therefore, the ocean along the coasts of Nova Zembla and Jelmorland, these lands are discoverable as far as the mouth of Chotanga, which is about the 73d degree, beyond which there is an unknown coast of about 200 leagues: we have only an account of them from the Muscovites, who have travelled by land into those climates; they state the country to be uninterrupted, have marked out the rivers

in

in their charts, and called the people *populi pa-
lati.* This interval of coasts, still unknown, extends from the mouth of Chotanga to that of
Kauvoina, in the 66th degree of latitude; the
ocean there forms a bay, whose most projecting
point in land is at the mouth of the Len, which
is a very considerable river. This bay is very
open, belongs to the Tartarian sea, and is called
the Linchidolin, where the Muscovites have a
whale fishery.

From the mouth of the Len we may follow
the coasts of Tartary more than 500 leagues
towards the east, to a peninsula inhabited by
the Schelates. This is the most northern extremity of Tartary, and is situate about the
72d degree of latitude. In this 500 leagues
the ocean makes no interruption by bays nor
arms, only a considerable elbow from the peninsula of the Schelates to the mouth of the river
Korvinea. This point of land also forms the
eastern extremity of the old continent, and
whose western is at Cape North in Lapland;
so that the old continent has about 1700
leagues northern coasts, comprehending the
sinuosities of the bays, from Cape North in
Lapland to the farthest point of land belonging

to the Schelates, and about 1100 leagues in a straight line.

Let us now take a view of the eastern coasts of the old continent, beginning at the farthest point of land which the Schelates inhabit, and descending towards the equator. The ocean at first forms. an elbow between the country of the Schelates, and the land inhabited by the people called Tschutschi, which projects a considerable way into the sea. To the south of this island it forms a small bay, called the Bay of Suctoikret, and afterwards another smaller bay, which projects like an arm 40 or 50 miles into Kamtschatka; the ocean then enters into the land by a long strait, filled with many small islands between the southern point of Kamtschatka and the northern point of Jesso, and forms a great mediterranean, which it is proper we should now trace throughout. The first is the sea of Kamtschatka, in which is a very considerable island, called Amour, or Love Island. This sea has an arm to the north-east; but this arm, and the sea of Kamtschatka itself, might possibly be, at least in part, formed by the rivers, which run therein, from the lands of Kamtschatka and from Tartary. Be this as it

will,

will, the sea of Kamtschatka communicates with the sea of Corea, which makes the second part of this mediterranean ; and all this sea, which is more than 600 leagues in length, is bounded upon the west and north by Corea and Tartary, and on the east and south by Kamtschatka, Jesso, and Japan, without having any other communication with the ocean than that of the fore-mentioned strait, for it is not certain whether that which is set down in some maps between Japan and Jesso really exists; and even if this strait does exist, the sea of Kamtschatka and Corea will still be regarded as forming a great mediterranean, divided from the ocean on every side, and could not be taken for a bay, for it has no direct communication with the ocean by its southern strait, but with the sea of China, which is rather a mediterranean than a gulph of the ocean.

It has been observed in the preceding article, that the sea has a constant motion from east to west ; and that consequently the great Pacific Sea made continual efforts against the eastern countries; an attentive inspection of the globe will confirm the consequences which we have drawn from this observation ; for from Kamtschatka to New Britain, discovered in

1700 by Dampier, and which is the 4th or
5th degree in the south latitude, the ocean appears to have washed away part of the land on
these coasts for upwards of 400 leagues, and
consequently the eastern bounds of the old continent formerly extended much farther than at
present; for it is remarkable, that New Britain
and Kamtschatka, which are the most projecting
lands towards the east, are under the same meridian.   All countries have their greatest extent
from north to south.   Kamtschatka reaches at
least 160 leagues from north to south, and that
point which is washed by the Pacific Sea on the
east, and on the other by the mediterranean sea
above mentioned, is divided in the direction
from north to south by a chain of mountains.

After these the lands of Jesso and Japan form
another extent of land, whose direction is also
north and south, extending upwards of 400
leagues, between the Great Sea and that of
Corea.   The chain of mountains of Jesso, and
of Japan, cannot fail of being directed from
north to south, since these lands, which are 400
leagues in this direction, are not more than 50
or 60 from east to west.   Therefore the lands
of Kamtschatka, Jesso, and the eastern part of
Japan, must be regarded as contiguous, and directed

rected from north to south. Still pursuing the same direction, after having passed Cape Ava at Japan, we meet with the island of Barnevelt, and three other islands, which are placed in the direction of north and south, and extend about 100 leagues. We afterwards meet with three other islands, called the islands of Callanos, then the Ladrones, which are fourteen or fifteen in number, all placed in the same direction from north to south, and all together occupying a space of more than 300 leagues in this direction, by so trifling a breadth, that its greatest does not exceed seven or eight leagues from east to west. It therefore appears to me that Kamtschatka, Jesso, eastern Japan, the islands of Barnevelt, the Callanos, and the Ladrones, are only the same chain of mountains, and the remains of an old country, which the ocean has at one time covered and gradually retired from. All these countries in fact appear to be only mountains, and the islands to be their points or peaks, while the low lands are covered with the ocean. What is related in Lettres Edifiantes, appears to be true, and that in fact a quantity of islands have been discovered, called the new Philippine Islands, and that their position is really such as is given by Father Gobien ; and it can-

not

not be doubted but that the most eastern of these islands are a continuation of the chain of mountains which forms the Ladrones, for these eleven eastern islands are all placed in the same direction from north to south, occupying a space of more than 200 leagues in length, the broadest of which is not more than 7 or 8 leagues from east to west.

But if these conjectures are thought too presumptuous, on account of the great intervals between the islands bordering on Cape Ava, Japan, and the Callanos, and between these islands and the Ladrones, and between the Ladrones and the new Philippines, the first of which is in fact about 160 leagues, the second 50 or 60, and the third near 120, I shall answer that the chains of mountains often extend much farther under the waters of the sea, and that these intervals are small in comparison of the extent of land which these mountains in the above direction present, which is 1100 leagues, computing them from the interior part of Kamtschatka. In short, if we wholly reject this idea, as to the quantity of land the ocean must have gained on the eastern coasts of the continent, and on that suit of mountains, still it must be allowed that Kamtschatka, Jesso, Japan,

the

the islands Bonga, Tanaxima, those of Great
Lequeo, King's Island, Formosa, Vaif, Basha,
Babuyane, Lucca, Mindano, Gilolo, &c. and
lastly, Guinea, which extends to New Britain,
and is situate under the same meridian as
Kamtschatka, do not form a continuation of
land of more than 2200 leagues, interrupted
only by small intervals, the greatest of which
perhaps is not more than 20 leagues, so that
the ocean has formed in the lands of the eastern
continent a great bay, which commences at
Kamtschatka and ends at New Britain. This
bay is interspersed with many islands, and has
every appearance of having been gained from
the land, consequently we may suppose, with
some probability, that the ocean, by its constant motion from east to west, has by degrees
acquired this extent on the eastern continent,
and has formed mediterraneans, such as Kamtschatka, Corea, China, and perhaps all the
Archipelago; for the earth and sea are there so
blended that it evidently appears to be an inundated country, of which we only see the eminences and high lands, while the lower are hid
under the waters of the ocean. This supposition appears to be in some measure confirmed
by the water being more shallow than in other

seas,

seas, and the innumerable islands resembling the tops of mountains.

If we particularly examine these seas, we shall find the sea of China forms a very deep bay in its northern part, which commences at the island of Fungma, and terminates at the frontier of the province of Pekin, about 50 leagues distance from that capital of the Chinese empire. This bay, in its most interior and narrowest part, is called the Gulph of Changi: It is very probable that this gulph, and a part of the sea of China, have been formed by the ocean, which has submerged all the ancient country, of which only the islands before-mentioned are now to be seen. In this southern part are the bays of Tonquin and Siam, near which is the peninsula of Malacco, formed by a long chain of mountains, whose direction is from north to south, and the Andaman islands, another chain of mountains in the same direction, and which appear to be only a succession of the mountains of Sumatra.

The ocean afterwards forms the great Gulph of Bengal, in which we may remark, that the peninsula of Indus forms a concave curb towards the east, nearly like the great bay of the eastern continent, which seems to have been

also

also produced by the same motion of the ocean from east to west. In this peninsula are the mountains of Gates, which have a direction from north to south, as far as Cape Comorin, and the Island of Ceylon seems to have been separated from this part of the continent. The Maldiva islands are only another chain of mountains, whose direction is also the same. After these follows the Arabian Gulph, which sends out four arms into the country; the two greatest on the western side, and the two smallest on the east. The first of these arms on the east side is the Bay of Cambaia, which is not above 50 or 60 leagues in length: this receives two very considerable rivers, viz. the Tapti and the Baroche, which Pietro de Valle calls the Mehi: the second arm, towards the east, is famous for the velocity and height of its tides, which are greater than in any other part of the world, and which extends for more than 50 leagues. Many rivers fall into this gulph, as the Indus, the Padar, &c. which have brought so great a quantity of earth and mud to their mouths as to raise the bottom almost to a level, the inclination of which is so gentle, that the tide extends to a very great distance. The first arm on the west side in the Persian Gulph,

which spreads more than 250 leagues on the
land; and the second is the Red Sea, which
extends more than 680, computing it from the
island Socotora. These two arms should be
regarded as two mediterranean seas, taking
them from beyond the straits of Ormuz and
Babelmandel: they are both subject to the
tides, but this is occasioned by their being so
near the equator, where the motion of the tides
is much greater than in any other climate;
and besides they are both very long and narrow. The motion of the tides is more rapid
in the Red Sea than in the Persian Gulph, because the Red Sea is near three times longer
and quite as narrow. The Red Sea does
not receive any river whose motion might
oppose the tides, whereas the Persian Gulph
receives three very considerable ones in its most
projecting extremity. It appears very apparently that the Red Sea has been formed by
an eruption of the ocean, for the bearing of
the lands are exactly similar, the coasts on each
side of the straits follow the same direction,
and evidently appear to have been cut by
waters.

At the extremity of the Red Sea is that
famous neck of land called the Isthmus of

Suez,

Suez, which forms a barrier to the Red Sea,
and prevents its communication with the Mediterranean. In a preceding article we noticed
the reasons which inclined us to think that the
Red Sea is higher than the Mediterranean, and
that if the Isthmus of Suez was cut, an inundation and an augmentation of the latter might
ensue. To which we shall subjoin, that if
even it should not be agreed that the Red Sea
is higher than the Mediterranean, it cannot
be denied that there is neither flux nor reflux
in the Mediterranean, adjoining to the mouths
of the Nile ; and that, on the contrary, in the
Red Sea the tides are very considerable, and
raise the water several feet, which circumstance
alone would suffice to send a quantity of water
into the Mediterranean if the Isthmus was
broken. Besides, we have an example on this
subject quoted by Varenius, who says in page
100 of his Geography : " Oceanus Germa-
" nicus, qui est Atlantici pars, inter Frisiam
" & Hollandium se effundens, efficit sinum,
" qui et si parvis sit respectu celebrium sinum
" maris, tamen & ipse dicitur mare, alluitque
" Hollandiæ emporium celeberrimum, Am-
" stelodamum. Non procul inde abest lacus
" Harlemensis, qui etiam mare Harlemense

D 2   " dicitur.

" dicitur. Hujus altitudo non est minor alti-
" tudine sinus illius Belgici, quem diximus
" & mittit ramum ad urbem Leidam, ubi in
" varias fossas divaricatur. Quoniam itaque
" nec lacus hic, neque sinus ille Hollandici
" maris inundant adjacentes agros (de naturali
" constitutione loquor, non ubi tempestatibus
" urgentur, propter quas aggeres facti sunt)
" pater inde, quod non sint altiores quam agri
" Hollandiæ. At vero Oceanum Germanicum
" esse altiorem quam terras hasce, experti sunt
" Leidenses, cum suscepissent fossam seu alveum
" ex urbe sua ad Oceani Germanici littora,
" prope Cattorum vicum perducere (distantia
" est duorum milliarum) ut, recepto per
" alveum hunc mari, possent navigationem
" instituere in Oceanum Germanicum, &
" hinc in varias terræ regiones. Verumenim-
" vero cum magnam jam alvei portem perfe-
" cissent, desistere coacti sunt, quoniam tum
" demum per observationem cognitem est,
" Oceani Germanici aquam esse altiorem
" quam agrum inter Leidam et litus Oceani
" istius; unde locus ille, ubi fodere desierunt
" dicitur, *Het malle Gat*. Oceanus itaque
" Germanicus est aliquantum altior quam
" sinus ille Hollandicus, &c." Therefore,

as the German Sea is higher than that of Holland, there is no reason why we should not believe the Red Sea may be higher than the Mediterranean. Herodotus and Diodorus Siculus speak of a canal of communication between the Nile, the Mediterranean, and the Red Sea, and M. Del'isle published a map in 1704, in which he traces one end of a canal to the most eastern part of the Nile, and which he judges to be a part of that which formerly joined the Nile with the Red Sea.*

In the third part of a book entitled, " Connoisance de l'Ancien Monde, or the Knowledge of the Old World," printed in 1707, we meet with the like sentiment; and it is there said, from Diodorus Siculus, that it was Neco, King of Egypt, who began this canal, that Darius, King of Persia, continued it, and that it was finished by Ptolemy II. who conducted it as far as the city Arsinoe, and that it could be opened and shut when they found it needful. Without desiring to deny these circumstances, I must own, that to me they appear doubtful. I do not know whether the violence and height of the tide in the Red Sea, would not be necessarily communicated to this canal; it appears to me,

* See Mem. de l'Acad. Sciences, 1734.

me, at least, that it would have required great precautions to confine the waters, to avoid inundations and to preserve this canal in good repair. Though historians assert that this canal was undertaken and finished, yet they do not tell us the length of its duration; and the remains which are pretended to be even now perceptible, are perhaps all that was ever done of it. The name of the Red Sea has been given to this arm of the ocean, because it has the appearance of that colour in every part where corals, or madrepores, are met with at the bottom. In the Histoire General des Voyages, vol. i. pages 198 and 199, it is said, " Before he quitted the Red Sea, D. Jean examined what might have been the reason why that name was given to it by the ancients, and if, in fact, this sea differed from others in its colour. He knew that Pliny had given several opinions on the origin of this name. Some derived it from a King named Erythros, who reigned in those parts, and which, in the Greek language, signifies red. Others imagined that the reflection of the sun produces a reddish colour on the surface of the water, and others that the water was naturally red. The Portuguese, who had made several voyages to the entrance of the straits,

straits, asserted that all the coasts of Arabia were very red, and that the sand and dust which the wind carries into the sea, tinged the water of the same colour.

" D. Jean, who examined the nature of the water, and the qualities of the coasts as far as Suez, asserts, that far from being naturally red, the water is of the same colour as in other seas, and that the sand and the dust having nothing red in themselves could not give this tinge to the water. The earth of both countries, he says, is generally brown; it is even black in some places, and in others white. On the coasts of Suaquem, where the Portuguese had not penetrated, he saw three mountains streaked with red, but they were of a very hard rock, and the neighbouring country was of the common colour.

" The truth is, that this sea is throughout of an uniform colour, which is easy to be demonstrated; but it must also be owned, that in some parts it appears to be red through chance, and in others green and white; the explanation of which phenomena is as follows: From Suaquem to Kossir, that is, for the space of 136 leagues, the sea is filled with shoals and rocks of coral; this name is given to them, by reason

that

that their form and colour render them so extremely like coral, that it requires great circumspection not to be deceived. There are two sorts of them, the one white and the other red; in many parts they are covered with a kind of gum, or glue, of a green, and in others with a deep orange. Now the water of this sea is so transparent that the bottom may be seen at 20 fathoms deep, especially from Suaquem to the extremity of the gulph; it appears, therefore, to take the colour of the matters it covers; as for example, when the rocks are covered with a green gum, the water above appears of a deeper green than the rocks themselves; and when the bottom is only sand, the water appears white: so likewise when the rocks are coral, the water seems to be tinged with red; and as these last coloured rocks are more frequently met with there than any other, D. Jean concludes, that the name of the Red Sea was affixed to the Arabian Gulph in preference to the Green or White. He applauds himself on this discovery, because the method by which he ascertained it left him no room for doubt. He caused a float to be moored against the rocks in the parts which were not deep enough to permit vessels to approach them, and the sailors could

often

often execute his orders with facility, without the sea being higher than the stomach at more than half a league from the rocks. The greatest part of the stones and pebbles they drew up, in those parts where the water appeared red, was also of that colour : in the water which appeared green, the stones were green, and if the water appeared white, the bottom was white sand, without any other mixture."

The direction of the coast of the Red Sea, from Cape Gordafu to the Cape of Good Hope, is pretty equal ; in the course of which there are no bays, excepting an arm on the coast of Melinda, that might be supposed as belonging to a large one provided the island of Madagascar joined the continent, which most probably was formerly the case, notwithstanding it is now divided by the straits of Mosambique. The coast bears the same direction from the Cape of Good Hope to Cape Negro on the west side of Africa ; it has the appearance of being a chain of high mountains, extends about 500 leagues, but contains scarcely any rivers of importance. Beyond Cape Negro however the land is much lower, and is supplied by several considerable rivers beside the Coanza and the Zaire ; and between that and Cape Gonsalvez, which is computed to be about 420 leagues, there are the mouths of no less than twenty-four large rivers; from this last Cape to Cape Trois-pointes it is an open bay, in about the centre of which is a considerable projection called Cape Formosa. On the southern side are the islands Fernanda, St. Thomas, and the Prince's Island, and which there is reason to suspect are part of a chain of mountains from Rio del Rey to the river Jamoer. The water turns somewhat into the land between Cape Trois-pointes to Cape Palmas, from the latter of which it is an open sea to Cape Tangrin; beyond this Cape there is a small bay towards Sierra Leona, and another in which are the islands of Bisagas. We then come to a considerable projection into the ocean called Cape Verd; of which the islands of that name are supposed to be a continuation, although it is more probable they are so of Cape Blanc, which is both higher and extends farther into the sea. From Cape Blanc to Cape Bajador is a mountainous and hard coast to which the Canary Islands seem to belong.

Turning from Africa we find an open bay extending to Portugal, and in about the centre of which are the straits of Gibraltar, through which the water runs with great rapidity into the Mediterranean,

diterranean, which flows almost 900 leagues into the interior part of land, and is the cause of many curious circumstances; 1st, it has no tides, at least that are visible, excepting in the Gulph of Venice and what are almost imperceptible at Marseilles and at Tripoli; 2dly, it surrounds a number of extensive islands, for instance, Sardinia, Sicily, Corsica, Cyprus, Majorca, and Italy, which is the largest known. It has also a fertile Archipelago; indeed it is from the Mediterranean Archipelago, that all collections of islands have been so denominated; this indeed has the appearance of belonging more to the Black Sea than the Mediterranean; nor is it in the least unlikely that Greece was at one time covered with the waters of the Black Sea, which empties itself into the Marmora, and from thence finds its way into the Mediterranean.

Some have asserted there was a double current in the Straits of Gibraltar, the one superior, which carries the water of the ocean into the Mediterranean, and the other inferior, which carries them in the contrary direction; but this opinion is evidently false, and contrary to the laws of hydrostatics: it has likewise been asserted to be the case in many other places, as in the Bosphorus, the strait of Sund, &c. and

E 2

Marsilli

Marsilli relates even experiments made in the Bosphorus, to prove the truth of these opposite currents ; but the experiments must have been badly made, since the matter is totally repugnant to the nature and motions of the waters ; besides Greaves in his Pyramidography, page 101 and 102, proves, by able experiments, that there is no such thing as a current in the Bosphorus, whose direction is opposite to the superior : what may have deceived Marsilli and others, is possibly the circumstance, that in the Bosphorus, the Straits of Gibraltar, and in all rivers which flow with rapidity, there is a considerable eddy along the shores, the direction of which is generally contrary to the principal current of the waters.

Let us now shortly trace all the coasts of the new continent. Cape Hold-with-Hope, lying in the 73d degree north latitude, is the most northern land we are acquainted with in New Greenland, and is not above 160 or 180 leagues distant from Cape North in Lapland. From this cape we may follow the coast of Greenland as far as the polar circle, where the ocean forms a broad strait between Iceland and Greenland. It is pretended that this country, adjacent to Iceland, is not the ancient Greenland which

the

the Danes formerly possessed as a province dependant on their kingdom; for in that there were civilized christians, who had bishops, churches, and several towns wherein they carried on their commerce. The Danes also visited it frequently, and as easily as the Spaniards can go to the Canaries: there still exists, as it is asserted, laws and ordinances for the government of this province, and those not very ancient: nevertheless, without attempting to divine how this country became absolutely lost, it is certain not the least trace of what we have related is to be met with in New Greenland. The people are wild and savage; there is no vestiges of any edifice; nor have they a word in their language which has an affinity with the Danish; in short, there is nothing which might give us room to judge that this is the same country. It is even almost a desert, and surrounded with ice for the greatest part of the year. But as these lands are of a vast extent, and as the coasts have been but little frequented by modern navigators, they may have missed the spot where the descendants of these polished people inhabit; or the ice having become more abundant in this sea, may prevent any approach to the shore near them: nevertheless, if we can

rely

rely on maps, this whole country has been coasted, and according to them it forms nearly a peninsula, and at the extremity of which are the two straits of Forbishers and of Friesland, where it is extremely cold, although they are not higher than the Orkneys, that is, at 60 degrees.

Between the west coast of Greenland and that of Labrador, the ocean forms a gulph, and afterwards a large mediterranean, which is the coldest of all seas, and the coasts of which are not perfectly known. By following this tract due north, we come to Davis's Strait, which leads to the Christian Sea, and is terminated by Baffin's Bay, which has the appearance of forming a kind of road into Hudson's Bay. Cumberland Strait, which as well as Davis's may lead to the Christian Sea, is narrower and more liable to be frozen: that of Hudson, though much more to the south, is also frozen during one part of the year. A very strong motion of the tide has been remarked in these straits, which is quite contrary to what is the case in the inland seas of Europe, as neither the Baltic nor Mediterranean have any; this difference seems to arise from the sea's motion, which always moving from east to west, occasions high tides in

the

the Straits, whose openings are turned towards the east; whereas in those of Europe, which open to the west, there is no motion; the ocean by its general motion enters into the first, and avoids the last; and this is the reason that there are such violent tides in the seas of China, Corea, and Kamtschatka.

Proceeding from Hudson's Strait towards Labrador, we come to a narrow opening, in which Davis, in 1586, sailed as far up as 30 leagues, and trafficked with the inhabitants, but no one has since attempted a discovery of this arm of the sea, and we are only acquainted with the country of the Esquimaux of all the adjacent land. The fort Pon Chartrin is the only and the most northern habitation of this country, which is separated from the island of Newfoundland by the little strait of Belleisle, which is not much frequented. As the eastern coast of Newfoundland is in the same direction as the coast of Labrador, we must regard the latter as a part of the continent, the same as Isleroyal appears to have been a part of Arcadia. There is no very considerable depth either on the great or other banks, where they fish for the cod; but as they slant for a distance under water, very violent currents are produced.

Between

Between Cape Breton and Newfoundland is a very broad Strait, by which we enter a small mediterranean, called the Gulph of St. Lawrence. This sea has an arm which extends far into the country, and seems to be only the mouth of the river St. Lawrence. The motion of the tides is extremely plain in this arm of the sea, and even at Quebec, which projects more into the country, the waters rise several feet. On quitting the Gulph of Canada, and following the coast of Arcadia, we meet with a small gulph called Boston-Bay, which forms a small square inlet into the land. But before we trace this coast farther, it is just to remark, that from Newfoundland to the most projecting Antille island, even to Guiana, the ocean forms a very great bay, which reaches as far as Florida, at least 500 leagues. This bay of the new continent is similar to that of the old, of which we have taken notice, where the ocean, after having made a gulph between Kamtschatka and New Britain, afterwards forms a vast mediterranean, which comprehends the seas of Kamtschatka, Corea, China, &c. so that in the new continent the ocean, after having formed a great gulph between Newfoundland and Guiana, forms a very large mediterranean,

mediterranean, extending from the Antilles to Mexico, which confirms our observations on the motion of the sea from east to west, for it appears that the ocean has equally gained on the eastern coasts of America and Asia. These great gulphs in the two continents are under the same degrees of latitude, and nearly.of the same extent.

If we examine the position of the Antilles, beginning at Trinidad, which is the most south, we cannot doubt but that Tobago, Trinidad, the Grenades, St. Vincent, Martinico, Mary Galante, Antigua, and Barbadoes, with every other island adjacent, at one time formed a chain of mountains, whose direction was from south to north, like that of the island of Newfoundland, and the country of the Esquimaux; afterwards the direction of the Antilles is from east to west, beginning at Barbadoes, then passing by St. Bartholomew, Porto Rico, St. Domingo, and Cuba, and nearly the same as Cape Breton, Acadia, and New England. All these islands are so adjacent to each other, that they may be looked upon as an interrupted tract of land, and as the summit of an overflown country now possessed by the sea. Most of them in fact are only points of mountains, and the sea which surrounds them is a real mediterranean where the motion of the flux and reflux is scarcely more sensible than in our Mediterranean, although the openings they present to the ocean are directly opposite to the motion of the waters from east to west, which must contribute to elevate the tides in the gulph of Mexico; but as this sea is very broad, the flux and reflux communicated to it by the ocean, dispersing over so large a space, becomes almost insensible at the coast of Louisiana, and many other places.

The old and new continent appear, therefore, both to have been encroached upon by the ocean in the same latitudes. Both have a vast mediterranean and a great number of islands, which are situated nearly in the same latitudes; the only difference is, that the old continent being much broader than the new, there is in the western part of it a mediterranean, of which nothing similar can be found in the new; but it appears that all which has happened to the eastern countries of the old world has also happened to the eastern part of the new, and that the greatest revolutions are

nearly

nearly in the middle and towards their equators, where the most violent motion of the ocean is made.

The coasts of Guiana, comprehended between the mouth of the river Oroonoko and the Amazones, presents nothing remarkable, but the latter, which is the broadest in the universe, forms a considerable extent of water near Coropa, before it arrives at the sea, by the two different mouths which surround the island of Caviana. From the mouth of the Amazones to Cape St. Roche, the coast runs almost straight east; from Cape St. Roche to St. Augustine it runs south, and from Cape St. Augustine to the Bay of All Saints it turns towards the west, so that this part of Brazil forms a considerable projection in the sea, which directly faces a like projection of land in Africa. The Bay of All Saints is a small arm of the ocean, running about 50 leagues into the land, and is much frequented by navigators. From this bay to Cape St. Thomas the coast runs direct south, and afterwards in a south-west direction as far as the mouth of the Plata, where the sea forms an arm projecting nearly 100 leagues into land. From thence to the extremity of

F 2

America,

America, the ocean forms a great gulph, terminated by the adjacent lands of Terra del
Fuega, as Falkland Island, Cape Assumption,
and the land discovered in 1671. At the bottom of this bay is the Straits of Magellan,
which is the longest in the world, and where
the tides flow extremely high. Beyond Magellan is that of La Maire, which is shorter,
and at last Cape Horn, which is the south point
of America.

We must remark on the subject of these
points that they all face the south, and most
of them cut by straits which run from east to
west; the first is that of South America, which
faces the southern pole, and is cut by the Strait
of Magellan; the second, that of Greenland,
which also directly faces the south, and is also
cut from east to west by Forbisher's Strait;
the third that of Africa, which also faces the
south; and beyond the Cape of Good Hope
are banks and shoals, that appear to have been
divided from it; the fourth, the peninsula of
India, which is cut by a strait that forms the
island of Ceylon, and facing the south like all
the rest. Hitherto we perceive no reason to be
given for this similarity, and can only remark
such are the facts.

From

From Terra del Fuega, all along the western coast of South America, the ocean very considerably penetrates into the land; and this coast seems exactly to follow the direction of the lofty mountains which cross all South America, from south to north, from the equator to the Arctic Pole. Near the equator the ocean forms a considerable gulph, beginning at Cape St. Francois, and reaching as far as Panama, the famous isthmus, which, like that of Suez, prevents the communication of the two seas, and without which there would be an entire separation of the old and new continents. From thence to California there is nothing remarkable. Between the latter and New Mexico an arm branches off, called Vermilion Sea, at least 200 leagues in length. In short, the western coasts of California have been followed to the 43d degree, at which latitude Drake, who was the first that made the discovery of the land to the north of California, and who called it New Albion, was obliged, through excessive cold, to change his course, and to anchor in a small bay which bears his name, so that these countries have not been discovered beyond the 43d and 44th degree, any more than the lands of North America beyond Moozemlaki

zemlaki under the 48th degree, and the Assiniboils under the 51st. The country of the first
savages extends much more to the west than the
east. All beyond, throughout an extent of more
than 1000 leagues in length, and as many in
breadth, is unknown, excepting what the Rus-
sians pretend to have discovered in their ex-
cursions from Kamtschatka to the eastern part
of North America.

The ocean, therefore, surrounds the whole
earth without any interruption, and the tour of
the globe may be made from the south point of
America; but it is not yet known whether the
ocean surrounds the northern part of the globe
in the like manner; and all mariners who have
attempted to go from Europe to China by the
north-east or north-west have alike miscarried
in their enterprises.

The lakes differ from the mediterraneans;
the first do not receive any water from the
ocean; on the contrary, if they have communication with the seas, they furnish them
with water. Thus the Black Sea, which some
geographers have regarded as an arm of the
Mediterranean, and consequently as an appen-
dix of the ocean, is only a lake, because, in
place of receiving water from the Mediterra-

nean,

nean, it supplies it with some, and flows with
rapidity through the Bosphorus into the lake
called the Sea of Marmora, and from thence
through the Strait of the Dardanelles into the
Grecian Sea. The Black Sea is about 250
leagues long by 100 broad, and it receives
a great number of rivers, as the Danube, the
Nieper, the Don, the Boh, the Donjec, &c.
The Don, which unites with the Donjec,
forms, before it arrives at the Black Sea, a
lake, called the Palus Meotis, which is more
than 100 leagues in length by 20 or 25 broad.
The sea of Marmora, which is below the Black
Sea, is a smaller lake than the Palus Meotis,
being not more than 50 leagues long and 8 or 9
broad.

Some ancients, and among the rest Diodorus
Siculus, have asserted that the Euxine, or Black
Sea, was formerly only a large river or lake,
and had no communication with the Grecian
sea; but being considerably increased with time
by the rivers which fell into it, the waters
forced a passage at first on the side of the
Cyanean islands, and afterwards on the side
of the Hellespont. This opinion appears to
be very probable, and the operation is easily
explained; for supposing the bottom of the
Black

Black Sea was formerly lower than it is at present, then the rivers which come into it would
have raised it by the mud and sand which they
brought with them, until the surface of the
water became higher than the land, when consequently it would have forced a passage for
itself, and as the rivers still continue to bring
sand and earth, and at the same time the quantity of water diminishes in the rivers, in proportion as the mountains from which they drew
their sources are lowered, it may happen in a
course of years that the Bosphorus will be
again filled up; but as these effects depend on
many causes, it is scarcely possible to give more
than mere conjectures thereon. From this
testimony of the ancients, Mr. Tournefort, in
his voyage to the Levant, says, on ancient
authority, that the Black Sea receiving the
waters of a great part of Europe and Asia, after
being considerably increased, opened itself a
passage by the Bosphorus, and afterwards
formed the Mediterranean, or so considerably
augmented it, that it became a great sea, and
forced itself a road through the strait of Gibraltar, by which the island of Atalantis, mentioned by Plato, was entirely overflowed.
This opinion has no foundation, since we are

certain

certain that it is the ocean which flows into the Mediterranean, and not the Mediterranean into the ocean. Besides, M. Tournefort has not combined two essential facts, both of which he mentions: the first is, that the Black Sea receives nine or ten rivers, not one of which but supplies it with more than the Bosphorus throws out: and the second, that the Mediterranean does not receive more water from rivers than the Black Sea, although it is seven or eight times larger, and that what the Bosphorus supplies it with does not make the tenth part of what falls into the Black Sea; how then could this tenth part of what falls into a small sea have formed not only a larger sea, but have also so greatly increased the waters, as to have broken down the lands at the strait of Gibraltar, and overflow an island larger than the whole of Europe? It is easy to perceive that this passage of M. Tournefort has not had due reflection. The Mediterranean receives at least ten times more water from the ocean than from the Black Sea, because the Bosphorus is only 800 feet broad in its narrowest part, whereas the strait of Gibraltar is more than 5000, and that, even supposing their velocity to be equal, still the depth of the straits of Gibraltar is by far the greatest.

M. de Tournefort, who ridicules Polybius on his predicting that the Bosphorus would be filled up in time, did not pay sufficient attention to circumstances, when he asserted that event to be impossible. This sea receives eight or ten great rivers, and as most of them bring sand and mud, must it not gradually be choaked up? Must not the winds and the natural current of the waters towards the Bosphorus, convey thither a part of these matters? It is, therefore, very probable that in a course of time the Bosphorus will be filled, when the waters of the rivers which come into the Black Sea shall be gradually diminished; now all rivers daily diminish, because the vapours collected by the mountains being the first sources of rivers, their quantity must decrease as the mountains diminish in height.

The Black Sea in fact receives more water from rivers than the Mediterranean, and the same author observes, " the greatest rivers in Europe fall into the Black Sea, by means of the Danube, in which the rivers of Suabia, Franconia, Bavaria, Austria, Hungary, Moravia, Corinthia,

Corinthia, Croatia, Bothnia, Servia, Tran-
silvania, Wallachia, empty themselves; those
of Black Russia and Podolia, go into the same
sea by the Niester; those of the southern and
eastern parts of Poland, of the northern parts
of Muscovy, and the country of the Cossacks,
enter therein by the Neiper or the Boristhenes;
the Tanais and Copa also fall into the Black
Sea by the Cimmerian Bosphorus; the rivers
of Mingrelia, of which Phasis is the principal,
also voids itself into the Black Sea, as does the
Casalmac, the Sangaris, and other rivers of
Asia Minor which have their course towards the
north; nevertheless the Thracian Bosphorus,
which is the only outlet from it, is not com-
parable to any of these great rivers."

These facts prove, that evaporation alone
carries off a very considerable quantity of water,
and it is from this great evaporation from the
Mediterranean that the ocean continually flows
thither through the straits of Gibraltar. It is
difficult to estimate the quantity of water any
sea receives; we should be acquainted with the
breadth, depth, and rapidity of all the rivers
which enter therein, how much they increase
and diminish in the different seasons of the year,
and how much it loses by evaporation; the

G 2

last

last of which is most difficult; for even supposing it proportional to the surfaces, it must be
more considerable in a hot than in a cold climate; besides, water mixed with salt and
bitumen, evaporates more slowly than fresh
water; a troubled sea more quickly than one
that is tranquil; and the difference of depth has
also some effect: in short, so many circumstances enter into this theory of evaporation
that it is scarcely possible to calculate any exact
estimations on it.

The water of the Black Sea appears to be
less clear and less saline than that of the ocean.
There are no islands in it, and its tempests
are more violent and more dangerous than in
the ocean, because the whole body of its waters
being contained in a bason, which has but a
small outlet, when they are agitated, they have
a kind of whirling motion which strikes the
vessels on every side with an insupportable violence.

Next to the Black Sea the greatest lake in
the universe is the Caspian Sea, whose extent
in length from north to south is about 300
leagues, and scarcely more than fifty broad.
This lake receives the Wolga and some other
considerable rivers, as the Kur, the Faie, and

the

the Gempo; but what is singular, it does not
receive any on its eastern side; the country
on that side being only a desert of sand almost
unknown. Czar Peter I. sent some engineers
there to design a chart of the Caspian Sea, who
discovered that its figure was quite different
from that given by former geographers, who
had represented it to be round, whereas it is
very long and narrow. The eastern coasts of
this sea, as well as the neighbouring country,
were unknown: even the existence of lake
Aral, which is 100 leagues distant from it towards the east, was doubtful, or at least thought
to be a part of the Caspian Sea, so that before
the discoveries of the Czar there was unknown
land in this climate upward of 300 leagues
long by 100 or 150 broad. Lake Aral is
nearly an oblong, and may be 90 or 100
leagues long, by 50 or 60 broad; it receives
two very considerable rivers, the Sideroias and
the Oxus, but as well as the Caspian has no
outlet for its waters; and it bears the further resemblance, for as the Caspian receives no
river on the east, so lake Aral receives none on
the west, from which we may presume, that
formerly these two lakes were but one, and that
the rivers having, by degrees, diminished, left

a great

a great quantity of sand and mud, and which forms the country that now divides them. There are some small islands in the Caspian, and its waters are much less saline than those of the ocean ; storms are here very dangerous, and large vessels are not used in it for navigation, because it has many sand banks, shoals and rocks scattered under the surface of the water. Pietro della Valle says, " The largest vessels employed on the Caspian Sea, along the coasts of Mazanda in Persia, where the town of Fer-habad stands, although they are called ships, appear smaller than our Tartanes. Their sides are high, and they draw but little water, having a flat bottom. They give this form to their vessels, not only because this sea is shallow, but because it is filled with shoals and sand banks ; so that if the vessels were not fabricated in this manner they could not be used with safety. Indeed, I was astonished, why at Fer-habad they fish only for salmon, which are found at the mouth of the river, some poor sturgeons, and other sort of fresh water fish, of little value : I attributed the cause of it to their ignorance of the arts of fishing and navigation until the Cham of Esterabad, whose residence is at a sea port, informed me that the waters are so shallow 20

and

and 30 leagues from shore that it was impossible to cast the nets with the chance of taking any fish, and that it was for this reason they gave the abovementioned form to their vessels, which are not mounted with any cannon, as but few corsairs and pirates ever visit this sea.

Struys and other travellers have asserted, that in the neighbourhood of Kilan, there were two gulphs wherein the rivers of the Caspian were ingulphed, and carried afterwards by subterranean canals into the Persian Gulph. De Fer and other geographers have even marked out these gulphs in their maps, nevertheless we are assured by the people sent by the Czar that they do not exist.*

The circumstance of willow leaves being seen in great quantities on the Persian Gulph, and which are supposed by the same authors to come from the Caspian Sea because there are no such trees on the Persian Gulph, is fully as improbable as their subterraneous gulphs, and which Gemelli Careri, as well as the Muscovites, asserts are entirely imaginary: in fact, the Caspian is near one third smaller than the Black Sea, which last also receives much more water by rivers than the former : the evaporation

* See Mem. Acad. Sciences, 1721.

tion therefore is sufficient to carry off all its water, nor is it necessary to suppose subterraneous gulphs in the Caspian any more than in the Black Sea.

There are lakes which do not receive any rivers, and from which none go out. There are others which both receive and discharge and some that only receive them. The Caspian Sea, lake Aral, and the Dead Sea, are of the last kind; they receive the waters of many rivers, and contain them. In Asia Minor there is a small lake of the like kind, and one much larger in Persia, on which the town of Marago stands; its figure is oval, and it is about ten or twelve leagues long, by six or seven broad; it receives the river Tauris, which is not very considerable. There is also a similar small lake in Greece, about 12 or 15 leagues from Lepanto, which are the only lakes of that kind known in Asia. In Europe there is not one which is considerable; in Africa there are many small ones, as those which receive the rivers Ghir, Zez, Touguedout, and Tasilet. These four lakes are pretty near each other, and situate towards the frontiers of Barbary near the deserts of Zara; there is another situate in the country of Kovar, which receives the river of Berdoa.

doa. In North America, where there are more lakes than in any other part of the world, not one of this kind is known, at least if we except two small collections of water formed by rivulets, the one near Guatimapo, and the other some leagues from Realnuevo, both in Mexico. But in South America, at Peru, there are two contiguous lakes, one of which, lake Titicaca, is very large, and receives a river whose source is not very remote from Cusco, and from which no river issues: there is one smaller in Tucuman, which receives the river Sala; and another larger in the same country, which receives the river Santiago, and three or four others between Tucuman and Chili.

The lakes which receive no rivers, and from which no rivers issue, are greater in number than those just spoken of; these lakes are kinds of pools where the rain water collects; or may proceed from subterraneous waters, which issue in form of springs, in low places, where they cannot afterwards find any drain. The rivers which overflow may likewise leave stagnate waters in the country, which may remain for a long time, and only be replenished by other inundations. The sea has often inundated lands

and formed saline lakes therein, like that at
Harleim, and many others in Holland, to which,
no other origin can be attributed; or by losing
its natural motion, might quit some land, and
leaving water in the lowest places may have
formed lakes, which have continued to be supported by rains. In Europe there are many
small lakes of this kind, as in Ireland, Jutland,
Italy, in the country of the Grisons, Poland,
Muscovy, Finland, and in Greece. But all
these lakes are very inconsiderable. In Asia
there is one near the Euphrates, in the desert
of Irac, more than 15 leagues long: another
in Persia nearly of the same extent, and on
which the towns of Kelat, Tetuan, Vastan, and
Van, are situated; another small one in Chora-
zän near Ferrior; another in Independent
Tartary, called Lake Levi; two in Muscovy
Tartary, another in Cochinchina, and one in
China very large, and not far distant from
Nankin; this last, nevertheless, communicates
with the adjacent sea, by a canal several leagues
in length. In Africa there is a small lake of
the same kind in the kingdom of Morocco;
another near Alexandria, which appears to
have been left by the sea; another very considerable one formed by the rain in the desert
Azarad,

Azarad, about the 30th degree latitude; this lake is eight or ten leagues long; another still larger on which the town of Gaoga is situate, in the 27th degree; another much smaller, near the town of Kanum, under the 30th degree; one near the mouth of the river Gambia; many more in Congo, about the 2d or 3d degree of south latitude; two more in the country of the Caffrees, one called the Lake Rufumbo, of no great length, and another in the province of Arbuta, which is perhaps the greatest lake of this kind, being about 25 leagues in length by seven or eight in breadth; there is also one of these lakes at Madagascar, near the east side, about the 29th degree of south latitude.

In America there is one of these lakes in the middle of the peninsula of Florida, in its centre is an island called Serope; the lake of Mexico is also of this kind, this is almost round, and about $10\frac{1}{2}$ leagues diameter; there is another still larger in New Spain, 25 leagues distant from the coast of Campeachy Bay, and another smaller in the same country near the coast of the South Sea. Some travellers have asserted that there was in the inland parts of Guiana a very great lake of that kind; it is

H 2

called

called the Golden Lake, or Lake Parima. They have related surprising things of the riches of the neighbouring country, and of the quantity of gold dust that is found in this lake. They give it an extent of more than 400 leagues in length, and 125 in breadth. No river, they say, goes out nor enters therein; although many geographers have marked this lake in their maps, it is not probable there is any such existing.

But the most general and largest lakes are those which receive and give rise to other great rivers: as their number is very great I shall speak only of the most considerable, or of the most remarkable. Beginning at Europe, we have in Switzerland the lake of Geneva, Constance, &c.; in Hungary, the lake Balaton; in Lavonia, a large lake, and which separates this province from Russia; in Finland, the lake Lapwert, which is very long, and is divided into many arms, and lake Oula, which is of a round figure; in Muscovy, lake Ladoga, more than 25 leagues long by above 12 broad. Lake Onega is as long, but not so broad. Lakes Ilmen and Belozo, from whence issue one of the sources of the Wolga; the Iwan-Osero, from whence issues one of the sources of the

Don;

Don: two other lakes from whence the Vit-zogda derives its origin; in Lapland, the lake from which issues the river Kimi; another much larger near the coast of Wardhus, and many others, from whence issue the rivers Lula, Pitha, and Uma. These are not very considerable. In Norway two more of nearly the same size as those of Lapland: in Sweden, lake Vener, which is as large a lake as Meler, on which Stockholm is situated; and two others less considerable; one is near Eveldal, and the other near Lincopin.

In Siberia, in Muscovy, and in Independent Tartary, there are a great number of these lakes, the principal of which is the great lake Baraba, which is more than 100 leagues long, and whose waters fall into the Irtis; the great lake Estraguel, the source of the same river: many other smaller, the sources of the Jenisca; the great lake Kita, the source of the Oby; another larger, the source of the Angara; lake Baical, which is more than 70 leagues long, and is formed by the same river Angara; lake Pehu, from which issues the river Urack, &c. In China and Chinese Tartary, lake Dalai, from whence issues the large river Argus, which falls into the river Amour; the lake of
the

the three mountains, the source of the river Helum; the lakes Cinhal, Cokmor, and Sorama, the sources of the river Honaho; two other lakes adjacent to the river Nankin, &c. In Tonquin, lake Guadag, which is very considerable. In India, the lake Chiamat, from whence issues the river Laquia, adjacent to the sources of the rivers Ava, Longenu, &c. This lake is more than 40 leagues broad by 50 long. There is another at the origin of the Ganges; and one bordering on Cashmere is the source of the river Indus, &c.

In Africa is lake Cayar, and two or three others adjacent to the mouth of Senegal river. Lakes Guarda and Sigismus make but one lake, of a triangular form, about 100 leagues long by 75 broad, and contain a very considerable island. In this lake the Niger loses its name, and takes that of Senegal, in the course of which, towards the source, we meet with another considerable lake, called Bournou, where the Niger again loses its name, for the river which comes therein is called Gambaru. In Ethiopia, at the sources of the Nile, is the great lake Gambia, upwards of 50 leagues long. There are also many lakes on the coast of Guinea, which appear to have been formed

by

by the sea, and there are only a few lesser lakes in the remaining part of Africa.

North America may be styled the country of lakes; the greatest are lake Superior, upwards of 125 leagues long by 50 broad; lake Huron, upwards of 100 leagues long by 40 broad; lake Illionois, which, comprehending the Bay of Puanto, is quite as extensive as lake Huron; lakes Erio, and Ontario, together upwards of 80 leagues long, from 20 to 25 broad; the lake Mistasin, to the north of Quebec, is about 50 leagues in length; and lake Champlain, to the south of it, is nearly of the same extent; lake Alemipigon, and the lake Christinaux, both to the north of lake Superior, are also very considerable; the lake Assiniboils contains many islands, and is upwards of 75 leagues long; there are also, independent of that of Mexico, two large lakes in that country, the one called Nicaragua, in the province of that name, which is upwards of 70 leagues long.

In South America there is a small lake, the source of the Maragnon, and another larger which is the source of the river Paraguay; also the lake Titicares, which falls into the river Plata; two smaller lakes which flow into the same

same river ; and some others, not very consi-
dierable, in the inland part of Chili.

All lakes from which rivers derive their origin, those which fall into the course of rivers,
and which carry their water thereto, are not salt.
Almost all those, on the contrary, which receive
rivers without others issuing thereout, are salt;
this seems to favour the opinion that the saltness of the sea arises from the salts which
rivers wash from the earth, and continually
convey into it; for evaporation cannot carry
off fixed salts, and consequently those which
rivers carry into the sea remain therein. Although river water appears to taste fresh, we
well know that it contains a small quantity of
salt, and in course of time might have acquired
such a considerable degree, as to occasion
the present saltness of the sea, and which must
still continue increasing. It is thus, therefore,
as I imagine, that the Black Sea, the Caspian,
lake Aral, &c. have become salt. With
respect to lakes, which do not receive any
river, nor from which does any issue, are either
fresh or salt, according to their different origins;
those near the sea are generally salt, and those
remote from it are fresh, because the one
has been formed by the inundations of the

sea,

sea, and the others proceed from springs of fresh water.

The lakes any ways remarkable are the Dead Sea, the waters of which contain much more bitumen than salt : it is called the Bitumen of Judea, but is no other than the Asphaltes, which has caused some authors to call it the Asphaltic Lake. The lands which border this lake contain a great quantity of this bitumen ; and many have supposed, as the poets feign of lake Avernus, that no fish could live therein, and birds which attempted to fly over it were suffocated ; but neither of these lakes produce such mortal events ; fish live in both, birds pass over them, and men bathe therein without the least danger.

At Boleslaw, in Bohemia, there is said to be a lake, wherein are holes, whose depth is unfathomable, from which impetuous winds issue, which are carried over all Bohemia, and in winter raise pieces of ice of an 100 weight in the air.

A petrified lake in Iceland is also mentioned ; and lake Neagh, in Ireland, has also the same property ; but these petrifactions are no other than incrustations, like those made by the water of Arcueil.

ARTICLE XII.

OF THE FLUX AND REFLUX.

WATER has but one natural motion; like other fluids it always descends from the higher into the lower places, unless obstructed by some intervening obstacle. When it reaches the lowest place it remains there calm and motionless, at least without some foreign cause agitates and disturbs it. All the waters of the ocean are collected in the lowest parts of the surface of the earth, of course the motions of the sea must proceed from external causes, the principal of which is the flux and reflux, which is alternatively made in a contrary direction, and from which results a general and continual motion in the sea from east to west. These two motions have a constant

and

and regular relation with the motions of the moon. When the moon is new, or at the full, this motion from east to west is more sensible, as well as that of the tides, which upon most shores ebb and flow every six hours and a half: that it is always high tide whenever the moon is at the meridian, whether above or below the horizon of the place; and low tide when the moon rises or sets. The motion of the sea from east to west is constant and invariable, because the ocean in its flux moves from east to west, and impels towards the west a great quantity of water, and the reflux seems to be made in a contrary direction, by reason of the small quantity of water then driven towards the west; the flux, therefore, must rather be regarded as a swelling, and the reflux as a subsiding of the water, which instead of its disturbing the motion from east to west, produces and continually restores it, although in fact it is stronger during the rise, and weaker during the fall, from the above reason.

The principal circumstances of this motion are, 1. That it is more sensible when the moon is new, or at the full, than in the quadratures: in spring and in autumn it is also more violent than at any other time of the

year;

year; and it is weaker in the soltsices, which is occasioned by the combination of the attraction of the moon and sun. 2. The wind often alters the direction and quantity of this motion, particularly that which constantly blows from the same quarter. It is the same with respect to large rivers which convey their waters into the sea and produce a current there, often extending several leagues, which is strongest when the direction of the wind agrees with the general motion. Of this we have an example in the Pacific Ocean, where the motion from east to west is constant and very perceptible. 3. We must remark that when one part of a fluid moves, the whole mass receives the motion; now in the motion of the tides a great part of the ocean moves in a very sensible manner, and consequently the ocean is agitated by this motion throughout its whole extent.

Perfectly to comprehend this we must attend to the nature of the power which produces the tides. We have observed that the moon acts upon the earth by a power called attraction by some, and by others gravity: this force penetrates through the globe, is exactly proportioned to the quantity of matter, and

decreases

decreases as the square of the distance increases.. Let us next examine what must happen to the waters. when the moon is at the meridian of any one place.—The surface of the waters being immediately. under the moon is then nearer that planet than any. other part of the globe; hence this part of the sea must be elevated towards the moon, by forming an eminence, the summit of which must be op-. posite to the moon's centre; for the formation of this eminence the waters at the bottom, as well as at the surface, contribute their share, in proportion to the proximity they are in of the moon, which acts upon them in the in-- verse ratio of the squares of their distances : thus the surface of that part of the sea is first raised.; the surface of the neighbouring parts will be likewise elevated, but to a less height, and the water at the bottom of all these parts will be raised by the same cause; so that all this part of the sea growing higher and form-ing an eminence, it is necessary that the water of the remote parts, and on which this force of attraction does not act, proceeds with precipi-tation to replace the waters which are thus elevated and drawn towards the moon. This is what produces the flux, or high tide, which

is

is more or less sensible on different coasts, and which agitates the sea not only at its surface but even to the greatest depths. The reflux, or ebb, happens afterwards by the natural inclination of the water, for when the moon no longer uses its power, the water which was raised by this foreign power retakes its level, and returns to the shores and places it had been forced to quit. When the moon passes to the antipode, or opposite meridian, the same effect ensues, though from a different cause. In the first case the waters rise because they are nearer the planet than any other parts of the globe; and in the second it is from the contrary reason, they rise because she is the most remote from them; and this it is easily perceived must produce the same effect, for the waters of this part being less attracted than those of the opposite hemisphere, they will naturally recede and form an eminence, the summit of which will answer to the point of the least action that is directly opposite to the moon's station, or where she was thirteen hours before. When the moon arrives at the horizon the tide is ebb, the sea is then in its natural state, and the water in a direct equilibrium; but when she is at the opposite meridian

ridian this equilibrium can no longer exist, since the waters of the part opposite to the moon being at the greatest distance possible from her, they are less attracted than the remaining part of the globe, and hence their relative weight, which always retains them in an equilibrium, impels them towards the opposite point to the moon. Thus in the two cases, when the moon is at the meridian of a place, or at the opposite meridian, the water must be raised nearly to the same height, and consequently fall and rise, when the moon is at the horizon either at her rising or setting. Thus a motion, such as we have just mentioned, necessarily disturbs the whole mass of the sea, and agitates it throughout its whole extent and depth ; and if this motion appears insensible in the open seas, it is nevertheless no less real; but as the winds cannot ruffle the bottom in an equal degree with the surface, the motion of the tides is necessarily more regular there, although directed alternately in the same manner as at the top.

From this alternative motion of flux and reflux there results, as already observed, a continual motion of the sea from east to west, be-

cause

cause the moon, which produces the tides, proceeds from east to west, and successively acting in the same direction, the water follows her course. This motion is most considerable in all sraits; for example, at the straits of Magellan the water rises nearly 20 feet, and continues so for six hours, whereas the reflux lasts only two*, and the water runs towards the west. This evidently proves that the reflux is not equal to the flux, and that from both there results a motion towards the west, much stronger in the time of the flux than in that of the reflux. This is the reason that in open seas, remote from land, the tides are only felt by the general motion of the waters from east to west.

The tides are stronger in the torrid zone between the tropics than in the rest of the ocean : they are also more sensible in places which extend from east to west, in long and narrow gulphs, and on the coasts where there are isles and promontories. The greatest known flux is at one of the mouths of the river Indus, where the water rises thirty feet. It rises also very remarkably near Malays, in the straits of

Sund,

* See Narborough's Voyage.

Sund, in the Red Sea, in Nelson's Bay, at the mouth of the river St. Lawrence, on the coasts of China, Japan, Banama, in the Gulph of Bengal, &c.

The motion of the sea from east to west is more sensible in particular places. Mariners have observed it in sailing from India to Madagascar and Africa; it is also very perceptible in the Pacific Sea, and between the Malaccas and Brazil: but this motion is most violent in the Straits; for example, the waters are carried with such great force in that direction through the Straits of Magellan that it is felt to a great distance in the Atlantic; and it is supposed that this caused Magellan to conjecture there was a strait by which the two seas had a communication. In the Manilla straits, and in all the channels which divide the Maldivian islands, the sea flows from east to west, as well as in the Gulph of Mexico, between Cuba and Jucatan. In the gulph of Paria this motion is so violent that the strait is called the Dragon's Mouth. In the Canadian and Tartarian Seas it flows also with violence, as well as in the Strait of Waigat, through which it conveys enormous masses of ice into the northern seas of Europe. The Pacific Ocean flows from east to west, through the Straits of Java; the sea of Japan flows towards China, the Indian Ocean flows towards the west, through the Straits of Java and other Indian islands; we cannot, therefore, doubt that the sea has a constant and general motion from east to west, and it is certain the Atlantic flows towards America, and that the Pacific Sea goes from it, as is evident at Cape Current between Lima and Panama.

In short, the alternatives of the flux and re-flux are regularly made in six hours and a half on most coasts, though at different hours, according to the climate and position of the lands: thus the sea coasts are continually beaten by the waves which at each time wash away some small parts of their matters, which they transport to a distance, and deposit at the bottom of the sea; so likewise the waves convey, and leave on the lower shores, shells, sands, &c. these by degrees form horizontal strata, which accumulating, become downs and hills, exactly similar to others, both as to form and internal composition. From this constant action, the sea naturally shuts itself out from the lowest coasts, and gains upon the highest.

To

To give an idea of the efforts of a troubled sea against coasts, I shall relate a fact which has been affirmed to me by a creditable person, and which I the readier gave credit to, having seen something nearly similar. In the principal islands of the Orkneys there are coasts composed of rocks perpendicularly divided to the surface of the sea, to the height of near 200 feet. The tides in this place rise very considerable, as is common in all parts where there are projecting lands and islands; but when the wind is very strong, and the sea swells at the same time, the motion is so great, and the agitation so violent, that the water rises to the summit of these rocks, and falls again in the form of rain: it throws to this great height gravel and stones from the foot of the rocks, and some of them even broader than the hand.

In the port of Livourne, where the sea is much more calm, I saw a tempest in December, 1731, wherein they were obliged to cut down the masts of some vessels that had been forced from their anchors by the wind, and driven into the road. The sea swelled above the fortifications, which were of a considerable height, and as I was on one of the most projecting works, I could not regain the town before I was wet-

ted

ted by the sea-water much more than I could have been by the most plentiful rain.

These examples are sufficient to shew with what violence the sea acts against some coasts. This continual agitation destroys and diminishes by degrees the land. The water carries away all these matters, and deposits them as soon as it arrives at a part where the troubled sea subsides into a calm. In tempestuous weather the water is foul, from the mixture of matters detached from the shore and bottom of the sea, which then casts on the coasts a number of things that it brings from a distance, and which are never met with but after storms; as amber-gris on the west of Ireland, and yellow amber on those of Pomerania, cocoa-nuts on the coasts of India, &c. and sometimes pumice and other singular stones. We can quote on this occasion a circumstance related in the new travels to the American Islands. " Being at St. Domingo, says the author, among other things they gave me some light stones, which the sea brought to the coast when there had been strong southerly winds; there was one two feet and a half long by eighteen broad, and one thick, which did not quite weigh five pounds: they are as white as snow, much

harder

harder than pumice, of a fine consistency, having no appearance of being porous, but when thrown into water, rebounded like a ball thrown on the ground, and it was with great difficulty they could be forced under the water with the hand." The stone must have been a very fine and close-grained pumice, which had issued from some volcano, and which the sea had conveyed, as it transports ambergris, cocoa-nuts, common pumice-stone, seeds of plants, rushes, &c. Observations of this kind have been generally made on the coasts of Ireland and Scotland. The sea by its general motion from east to west must convey the productions of our coast to those of America; and it is by some irregular motions that the productions of the East and West Indies, as well as the northern climates, are brought upon our shores. There is a great appearance that the winds cause those effects; large spots have often been observed in the high seas, far from shore, covered with pumice-stones; they could only come from the volcanoes in islands or on the continent, and which the current had transported to the middle of the seas. Before the southern part of America was known, and in the time when the India Sea was thought to

have

have no communication with our ocean, appearances of this kind afforded the first supposition of it.

The alternative motion of the flux and reflux, and the constant motion of the sea from east to west, presents different phenomena in different climates, according to the bearing of the land and the height of the coasts. There are parts where the general motion from east to west is not perceptible; there are others where the sea has even a contrary motion, as on the coast of Guinea. But these contrary motions are occasioned by the winds, by the position of the lands, by the waters of large rivers, and by the disposition of the bottom of the sea; all these causes produce currents which alter, and often change the general motion in many parts of the sea; but as the motion from east to west is the greatest, most general and constant, it must also produce the greatest effects, and all taken together, the sea must gain ground towards the west, and lose it towards the east; although it may happen that on those coasts where the west winds blow during the greatest part of the year, as in France and England, the sea may gain on the east, yet these particular exceptions do not destroy the effect of the general cause.

ARTICLE XIII.

OF THE INEQUALITIES AT THE BOTTOM OF THE SEA, AND OF CURRENTS.

THE coasts of the sea may be distinguished into three kinds, 1st, the elevated coasts, which are rocks and hard stones, generally divided perpendicularly, and which rise sometimes to the height of 7 or 800 feet. 2d, The low coasts, some of which are almost level with the surface of the water, and others rising with a moderate elevation, often bounded by rocks at the water's edge, forming shelves and breakers, which render the approach to shore very difficult and dangerous. 3dly, Downs, which are coasts formed by sand which the sea accumulates, or brought or deposited by

rivers ;

rivers; these downs form hills more or less elevated, according to the accumulated sand.

The coasts of Italy are bordered by several sorts of marble and stone; these rocks appear at a distance as so many pillars of marble perpendicularly divided. The coasts of France from Brest to Bourdeaux are almost surrounded with rocks just at the water's edge, which occasion dangerous breakers. The coasts of England, Spain, and many others, are also bordered with rocks and hard stone; excepting some parts which are made use of for bays, ports, and havens.

The depth of water along the coasts is in proportion to their elevation. The inequalities at the bottom of the sea near the coasts, correspond also with the inequalities of the surface of the ground along the shore. A celebrated navigator has made the following observations on this subject.

" I have constantly remarked, that where the coasts are defended by steep rocks, the sea is there very deep, and seldom affords a probability of anchoring; and, on the contrary, where the ground inclines from the coast to the sea, however elevated it may be further

inland

inland, the bottom is good there, and consequently admits of anchorage.

"According to the declivity of land, as it
approaches the water's edge, so we generally
find our anchor ground, and either approach
or keep at a distance from shore agreeable to
the steepness of the land; for I never saw or
heard of a coast where the land is of a continual height, without some vallies lying inter-
mixed with the high-lands; they are the subsiding of low lands, and afford good anchoring,
the earth being lodged deep under water; for
this reason it is we find good harbours upon
coasts which abound with steep cliffs, because
the land has subsided between them. But
where the declensions from the hills is not within
land but towards the main sea, as at Chili and
Peru, and the coasts are nearly perpendicular,
as in the countries running from the Andes, it
is very deep, and has scarcely any creeks or
harbours. The coasts of Gallicia, Portugal,
Newfoundland, the islands of Juan Fernando
and St. Helena, &c. are somewhat similar to
those of Peru, yet good harbours are not so
scarce, as there is always good anchorage where
there are short ridges of land. In general the
land under water seems to be exactly pro-

portioned to the rising of the contiguous part above, and therefore, where the lands upon the shores are steep, there is but little security for ships, they being very easily driven from their moorings; yet although steep cliffs denote this disadvantage, they assure us of this benefit also, that we can sail close to them with safety, besides being able to see them at a considerable distance; whereas low lands are frequently not discovered until we are near, and always experience the hazard of running aground. This fact of good anchorage where the lands on the coast are low, might be illustrated by many instances in the bays of Campeachy, Honduras, Panama; the coasts of Portobella, Carthagena, Guinea, Callifornia, China, Coromandel, &c. but going into particulars would be almost endless, as I very seldom found it otherwise than that deep waters and high shores went together, as well as low lands and shallow seas."

The fact therefore of there being considerable mountains, and other inequalities, at the bottom of the sea is fully confirmed by the observations of navigators. Divers also assure us, there are smaller inequalities formed by rocks, and that it is much the coldest in the vallies of

the

the sea. In general the depths in great seas, as we have already observed, increase proportionably to their distance from shore. By Mr. Buache's chart of that part of the ocean between the coasts of Africa and America, and by the divisions he has given of the sea from Cape Tagrin to Rio-Grande, there appears to be similar inequalities in the ocean to those on land. That the Albrolhos, where there are some rocks at the surface of the water, are only the tops of very large and lofty mountains, of which Dolphin island is one of the highest peaks. That the islands of Cape de Verd are also the tops of mountains; that there are a great number of shoals in the sea, which round the Albrolhos descends even to unknown depths.

With respect to the quality of the different soils which form the bottom of the sea, as we must rely on divers and the plumb, we can say nothing exact or precise concerning it; we only know that there are parts covered with mud to a considerable thickness, on which anchors have no hold; in these parts probably the mud of rivers are deposited. In other parts are sands similar to those on land. In others are shells, heaped up together, madre-

pores,

pores, corals, and other productions of insects, which begin to unite and appear like stones; in others are fragments of stones, gravel, and often entire stones and marble. For example, in the Maldivian islands the buildings are made of a hard stone weighed up from several fathoms under water. At Marseilles very good marble is obtained from the bottom of the sea, which, so far from wasting and spoiling stone and marble, in our discourse on minerals, we shall prove they are formed and preserved therein; whereas the sun, earth, air, and rain water, corrupts and destroys them.

The bottom of the sea must be composed of the same matters as our habitable land, because the very same substances are contained in the one as the other; places are found at the bottom of the sea, covered with shells, madrepores, and other productions of sea matters, as we meet with on earth an infinity of quarries and banks of chalk and other matters replete with the same sort of shells, madrepores, &c. so that in all respects the dry parts of the globe resemble those covered by the water, both in composition of matters, and inequalities of the superfices.

It

It is to these inequalities at the bottom of
the sea, we must attribute the origin of currents,
for if the bottom was equal and level, there
would be no other current than the general motion from east to west, and a few others which
might be caused by the action of the winds ;
but a certain proof that most currents are
produced by the flux and reflux, and directed
by the inequalities at the bottom of the sea, is,
that they regularly follow the tides, and change
their direction at each ebb and flow. See
Pietra della Valle on the subject of the currents
of the gulph of Cambay, and the accounts of
all navigators, who unanimously assert that in
those parts where the flux and reflux of the sea
is the most violent, the currents are also most
rapid.

Therefore it cannot be doubted but that the
tides produce currents whose direction always
answers that of the opposite hills and all mountains between which they flow. Currents produced by winds, also follow the direction of
those hills which are under the water, seldom
running opposite to the wind which produces
them, any more than those which are occasioned
by the tides follow the direction of their original
cause.

To

To give a clear idea of the productions of currents, we shall first observe they are to be met with in every sea; that some are rapid, and others slow; that some are of great extent, both in length and breadth, and others short and narrow; that the same cause, whether the wind or tides, which produces these currents, frequently gives to each of them a velocity and direction very different; that a north wind, for example, which should give the water one general motion towards the south, on the contrary, produces a number of currents, separated from each other, and very different both in extent and direction; some flowing towards the south, others south-east, and others south-west; some are very rapid, others slow; some long and broad, others short and narrow; in fact, their motions are so various that we have no idea left of their original cause. When a contrary wind succeeds, all these currents take an opposite course, and follow in a contrary direction, precisely in the same manner as would be the case upon land between two opposite and adjacent hills, provided it was covered with water, as is seen at the Maldiva and all the islands of the Indian seas, where the currents run, and the winds blow, for six months in a

contrary

contrary direction. The same remark has been made on currents between shoals and sand-banks. In general all currents, whether caused by the motion of flux or reflux, or the action by the wind, have the same extent and direction throughout their whole course, yet differ from each other in most respects, which can proceed only from the inequalities of the hills, mountains, and vallies, at the bottom of the sea, it being certain that the current between two islands follows the direction of the coasts; and the same is observable between banks of sand, shoals, &c. we must, therefore, look on the hills and mountains of the bottom of the sea as banks which direct the current; and hence a current is a river, the breadth of which is determined by that of the valley through which it flows: its rapidity depends on the force which produces it, combined with the breadth of the interval through which it must pass: and its direction is traced by the position of the hills and inequalities between which it must take its course.

We shall now give a reason for the singular correspondence between the angles of mountains and hills, which are to be met with in every part of the world. We have already

remarked

remarked that when a river, &c. forms an elbow, one of the borders forms on one side a projection inland, and the other forms a point from land, and that through all the sinuosities of their course this correspondence is always found. This fact is founded on the laws of hydrostatics. It would be easy to demonstrate the cause of this effect; but it is sufficient that it is general and universally known, and that all the world may be convinced of it by their own eyes, that when the banks of a river form a projection inland to the left hand, the other shore forms a projection from land to the right.

Hence the currents of the sea must be looked upon as great rivers, subject to the same laws as those on land, and will, like them, form in the extent of their course many sinuosities, whose projections or angles will correspond; and as the banks of currents are hills and mountains, above or below the surface of the water, they will have given these eminences the same form as is remarked on the shores of rivers; therefore we must not be astonished that our hills and mountains, which have been formerly covered by the sea, and formed by the sediments which the waters have left, should,

by

by the motion of its currents, have taken this
regular figure, and all the angles are alternately
opposite ; they have been the shores of the
currents or rivers of the sea, and have therefore
necessarily taken a figure and direction similar
to those of the shores of the rivers of the
earth.

This alone, independent of the other proofs
we have given, would be sufficient to evince
that the earth of our continent and islands have
been covered with waters of the ocean, and
doubtless throws great light upon the Theory
which I have endeavoured to prove well founded ; for it was not sufficient to have proved
that the strata of the earth were formed by the
sediments of the sea ; that the mountains were
elevated by the successive accumulation of such
sediments ; and that they were composed of
shells and other marine productions ; but it required also a reason why the angles of mountains so exactly correspond ; this could only be
done by an investigation into the real cause,
which had not hitherto been attempted, and
which, being united with the rest, forms a body
of proofs as complete as may be had in physics,
and establishes my Theory to be founded on
facts, independent of all hypothesis.

 M The

The principal currents of the ocean are those observed in the Atlantic Sea, near Guinea. They extend from Cape Verd to the Bay of Fernandes. Their motion is from west to east; that is contrary to the general motion of the sea. These currents are so rapid that vessels sail in two days from Moura to Rio de Benin, a course of 150 leagues; but they require six or seven weeks to return; nor would it be possible to get out of these climates if advantage was not taken of the tempestuous winds which suddenly rise in them; but there are entire seasons during which vessels cannot stir, the sea being continually calm, excepting what arises from the currents, which is always directed towards the coasts, and never extend more than 20 leagues from shore. Near Sumatra there are rapid currents, which flow from south to north, and which probably formed the gulph at Malacca. There are also considerable currents between Java and Magellan, the Cape of Good Hope, and the island of Madagascar, especially on the coast of Africa, between Natal and the Cape. In the Pacific Sea, on the coast of Peru, and the rest of America, the sea moves from south to north, and a south wind continually blowing there seems to be

the

the cause. The like motion is observed on the coasts of Brazil; from Cape St. Augustine to the Antilles; from the mouth of the Manilla strait to the Philippine islands; and in the port of Kubuxiu at Japan*.

There are violent currents in the sea adjacent to the Maldivian islands; and between those islands these currents flow, as already observed, constantly for six months from east to west, and during the other six months they follow the direction of the monsoons, and it is probable they are produced by those winds.

We speak here only of currents, whose extent and rapidity are very considerable, for in every sea there are an infinity of currents, though of no great importance. The flux and reflux, the winds, and all other causes which agitate the waters, produce currents, more or less perceptible, in different parts. We have observed that the bottom of the sea, like the surface of the earth, is overspread with mountains intersected with inequalities and divided by banks of sand. In all mountainous places currents will be violent; in all places where the bottom of the sea is level they will be almost imperceptible; the

M 2

rapidity

* See Varen. Geography, page 140.

rapidity of the current will increase in proportion to the obstacles the water meets with, or rather to the contraction of the spaces through which they incline to pass. Between two chains of mountains the current will be so much the stronger as the mountains are near. It will be the same between two banks of sand, or two neighbouring islands. It is also remarked in the Indian ocean, which is divided with an infinity of islands and banks, there are rapid currents throughout, which render the navigation of that sea dangerous.

It is not inequalities at the bottom of the sea alone which form currents, but the coasts themselves have a similar effect, as the water is repelled at greater or lesser distances: this repulsion of the waters is a kind of current which circumstances can render continual and violent; the oblique position of a coast, the vicinity of a bay, or of some great river, a promontory; in one word, every particular obstacle which opposes the general motion, will always produce a current. Now, as nothing is more irregular than the bottom and borders of the sea, we must cease from being surprised at the great number of currents which every where appear.

All

All currents have a determinate breadth, which depends on that of the interval between the two eminences which serves it for a bed. The currents flow into the sea as rivers flow on land, and they produce similar effects. They form their bed, and give to eminences corresponding angles. In one word, it is these currents which hollowed our vallies, formed our mountains, and gave to the surface of the earth, when it was under water, the form it now retains.

If any doubt of the correspondence of the angles of mountains remains, I appeal to the sight of every man who makes the observation. Every traveller, with the smallest attention, will perceive that the opposite sides of a hill exactly correspond. Whenever the hills to the right of the valley form a projection, those opposite recede to the left. These hills have also nearly the same elevation, and it is very rare to see any great inequality of height in the two hills separated by a valley. I can assert, that the more I have looked on the circumference and heights of hills, the more I have been convinced of the correspondence of the angles, and of the resemblance they have with the beds and borders of rivers; and it is by reiterated observations

observations on this surprising regularity and resemblance that my first ideas of this Theory of the Earth arose. Let us add to these observations that of the parallel and horizontal situation of the strata, that of the shells being dispersed throughout the earth, and incorporated in every matter; and it must be admitted, that on a subject like this we cannot have a greater degree of probability.

ARTICLE XIV.

OF REGULAR WINDS.

NOTHING can appear more irregular and variable than the force and direction of winds in our climates; but there are countries where this irregularity is not so great, and others where the winds constantly blow in one direction, and with almost the same degree of strength.

Although

Although the motion of the air depends on a great number of causes, there are nevertheless principal ones, of which it is difficult to estimate the effects, because of the modifications from secondary causes. The most powerful cause is the heat of the sun, which produces successively a considerable rarefaction in different parts of the atmosphere, and gives rise to an east wind that constantly blows between the tropics, where rarefaction is the greatest.

The force of the sun's attraction, and even that of the moon on the atmosphere, are inconsiderable in comparison with that just mentioned; it is true, this force produces in the air a motion similar to that of the flux and reflux in the sea, yet it must not be supposed that the air, because it has a spring, and is 800 times lighter than water, receives, by the action of the moon, a more considerable motion than that of the waters of the sea; for the distance of the moon being the same, a sea of any fluid matter will have nearly the same motion, because the force which produces it penetrates the matter, and is proportional to its quantity; thus a sea of water, air, or quicksilver, would elevate itself nearly to the same height, by the action of the sun and moon; hence we see that

the

the influence of the planets in the atmosphere
is not considerable, and although it must cause
a slight motion of the air from east to west,
this motion is insensible in comparison with
that produced by the heat of the sun ; but as
the rarefaction will be always greatest when the
sun is at the zenith, the current of air must
follow the sun, and form a constant wind from
east to west. This wind blows continually
over the sea in the torrid zone, and in most
parts of the land between the tropics ; it is this
wind we feel at the sun's rising ; and in general the east winds are more frequent and impetuous than the west ; this general wind from
east to west extends even beyond the tropics,
and blows so constantly in the Pacific Sea, that
vessels which sail from Acapulco to the Philippines, perform their voyage, which is more
than 2700 leagues, without any risque, and almost without any need of directing their course.
In the Atlantic, between Africa and Brazil,
this wind is also constant : it is felt also between the Philippines and Africa, but not in
so constant a manner, by reason of the islands,
and different obstacles that are met with in
that sea ; for during the months of January,
February, March, and April, it blows between

the

the Mozambique coast and India, but during the other months, it gives place to different winds: and although this east wind is less felt on the coasts than in the open sea, and still less in the middle of continents than on the coasts; nevertheless there are places where it blows almost continually, as on the east coasts of Brazil, on the coasts of Loango, in Africa, &c.

This east wind continually blowing under the line, is the cause, that sailing from Europe to America, the course of the vessel is directed from the north to the south, along the coasts of Spain and Africa, to within 20 degrees of the equator, where this east wind is met with, which carries them directly to the coasts of America. The voyage from Acapulco to the Philippine islands, is made in two months by the favour of this east wind: but the return from them to Acapulco is longer and more difficult. At 28 or 30 degrees on this coast from the line, the western wind is nearly as constant, which is the reason that vessels returning from the East Indies to Europe, do not follow the same track as in going; those from New Spain sail north along the coasts till they arrive at the Havannah, and from thence they continue northward, until they meet with the westerly winds which carry them to the Azores and afterwards to Spain. So likewise in the South Sea, those which return from the Philippines, or China, to Peru, or Mexico, sail north as far as Japan, and navigate under that parallel to a certain distance from California, from whence, coasting along New Spain, they arrive at Acapulco. These winds do not always blow from one point, but in general from the south-east from April to November, and from the north-east from November to April.

The east wind, by its action, increases the general motion of the sea from east to west; it also produces currents which are constant, some flowing from east to west, others from west to east; and from the east to the south-west or north-west, following the direction of the eminencies and chains of mountains at the bottom of the sea, the vallies that divide them serving as channels to these currents. The alternative winds which blow sometimes from the east, and sometimes from the south, produce also currents which change their direction at the same time with these winds.

The winds which blow continually for some months, are generally followed by contrary winds,

winds, and therefore mariners are obliged to wait for that which is favourable to their voyage. When these winds change, a calm or dangerous tempest generally ensues, and which continues for several days, sometimes a month, and has been known for more than two.

These general winds caused by the rarefaction of the atmosphere, are differently combined and modified by different causes in different climates. In that part of the Atlantic, under the temperate zone, the north wind blows almost constantly during the months of October, November, December, and January, which makes those months the most favourable to embark from Europe to India, in order to pass the line by the aid of these winds; and it is known by experience, that ships which quit Europe in the month of March frequently do not arrive sooner at Brazil than those which sail in the October following. The north wind almost continually reigns during winter in Nova Zembla, and other northern coasts. The south wind blows during the month of July at Cape de Verd, when the rainy season, or winter of these climates sets in. At the Cape of Good Hope the north-west wind blows during the month of September. At Patna,

in

in the East Indies, the north-west wind blows during the months of November, December, and January, and produces heavy rains; but the east wind blows during the other nine months. In the Indian ocean, between Africa and India, as far as the Malacca islands, the monsoons reign from east to west from January to the beginning of June, the west winds begin in the months of August or September; during the interval of June and July, there are dreadful tempests generally from the north winds; but on the coasts these winds vary much more than in the open sea.

In the kingdom of Guzarat, and on the coasts of the neighbouring sea, the north winds blow from March till September, and during the other months south winds almost always reign. The Dutch, to return from Java, generally set sail in the month of January or February, when they have the assistance of an easterly wind which is felt as far as the 18th degree of South latitude; afterwards they meet with the south winds which carry them to St. Helena *.

There are regular winds produced by the melting of snows, which the ancient Greeks

· have

* See Varen. Geography, gener. cap. 20.

have noticed. During summer a north-east
wind, and in winter one from the south-east,
were noticed in Greece, Thrace, Macedonia,
the Egean sea, and as far as Egypt and Africa;
the same kind of winds have been remarked
at Congo, at Guzarat, and at the extremity
of Africa, which are all produced by the melting of the snows. The flux and reflux of the
sea also produce regular winds which remain
only a few hours, and in many places winds
are observed to blow from the land during
night, and from the sea during the day, as on
the coasts of New Spain, Congo, the Havannah, &c.

The north winds are pretty regular in the
polar circles; but the nearer we approach the
equator, the weaker they become: a circumstance equally common to the two poles.

In the Atlantic and Ethiopian ocean within
the tropics there is an east wind which blows
all the year without any considerable variation,
excepting some few small places, where it
changes according to circumstances and the
position of the coasts. First, near the coasts
of Africa, having passed the Canary islands,
about the 28th degree of north latitude, a fresh
wind blowing from the north-east or north-

north-

north-east, is sure to be met with; this wind accompanies the vessels to the 10th degree of the same latitude; about 100 leagues from the coast of Guinea; where at the 4th degree north latitude they meet with calms and tornadoes. Secondly, in going to America by the Caribbee islands, this wind is found to veer more and more to the east, in proportion as they approach the coast. Thirdly, the limits of these variable winds in the Atlantic, are greater on the American coasts than on those of Africa. A south or south-west wind blows continually all along the coast of Guinea for a space of 500 leagues from Sierra Leona to the island of St. Thomas; the narrowest part of that sea is from Guinea to Brazil, being not more than 500 leagues across. Nevertheless, ships which sail from Guinea do not direct their course straight to Brazil, especially when they sail in the months of July and August, for the purpose of taking advantage of the south-east winds which reign at that time *.

In the Mediterranean the east wind blows from the land in the evening at the sun's setting, and the west wind from the sea at its rising in the morning. The south wind, which is commonly

monly

* See Abridg. Phil. Tran. vol. 11, page 129.

monly attended with rains, and which generally blows at Paris, Burgundy and Champagne about the beginning of November, gives place to mild and temperate breezes that produce that fair weather vulgarly called the summer of St. Martin's.

Doctor Lister pretends that the east wind that blows between the tropics all the year, is produced by the vapour of the plant called sea lentil, which is extremely plentiful in those climates, and that the difference of the winds on the land proceeds only from the different disposition of the trees and forests; and he very seriously gives this ridiculous imagination for a cause of the wind, by saying, that at noon the wind is strongest because the plants are hotter and respire the most, and that it blows from east to west, because all plants, somewhat like sun-flowers, turn and respire with the sun.

Other authors have mentioned the motion of the earth on its axis as the cause of this wind : this opinion is specious; and every person, even but little initiated in mechanics, must comprehend, that no fluid which surrounds the earth can have a particular motion from the rotation of the globe ; that the air can have no other motion than that of the earth,

and

and that all turning together at one time, this rotative motion must be as insensible in the atmosphere, as it is on the surface of the earth.

The principal cause of the winds, as we have observed, is the heat of the sun; on this subject we refer to Halley's Treatise in Phil. Trans. All causes which occasion rarefaction or condensation in the air will produce winds, whose directions will be opposite to the places where is the greatest rarefaction or condensation.

The pressure of the clouds, the exhalations of the earth, the inflammation of meteors, &c. are causes which also produce considerable agitations in the atmosphere. Each of these causes combining in different manners, produces different effects. It appears to me, therefore, a vain attempt to assign a theory of the winds, for which reason I shall limit myself to the study of their history.

If we could have a course of observations on the direction, power, and variation of the wind in different climates; if this course of observations was exact and extensive enough for us to perceive the result of these vicissitudes of the air in every country, we should arrive

at

at that degree of knowledge, from which at present we are very remote; but a short time has passed since meteorological observations have been made, and possibly much more will pass before we know how to employ the results of them, although they are the only means that we have to arrive at some positive knowledge on this subject.

On the sea the winds are more regular than on land, because the sea is an open space, in which nothing opposes their direction, while on land mountains, forests, and towns, form obstacles which change their course. Winds reflected by the mountains are often as impetuous as in their first direction: these winds are very irregular, because their course depends on the size, height, and situation of the mountains which reflect them. The sea winds blow with greater power than the land winds, are not so variable, and last longer. Land winds, however violent, have moments of remission, and sometimes of quiet, but at sea their currents are constant and continual, without any interruption.

In general on the sea the east wind, and those which come from the poles, are stronger than the west and those which proceed from the equator. On the land the west and south winds are more or less violent, according to the situation of the climates. In spring and autumn all winds are more violent than in summer or winter, and for these reasons; first, in spring and autumn are the highest tides, and consequently the winds that these tides produce are most violent at those seasons; secondly, the motion which the action of the sun and moon produce in the air is also greater in the season of the equinoxes; thirdly, the melting of the snows in spring, and the condensation of the vapours that the sun raises during summer, which refall in plentiful rains during autumn, produce, or at least increase the wind; fourthly, the change from heat to cold, or from cold to heat, cannot be made without increasing and diminishing consequently the volume of air, which alone must produce very high winds.

Contrary currents are often observed in the air; some clouds move in one direction, while others, which are higher or lower, move in a directly opposite one; but this contrariety of motion does not remain, being commonly produced by the resistance of some large clouds

that

that force the wind into another course, but which returns again as soon as the obstacle is dissipated.

The winds are more violent in mountainous places than in plains, and increase until we reach the common height of the clouds, that is to say, to about one quarter, or one third of a league perpendicular height; beyond that height the sky is generally serene, at least during the summer, and the wind gradually diminishing. It is even asserted to be quite insensible at the summit of the highest mountains; but these summits being covered with snow and ice, it is natural to suppose that this region of air is agitated by the wind when the snow falls, and only during summer that the winds are not to be perceived. In summer the light vapours which are raised above the summit of these mountains fall in the form of dew, whereas in winter they condense and fall in snow or ice, which in winter may raise considerable winds, even at that height.

A current of air increases in velocity where the space of its passage is straitened: the same wind which was moderate in an open plain becomes violent in passing through a narrow passage in a mountain, or between two

lofty

lofty buildings; and its most violent action is at the top of these structures or mountains, for air being compressed by these obstacles, its density and mass becomes increased, and as the velocity remains, the force or momentum of the wind naturally becomes much stronger. This is the cause that near a church or castle the winds seem to be stronger than at a distance from them. I have often remarked, that the wind reflected from a lone building is more violent than the direct wind which produced it. This can only be occasioned by the impelled air being compressed against the building, and by that means adds to its force.

The density of the air being greatest at the surface of the earth, we might be led to imagine that the greatest action of the wind should be there also; and I indeed think this is really the case when the sky is serene; but when it is covered with clouds, the most violent action of the wind is at the height of these clouds, which generally fall in rain or snow. The strength of the wind, therefore, must be estimated, not only by the velocity, but also by the density of the air; for it will often happen that one wind, which shall have no more velocity than another, will, nevertheless, root up trees and overturn buildings,

buildings, only from the air impelled by this wind being denser; and this evinces the imperfection of the machines invented to measure the velocity of the wind.

Particular winds, whether direct or reflected, are more violent than general ones. The interrupted action of land-winds depends on the compression of the air, which renders each blast much more violent 'than if the wind blowed uniformly. A strong continued wind never occasions such disasters as the rage of those produce which blow, as it were, by fits; but we shall give examples thereof in the following article.

We may consider the winds, and their directions, under general points of view, from which possibly we may derive useful instructions; for example, we might divide the winds into zones. The east wind, which extends to about 25 or 30 degrees on each side the equator, exerts its action round the globe in the torrid zone; the north wind almost always as constantly in the frigid zones. Therefore it may be said that the east wind occupies the torrid zone, the north wind the frigid zones, and with respect to the temperate zone, the winds which reign there are merely currents

of

of air produced by these two winds, whose direction tends to the eastern points. With respect to the westerly winds, which often reign in the temperate zones, both in the Pacific and Atlantic Oceans, they may be regarded as winds reflected by the lands of Asia and America, deriving their origin from the east and north winds.

Although we have said that, generally speaking, the east winds reign around the globe to about 25 or 30 degrees on each side the equator, it is nevertheless certain, that in some parts they do not extend so far, and their direction is not always from east to west, for on this side the equator it is east-north-east, and beyond the equator it is east-south-east, and the further we remove from the equator the more the direction is oblique. The equator is the line under which the direction of the wind from east to west is the most exact; for example, in the Indian ocean, the general wind from east to west scarcely extends beyond 15 degrees. Sailing from Goa to the Cape of Good Hope this wind is not felt till we have past the equator; but after arriving at the 12th degree south latitude, it continues to the 28th degree. In the sea which divides Africa from

America

America there is an interval from the 4th degree north latitude to the 10th or 11th degree south, where this general wind is not perceivable; but beyond the 10th or 11th degree it reigns as far as the 30th.

There is also much exception with regard to the trade winds, whose motion is alternative. Some remain a longer or a shorter time, others extend to greater or less distances; others are more or less regular, and more or less violent. Varenius speaks thus of a principal phenomena of these winds. " In the ocean between Africa and India, as far as the Malaccas, the east winds begin to reign in January and last to the beginning of June; in August or September the west winds begin and continue during three or four months. In the interval of these monsoons, that is from the end of June to the beginning of August, there is no wind on that sea, but they have violent storms which come from the north.

" These winds are subject to the greatest variations near the land, for ships cannot depart from the Malabar coast, nor other western ports on the coasts of the peninsula of India, to sail to Africa, Arabia, or Persia, but from January to April or May; for from the end of

May,

May, and during the months of June, July, and August, there are such violent tempests from the north or north-east that ships are not able to keep the sea. On the other side of this peninsula, in the sea which bathes the Coromandel coast, these tempests are not known.

" To sail from Java, Ceylon, and many other places, to the Malacca islands, the month of September is the most proper time, because the west wind begins to blow in these parts ; nevertheless, at 15 degrees south of the equator, we lose this west wind and meet with the general winds, which blow south-east. To sail from Cochin to Malacca they depart in March, because the west winds begin to blow at that time ; therefore these westerly winds blow at different times in different parts of the Indian sea ; and it is necessary to sail at different periods in going from Java to the Malaccas, from Cochin to Malacca, from Malacca to China, and from China to Japan.

" At Banda, the west winds finish at the end of March, calms reign during April, in May the east winds begin again with great violence. At Ceylon, the west winds begin about the middle of March, and remain till the beginning of October, when the east or rather north-

east

east wind returns. At Madagascar, from the middle of April to the end of May, the north and north-west winds are constant; but in February and March, the east and south winds reign. From Madagascar to the Cape of Good Hope, the north and collateral winds blow during March and April. In the Gulph of Bengal, the south wind prevails after the 20th of April, before which time the south-west or north-west winds are predominant. The west winds are also violent in the sea of China, in June and July, which is likewise the most suitable season to go from China to Japan; but to return from Japan to China, February and March are preferred, because the east or north-east winds prevail.

" There are winds which may be regarded as peculiar to certain coasts; for example, the south wind is almost continually on the coasts of Chili and Peru; it begins at the 46th degree south latitude, and extends beyond Panama, which renders the voyage from Lima to Panama much easier performed than the return. The west wind blows continually on the Magellanic coasts, and in the straits of Le Maire. The north and north-west winds almost continually reign on the Malabar coast. The

north-west wind is very frequent on the coast
of Guinea. The westerly winds reign on the
coasts of Japan, in the months of November and
December."

The alternative, or periodical winds, which
we have just been speaking of, are sea winds;
but there are also land winds which are periodical, and return either at a certain season,
or in certain days, or even at certain hours;
for example, on the Malabar coast, from September to April a land wind blows from the
eastern side; it generally commences at midnight, and finishes at noon, and is not felt beyond 12 or 15 leagues from the coast; and from
noon till midnight a gentle wind blows from
the west. On the coast of New Spain, in America, and on that of Congo, in Africa, land
winds reign during the night, and sea winds
during the day. At Jamaica the winds blow
from all parts of the coast at once during the
night, and therefore vessels cannot go in, nor
depart from it with safety, but in the day time.

In winter the port of Cochin is not to be
entered, nor can any vessel quit it, because the
winds blow with such impetuosity, that ships
cannot remain at sea; and besides the west
winds, which blow with such fury, bring to
                                        the

the mouth of the river so great a quantity of sand as prevents the possibility of ships of any size from entering it during six months of the year; but the east winds which blow during the other six months repel these sands, and render the entrance of the river free. At the strait of Babelmandel there are south-east winds which reign throughout the season, and are always succeeded by north-east. At St. Domingo there are two different winds which regularly rise almost every day, the one a sea wind proceeding from the east, and commences at 10 o'clock in the morning; the other a land wind comes from the west, rises at six or seven o'clock in the evening, and remains all night. There are many other facts of this nature to be extracted from travellers, the knowledge of which might perhaps lead to a history of the winds, which would be a useful work equally to navigation and physics.

ARTICLE

ARTICLE XV.

OF IRREGULAR WINDS, HURRICANES, AND OTHER
PHENOMENA, CAUSED BY THE AGITATION OF
THE SEA AND AIR.

THE winds are more irregular on the land than on the sea, and in high places than in low. The mountains not only alter the direction of winds, but even produce some which are either constant or variable according to different causes. The melting of snow upon the summits of mountains, generally produces constant winds, which sometimes remain a considerable time; the vapours that are stopt by mountains accumulate there, and produce variable winds, very frequent in all climates: and there are as many variations in the motions

of

of air, as there are inequalities on the surface of the earth. We can therefore give only examples, and relate circumstances which are attested; and as we are deficient in a course of observations on the variation of winds, and even of the seasons in different countries, we do not pretend to explain all the causes of these differences, but confine ourselves to those which appear the most probable.

In straits, on all projecting coasts, at the extremity of all promontories, peninsulas and capes, and in all narrow bays, storms are frequent; but without these there are some seas much more tempestuous than others. The Indian ocean, the Japan and the Magellan seas, that of the African coast beyond the Canaries, and on the other side towards the coast of Natal and the Red Sea, are very liable to storms. The Atlantic is more stormy than the ocean, which from its tranquillity is called the Pacific Sea; this sea, however, is not absolutely tranquil, except between the tropics, for the nearer we approach the poles, the more we are subject to variable winds, whose sudden changes are frequently the cause of tempests.

All

All continents are subject to variable winds, which often produce singular effects; in the kingdom of Cassimir, which is surrounded by the mountain of Caucasus, at the mountain Pirepinjale, extraordinary and sudden changes are experienced; we pass, in less than an hour's travelling, from summer to winter; at this place are two winds, a north and south, and which, according to Bernier, we successively feel in less than 200 feet distance from each other; the position of this mountain must be singular, and merit observation. In the peninsula of India, which is crossed from north to south by the mountains of Gate, it is winter on one side, and summer on the other at the same time. The like difference is met with on the two sides of Rozalgate Cape in Arabia; the sea to the north of the cape is perfectly tranquil, while in the south violent tempests are experienced. It is the same in the island of Ceylon; winter and high winds are experienced in the northern parts of the island, while in the southern there is fine summer weather. This contrariety of seasons at the same time not only happens in many parts of the Indian continent, but also in many islands; for example, at Cerem, a

long

long island in the vicinage of Amboyna, they have winter in the northern part, and summer at the same time in the southern, and the interval that divides the two seasons is not above three or four leagues.

In Egypt they have a south wind in summer, so hot as to prevent respiration, and raises such great quantities of sand, that the sky seems covered with thick clouds; this sand is so fine, and driven with such force, that it penetrates even into the closest chests. When these winds last many days they cause epidemical diseases, which are often followed by a great mortality. It seldom rains in Egypt, nevertheless every year there are some days of rain in the months of December, January, and February. Thick mists are more frequent there than rain, especially in the environs of Cairo; these mists begin in November, and continue all the winter; and during the whole year there falls so plentiful a dew, even when the sky is serene, that it might be taken for a slight rain.

In Persia winter begins in November and lasts till March: the cold is intense enough to form ice: much snow falls on the mountains, and often a little in the plains. From March

to

to May the winds blows with great violence, and bring heat with them. From May to September, the sky is serene, and the heat moderated by fresh breezes, which rise every evening and remain till morning. In autumn they have violent winds, like those of the spring; nevertheless, although these winds are very violent they scarcely ever produce tempests or hurricanes; but in summer there often arises along the Persian Gulph a very dangerous wind, called by the natives Samuel; it is still hotter and more terrible than that of Egypt. This wind is mortal, and acting like an inflamed vapour, it suffocates every person unfortunately enveloped within its vortex. In summer there also rises a wind of the same kind along the Red Sea, which suffocates men and cattle, and which conveys so great a quantity of sand that many persons conceive this sea will in time be choaked up with what falls therein. There are often clouds of sand in Arabia which darken the air and form dangerous whirlwinds. At Veru Cruz, when the hot north winds blow, the houses of the town are almost buried under the sand. In summer hot winds rise also at Negapatam, in the peninsula of India, likewise at Petapouli and Masulapatan.

patan. These burning winds, which destroy people, are fortunately of short duration, but they are very violent, and the greater swiftness they come with the more dreadful are their heats, whereas all other winds refresh so much the more as their velocity is greater. This difference proceeds from the degree of heat in the air, for while the heat of the air is not so great as that of the body of animals, the motion of the air is refreshing; but if the heat of the air exceeds that of the body, then its motion heats and burns. At Goa the winter, or rather the rainy and tempestuous season, is May, June, and July, and without which rains the heat would be perfectly unsupportable in that country.

The Cape of Good Hope is famous for its tempests, and the singular cloud which produces them. This cloud appears at first like a small round spot in the sky, called by the sailors the Ox's Eye. Probably its appearing so minute is owing to its exceeding great height.

Of all travellers who have spoken of this cloud, Kolbe appears to have the most examined it with attention; his words are, " The cloud seen on the mountains of the Table, or

of the Devil, or of the Wind, is composed, if I
am not deceived, of an infinity of small particles, impelled first against the mountains of the
Cape towards the east, by the easterly wind
which blows during almost the whole year in the
torrid zone; these particles are stopt in their
course by these high mountains, and collect on
their eastern side; they then become visible and
form these assemblages of clouds, which being
incessantly driven by the east wind, rise to the
summit of these mountains; they do not long
remain there at rest, but being obliged to advance,
they ingulph themselves between the hills before
them, where they are bound and confined as in
a canal; the wind presses them from above, and
the opposite sides of the two mountains retain
them in a direct line: in advancing they arrive
at the foot of a mountain, where the country is
a little more open, they then expand, and become
again invisible; but they are shortly driven
against other mountains, by clouds which are
behind them, and thus proceed with much impetuosity, until they arrive at the highest mountains of the Cape, which are those of the Wind,
or Table, where they have to encounter a wind
blowing in an exact contrary direction; this
occasions a dreadful conflict, for the vapours

being

being impelled behind and repelled before, produce horrible whirlwinds either on the high mountains of the Table, or adjacent vallies. When the north-west wind yields, the south-east increases and continues to blow with more or less violence for six months, it reinforces itself while the cloud of the Ox's Eye is thick, because the vapours collected behind press forward, and it diminishes as soon as its thickness is lessened, because there are fewer particles and less pressure, and it is entirely lowered when the Ox's Eye is no longer apparent, because no new or not sufficient vapours any longer come from the east.

" All the circumstances attending this phenomenon lead to an hypothesis, which well explains every part of them: First, behind the mountain of the Table we remark a train of light white mists, which commencing on the eastern descent of this mountain, incline to the sea, and occupy the mountains of Stone throughout all their extent; I have often contemplated this train, which according to my opinion was caused by the rapid passage of the vapour abovementioned, from the mountains of Stone to that of the Table.

Q 2   " Secondly,

" Secondly, These vapours must be extremely embarrassed in their road, by the frequent
shocks and counter shocks caused, not only by
the mountains, but also by the south and east
winds which reign at places circumjacent to
the Cape : I have already spoken of the two
mountains called Hanging Lip and Norvege,
situate on the points of False Bay ; when the
particles which I conceive are impelled on these
mountains by the easterly winds, they are repelled from them by the south, which carry
them on the neighbouring mountains ; they are
stopt there and appear like clouds, which is
often the case upon the mountains of False Bay.
These clouds are frequently very thick above
the land which the Dutch are in possession of,
on the mountains of Stenltenborch, of Draken-
stein, and Stone, but particularly on the mountains of the Table, and of the Devil.

" In short, what confirms me in my opinion
is, that constantly two or three days before the
south-east wind blows on the Lion's Head,
small black clouds are perceived above it ; these
clouds, according to my opinion, are composed
of the particles or vapours which I have spoken
of.   If the north-west wind prevails when they

arrive

arrive there, they are stopped in their course, but are never driven to a great distance till the south-east winds commence."

The first mariners who approached the Cape of Good Hope were ignorant of the effects of these clouds, which appear to form in the air so slowly, and without any motion, but which in a moment excite the most dreadful storms that precipitate the largest vessels to the bottom of the sea. In the country of Natal, a small cloud similar to the Ox's Eye at the Cape, produces the like effects. In the sea between Africa and America, especially near the equator, these kind of tempests very often arise. Near the coast of Guinea, three or four of these storms sometimes happen in a day; they are also caused and announced by small black clouds; the rest of the sky being generally serene, and the sea perfectly calm. The first blast which issues from these clouds is furious, and would sink ships in open sea, if they did not take the precaution to furl the sails. It is principally in April, May, and June these tempests are experienced on the coast of Guinea, because no regular wind blows there. The stormy season on the coasts of Loango is in January, February, March, and April. On the other side of Africa,

at

at Cape of Gardafu, these kinds of tempests rise
in May, and the clouds which produce them are
generally in the north like those of the Cape of
Good Hope.

All these tempests are produced by winds
which issue from a cloud, and which have directions either from north to south, or north-
east to south-west, &c. but there are other
kinds which are still more violent, and in
which the winds seem to proceed from every
quarter at once; they have a whirling motion,
which nothing can resist. A calm generally
precedes these horrible tempests; but in an
instant the fury of the winds raises the waves as
high as the clouds. There are parts of the
sea which cannot be approached, from there
being constantly calms and hurricanes in them.
The Spaniards have called these places Calms
and Tornados; the most considerable are near
Guinea, at two or three degrees north latitude;
they are 300 or 350 leagues in length by as
many in breadth, which forms a space of more
than 100,000 leagues square.

When contrary winds come all at once in
the same place, as to a centre, they produce
whirlwinds by the contrariety of their motions;
but when these winds meet with others in opposition,

position, which counterbalance their action, they then revolve in a considerable circle, and occasion a dead calm, through which it is impossible for vessels to make their way. These places of the sea are marked in Senex's globes. I am inclined to think that the contrariety of the winds alone could not produce this effect if the direction of the coasts, and the particular form of the bottom of the sea, did not contribute thereto. I imagine that the currents caused by the winds, but directed by the form of the coasts and the inequalities of the bottom of the sea, end at these places, and that their opposite and contrary direction, in a plain surrounded on all sides by a chain of mountains, is the real cause of these tornados.

Whirlpools appear to be no other than the eddies of the water formed by the action of two or more opposite currents. The Euripus, so famous for the death of Aristotle, alternately absorbs and rejects the water seven times in twenty-four hours. This whirlpool is near the Grecian coast. The Charybdis, which is near the straits of Sicily, rejects and absorbs the water thrice in twenty-four hours. We are not quite certain as to the number of alternative motions in these whirlpools. Doctor Placentia,

centia, in his treatise, says, that the Euripus has irregular motions for eighteen or nineteen days every month, and regular ones for the other eleven; that in general it swells about one foot, and seldom two: he says likewise that authors do not agree as to the tides of the Euripus; that some assert it is twice, some seven, others fourteen times in twenty-four hours, but that Loirius having examined it attentively, observed it rose regularly every six hours, and with so violent a motion, that it was sufficient to turn the wheel of a mill.

The greatest known whirlpool is that in the Norway sea, which is affirmed to be upwards of twenty leagues in circumference. It absorbs for six hours water, whales, ships, and every thing that comes near it, and afterwards returns them in the same quantity of time as it drew them in.

It is not necessary to suppose there are holes and abysses in the bottom of the sea which swallow up the waters continually; to assign a reason for whirlpools, it is well known that when water has two contrary directions, the combination of these motions produce a whirling, and seem to form a void place in the centre. It is the same with respect to whirl-

pools

pools in the sea, they are produced by two or three contrary currents; and as the flux and reflux, which run every six hours in contrary directions, are the principal cause of currents, it is not astonishing that whirlpools, which result from them, attract and swallow up all that surrounds them, and afterwards reject all they have absorbed in the same portion of time.

Whirlpools, therefore, are produced by opposite currents, and likewise by the meeting of contrary winds. These whirlwinds are common in the sea of China and Japan, near the Antilles, and in many other parts of the sea, particularly near projecting lands and high coasts; but they are still more frequent upon land, and their effects are sometimes prodigious. " I have seen," says Bellarmin, " an " enormous ditch dug up by the wind, and the " earth thereof carried to a distance; so that " the place from whence it had been taken ap- " peared a frightful hole, and the village upon " which it was dropped was entirely buried " with it."

In the history of the French Academy, and in the Philosophical Transactions, are the detail of the effects of many hurricanes, which appear inconceivable and scarcely credible, if the facts were not attested by a great number of intelligent testimonies.

It is the same with respect to water-spouts, which mariners never see without fear and amazement; these are very frequent near certain coasts of the Mediterranean, especially when the sky is cloudy and the wind blows at the same time from various coasts. They are more common near the coasts of Laodicea, Grecgo and Carmel, than in other parts of the Mediterranean. Most of them are large cylinders of water which fall from the clouds, although it appears, when we are at some distance, that the water of the sea rises up to the clouds.*

But there are two kinds of water-spouts, the first of which, alluded to above, is no other than a thick compressed cloud, reduced to a small space by contrary winds, which, blowing at the same time from many corners, give it a cylindric form, and causes the water to fall by its own weight. The quantity of water is so great, and the fall so sudden and precipitate, that if unfortunately one of these spouts breaks on a vessel, it shatters it to pieces and sinks it in an instant. It is asserted, and possibly with foundation, that these spouts may be broken
and

* See Shaw's Travels, vol. 2. p. 56.

and destroyed by the commotion which the firing of cannons excites in the air; which answersto the effect of dispersing thunder-clouds by the ringing of bells.

The other kind of water-spout is called a typhon, which many authors have confounded with the hurricane, in speaking of the storms of the Chinese sea, which is in fact subject to both. The typhon does not descend from the clouds, but rises up from the sea with great violence. By whirlwinds, sands, earth, houses, trees, and animals, are raised in the air, and transported to different parts ; but typhons, on the contrary, remain in the same place, and can only have subterraneous fires for their origin ; for the sea is then in the greatest agitation, and the air so strongly filled with sulphurous exhalations, that the sky appears covered with a copper-coloured crust, although there are no clouds, and the sun or stars may be seen through the vapour. It is to these subterraneous fires the warmth of the sea of China in winter must be attributed, as these typhons are there very frequent.*

Thevenot, in his voyage to the Levant, says, " we saw water-spouts in the Persian gulph,

R 2

between

---

* See Acta Eud. Lips. Supplementum, vol. 1. p. 405.

between the islands Quesomo, Lareca, and Ormutz. I think few people have considered water-spouts with so much attention as I have done. I shall mention my remarks with all possible simplicity, in order to render them plain and easy to be comprehended.

" The first that we saw appeared on the northern coast, between us and the island Quesomo, about a gun-shot from the ship: we directly perceived the water boiled on the surface of the sea, and was raised about a foot: it was whitish, and the top appeared like a thick black smoke, so that it properly resembled some burning straw, which only smoked. It made a noise like a torrent that runs with rapidity into a deep valley. This noise was mixed with another, similar to the hissing of serpents: a little afterwards we perceived something like a dark pipe, which resembled smoke ascending towards the clouds, turning round with great velocity: this appeared about the thickness of my finger, and the same noise still continued. After this it disappeared, having remained somewhat less than a quarter of an hour. This over, we perceived another on the south side, which began in the same manner as the preceding:

directly

directly after a third made its appearance on
the west, and then a fourth by its side. The
farthest of them was not more than a musket-
shot from us. They all appeared like burning
heaps of straw, a foot and a half or two feet
high, and were attended with the same noise as
the first. We afterwards saw three pipes or
canals descending from the clouds to the water.
They were broad at the top and lessened down-
wards, something in the shape of a trumpet,
or as the paps of an animal, drawn perpendicularly down by a heavy weight. These canals
appeared of a darkish white, occasioned, as I
think, by the waters which were in them; for
apparently they were formed before the water
entered, as when they were empty they were
no longer to be seen, like as a clear glass tube
placed at some distance before our eyes, is not
perceptible if it is not filled with some coloured
liquor. These pipes were not strait but crooked
in some places; they were not even perpendicular, but from the clouds, where they were
joined, to the parts which drew in the water,
they were very much bent; and what is more
particular, the cloud, to which the second of
the three was fastened, having been driven by
the wind, this pipe followed it without break-

ing

ing or quitting the place where it drew in the water, and passing behind the first, they had for some time the form of St. Andrew's cross. At the beginning neither of them was more than an inch in thickness, excepting just at the top, but afterwards the first of the three increased considerably. The two others scarcely remained longer than that which we saw on the north side. The second, on the south side, remained about a quarter of an hour, but the first on that side remained longer, and gave us some apprehensions. At first it was not bigger than my finger, afterwards it swelled as thick as my arm, then as my leg, and at last as the trunk of a large tree, which a man might encompass with both his arms. We distinctly perceived water through this transparent body, which ascended in a serpentine manner. Sometimes it diminished in size at the top, and sometimes at the bottom, then it exactly resembled a tube with some fluid matter pressed with the fingers, either above to make this liquor descend, or at bottom to cause it to ascend; and I am persuaded that it was the violence of the wind which caused these changes, pressing the pipe in a similar manner. After this it diminished less than my arm, then

returned

returned as large as my thigh, and then again became very small; at last I saw the water that was raised from the surface began to lower, and the end of the pipe divided from it, when, by the change of light from a cloud, it was lost to our sight; I continued, however, to observe whether it returned, because I had remarked that the pipe of the second had appeared to be broken in the middle, and directly after we saw it whole. This we found was occasioned by the light which hid the half from us, but the last we saw no more.

" These water-spouts are very dangerous, for if they fall on a vessel they entangle in the sails so much that sometimes they raise it up, and afterwards let it fall with such violence as to sink it; at least if they do not lift the vessel up, they tear all the sails, or let the water they contain fall on it, and which often sinks it to the bottom. There cannot be the least doubt but it is by similar accidents that many ships, of which we have heard no accounts, have been lost, since there are but few examples of those that we have known, from certainty, to have perished in this manner."

I suspect there are many optical illusions in the above account, but I have recounted them as related, in order that we might compare them with those of other travellers. The following description is by M. Gentil, in his voyage round the world. " At eleven o'clock in the morning, the air being filled with clouds, we perceived about our vessel, at a quarter of a mile distant, six water-spouts, which made a noise similar to that of water flowing in sub-terraneous canals, and increased until it resembled the whistling which an impetuous wind makes among the cordage of a ship. We at first observed the water to boil up about a foot and a half above the surface. Above this boiling there appeared a mixed or rather a thick smoke, which formed a kind of canal, that ascended to the clouds. These canals inclined according as the wind moved the clouds to which they were attached, and in spite of the wind's impulsion they not only adhered to them, but even lengthened and shortened themselves in proportion as the clouds rose higher or lower in the atmosphere.

" These phenomena terrified us greatly, and our sailors, instead of being bolder, fomented their fears by the dismal tales they told each other. If these spouts, said they, fall on our vessel, they will lift her up, and then she will

sink

sink by the violence of her fall. Others con-
tended in a decisive tone, that they would not
raise the vessel up, but if they met it in their
course, being full of water, the ship would
break the communication they had with the sea,
and the whole body of the water would fall perpendicularly on the deck of the vessel and split
her to pieces.

" To prevent this misfortune the cannon
was loaded, the sailors pretending the report of
a cannon, by agitating the air, dissipated these
phenomena ; but we had no need of having recourse to this remedy, for when they had run
about ten minutes about the ship, some at a
quarter of a league, others at a less distance,
we perceived the canals to grow narrower by
degrees, till they got loose from the surface of
the sea and then dissipated."

It appears from the description given by
these two travellers, that water-spouts are produced, at least in part, by the action of a fire
or smoke which rises from the bottom of the
sea with great force, and that they are quite
different from those produced by contrary
winds.

" The water-spouts, says Mr. Shaw, which
I had an opportunity of seeing, appeared as so

many cylinders of water, which fell from the clouds, although by the reflection of the columns which descend, or by the drops which detach themselves from the water they contain, it sometimes seems, especially when we are at some distance, that the water is drawn up from the sea. To render a reason for this phenomena we may suppose that the clouds being collected in one part by opposite winds, they force them by pressing them with violence to condense and descend in this manner."

There still remain many facts to be acquired before we can give a complete explanation of these phenomena; it appears to me, that if there are under the waters of the sea, at particular places, soils mixed with sulphur, bitumen, and minerals, these matters may be inflamed and produce a great quantity of air, which being newly generated and prodigiously rarefied, ascends with rapidity, and may raise these water-spouts from the sea to the sky; so likewise if, by inflammation, the sulphurous matters which a cloud contains, a current of air is formed, which descends perpendicularly from the clouds towards the sea, all its water may follow the current of air, and form a water-spout which will fall from the sky upon

the

the sea ; but it must be allowed that the explanation of this kind of water-spout, no more than that we have given of those produced by contrary winds, is not satisfactory ; and it might be asked why these kinds of water-spouts, which fall perpendicularly from the clouds, are not as often seen on the land as on the sea ?

The History of the Academy, anno 1727, mentions a land water-spout which appeared at Capestan, near Beziers; it descended from a cloud like a black pillar, which diminished by degrees, and at length terminated in a point upon the surface of the earth. It obeyed the wind which blew from west to south-west. It was accompanied with a very thick smoke, and made a similar noise to that of a troubled sea. It tore up and carried away trees to the distance of forty or fifty feet, marking its way by a large track, on which three carriages might have passed each other. There appeared another pillar of the same kind, but which soon joined the first; and after the whole had disappeared, a great quantity of hail fell on the earth.

This kind of water-spout appears to be still different from the other two : it is not mentioned to have contained water ; and it seems, by what I have related, and by the explanation

S 2

given

given thereof by M. Andoque, to the academy, that this water-spout was only a whirlwind, rendered visible by the dust and condensed vapours which it contained.

In the same history, anno 1741, a water-spout is spoken of, seen on the lake of Geneva; the upper part was inclined to a very black cloud, and the lower, which was narrower, terminated a little above the water. This phenomenon remained only a few minutes, and, at the moment it was dissipated, a thick vapour was perceived at the part where it first appeared; the waters of the lake boiled and seemed to make an effort to rise up. The air was very calm during the whole time; and when it disappeared neither wind nor rain ensued. "After all we are acquainted with," says the historian of the academy, "concerning water-spouts, is not this another proof that they are not formed by the conflict of the winds, but almost always produced by volcanos or subterraneous vapours, from which we know the bottom of the sea is not exempt? Whirlwinds and hurricanes, which we commonly thought to be the cause of these appearances, may possibly be only the effect, or an accidental event thereof."

ARTICLE

ARTICLE XVI.

OF VOLCANOS AND EARTHQUAKES.

THE burning mountains, called volcanos, contain in their bowels, sulphur, bitumen, and other matters of an inflammable nature, the effects of which are more violent than that of gunpowder, or even thunder, and have from the earliest ages terrified mankind, and desolated the country. A volcano is an immense cannon, whose orifice is often more than half a league: from this wide mouth are vomited forth torrents of smoke and flames, rivers of bitumen, sulphur, and melted metals, clouds of cinders and stones, and sometimes it ejects enormous rocks to many leagues distance, which human powers united could not move; the conflagration is so terrible, and the quantity of burnt, melted,

calcined,

calcined, and vitrified matters which the mountain throws out, is so great, that they destroy cities and forests, cover fields an hundred and two hundred feet in thickness, and sometimes form hills and mountains, which are only heaps of these matters piled up together. The action of this fire, and the force of its explosion, is so violent, that it produces by its re-action, succussions which shake the earth, agitate the sea, overthrow mountains, and destroy the most solid towers and edifices, even to very considerable distances.

These effects, although natural, have been looked upon as prodigies; and although we see in miniature, by fire, effects nearly similar to those of volcanos, yet there is something in grandeur, of whatever nature it may be, that invariably strikes the imagination and influences the mind, and therefore I am not surprised that some authors have taken them for the vents of a central fire, and ignorant people for the mouths of Hell. Astonishment produces fear, and fear is the mother of superstition. The natives of Iceland imagine the roarings of the volcano are the cries of the damned, and its eruptions the effects of the rage of devils, and the despair of the wretched.

All

All its effects, however, arise from fire and smoke : veins of sulphur, bitumen, and other inflammable matters, are found in the bowels of mountains, as well as minerals and pyrites, which ferment when exposed to air or humidity, and cause explosions proportionate to the quantity of inflamed matters. This is the just idea of a volcano, and it is easy for a philosopher to imitate the action of these subterranean fires ; for by mixing together a quantity of brimstone and iron filings, and burying them in the earth to a certain depth, a small volcano may be produced, whose effects will be exactly similar ; for this mixture inflames by fermentation, throws off the earth and stones with which it is covered, and smokes, flames, and explodes like a real volcano.

In Europe are three famous volcanos, Mount Ætna, in Sicily, Mount Hecla, in Iceland, and Mount Vesuvius, near Naples, in Italy. Mount Ætna has burnt from time immemorial, its eruptions are very violent, and the quantity of matter it throws out is so great that after digging 68 feet deep, marble pavements, and the vestiges of an ancient town have been found buried under this thickness of matter, in the same manner as the city of Herculaneum has

been

been covered by the matter thrown out from Vesuvius. New mouths in Ætna were opened in 1650, 1669, and at other times. We see the flame and smoke of this volcano from Malta, about 60 leagues distance; it smokes continually, and there are times when it vomits flames, stones, and matters of every kind with impetuosity. In 1537, there was an eruption of this volcano, which caused an earthquake in Sicily that continued for 12 days, and which overthrew a number of houses and public structures; it ceased by the opening of a new mouth, the lava from which burnt every thing within five leagues of the mountain. The cinders thrown out by the volcano were so abundant, and ejected with so much force, that they were driven as far as Italy; and vessels at some distance from Sicily were incommoded by them. Farelli says the foot of this mountain is 100 leagues in circumference.

This volcano has now two principal mouths, one narrower than the other; smoke comes continually from them, but flames never issue but during the time of eruptions; it is pretended that large stones have been thrown out by them to the distance of 60,000 feet.

In

In 1683 a violent eruption caused a terrible earthquake in Sicily; it entirely destroyed the town of Catanea, and killed more than 60,000 persons in that town, besides those which were destroyed in the neighbouring towns and villages.

Hecla throws out its fires through the ice and snow of a frozen land; its eruptions are nevertheless as violent as those of Ætna, and other volcanos of southern countries. It throws out cinders, lava, pumice stones, and sometimes boiling water: it is not inhabitable within six leagues of this volcano, and the whole island of Iceland is very abundant in sulphur. The history of the violent eruptions of Hecla are recorded by Dithmar Bleffken.

Mount Vesuvius, according to the historians, did not begin burning till the seventh Consulate of Titus Vespasian and Falvius Domitian; the top being opened, it at first threw out stones and rocks, afterwards fire and lava, which burnt two neighbouring towns, and emitted such thick smoke that it obscured the light of the sun. Pliny the elder, desirous of examining this conflagration nearer, was suffocated by the smoke.*

VOL. II.   T   Dion

* See the Epistle of Pliny, jun. to Tacitus.

Dion Cassius relates, that this eruption was so violent, that cinders and sulphurous smoke were driven as far as Rome, and even beyond the Mediterranean into Africa. Heraclea was one of the two towns burned by this first conflagration of Vesuvius, which in these latter times has been discovered at more than 60 feet deep, the surface above which was become, by length of time, arable land and fit for culture. The relation of the discovery of Heraclea is in the hands of the public, and we can only wish that some person, versed in Natural History, would examine the different matters which compose this soil of 60 feet, attending to their disposition and situation, the alterations they have produced or suffered, the direction they have taken, and the hardness they have acquired.

There is an appearance that Naples is situate on a hollow ground, filled with burning materials, for Vesuvius and Solfatera seem to have interior communications. When Vesuvius casts out lava Solfatera emits flames, and when the one ceases the other is extinguished. The city of Naples is situate nearly between them.

One

One of the last and most violent eruptions of Mount Vesuvius was in the year 1737.* The mountain vomited, by several mouths, large torrents of burning metallic matters, which dispersed themselves over the country, and flowed into the sea. Mons. Montealegre, who communicated this relation to the Academy of Sciences, observed, with horror, one of these rivers of fire, whose length, from the mountain to the sea, was about seven miles, its breadth about 60 feet, its depth 25 or 30 palms, and in bottoms or vallies 120: the matter which flowed was like the scum which issues from the furnace of a forge, &c.†

In Asia, particularly in the islands of the Indian ocean, there are many volcanos; one of the most famous is Mount Albours, near Mount Taurus, eight leagues from Herat; its summit continually smokes, and it frequently throws out flames and burning matter in such quantities that the surrounding country is covered with cinders. In the island of Ternate there is a volcano which throws out matter

T 2 like

* It should be remembered, as noticed by Mr. Smellie, that the original of this work was published by our author in 1749, since when Vesuvius has undergone several eruptions.

† See the Hist. Acad. an. 1737.

like pumice-stones. Some travellers assert
that this volcano is most furious at the time of
the equinoxes, because certain winds then reign
there, which inflame the matter that feeds, and
has fed this fire for a number of years.*

The island of Ternate is but seven leagues
round, and is only the summit of a mountain;
it gradually ascends from the shore to the
middle of the island, where the volcano rises
to a considerable height, to the top of which
it is very difficult to attain. Many rills of
sweet water descend along the ridge of this
mountain, and when the air is calm, and the
season mild, this burning gulph is in less agitation than during storms and high winds.†
This confirms what I have said in a former
article, and seems to prove that the fire of
volcanos does not proceed from any considerable depth, but from the top, or at least not
far distant from the summit of the mountain;
for if it was not so, the high winds could not
increase their combustion. There are other
volcanos in the Malaccas. In one of the
Mauritius islands, 70 leagues from the Malaccas, there is a volcano, whose effects are as

violent

* See Argensola's Travels, vol. 1, page 21.
† See the Travels of Schuten.

violent as those of Mount Ternate. Sorca island, one of the Malaccas, was formerly inhabited. In the middle of this island there is a lofty mountain, with a volcano at the top. In 1693 this volcano vomited bitumen and inflamed matters in such a great quantity as to form a burning lake, and which covered the whole island.*

At Japan, and in the adjacent islands, there are several volcanos, which emit flames during the night and smoke in the day. At the Philippine islands there are also burning mountains. One of the most famous volcanos of the islands in the Indian ocean, and the most recent, is that near the town of Panarucan, in the island of Java; it opened in 1586, and at the first eruption, it threw out an enormous quantity of sulphur, bitumen, and stones. The same year Mount Gounapi, in the island of Banda, which continued only seventeen years, opened and ejected, with a frightful noise, rocks and matters of every kind. There are also some other volcanos in India, as at Sumatra, and in the north of Asia, but those are not considerable.

In

* See Phil. Trans. ab. vol. II page 391.

In Africa, there is a mountain, or rather a cavern, called Beniguazeval, near Fez, which always emits smoke, and sometimes flames. One of the islands of Cape de Verd, called the Fuogo, is only a large mountain which burns continually; this volcano throws out cinders and stones; and the Portuguese, who have attempted several times to erect habitations in this island, have been constrained to abandon the project through dread of the volcano. The Peak of Teneriffe, considered as one of the highest mountains of the earth, throws out fire, cinders, and large stones; from its top rivulets of melted sulphur flow across the snow, where it forms veins that are distinguishable at a great distance.

In America there are a great number of volcanos, particularly in the mountains of Peru and Mexico; that of Arequipa is one of the most famous; it often causes earthquakes, which are more common in Peru than in any other country in the world. The volcano of Carrappa and that of Malahallo are, according to the report of travellers, the most considerable, next to that of Arequipa; but there are many others in these parts of which we have no exact knowledge. M. Bouguer, in his voyage to Peru,

published

published in the Memoirs of the Academy of the year 1744, mentions two volcanos, called Cotopaxi and Pichincha ; the first at some distance from, the other near the town of Quito ; he was witness of a conflagration of Botopaxi in 1742, and of the orifice which was made in that mountain ; this eruption did no other damage than melting the snow and producing such torrents of water, that in less than three hours inundated a tract of country 18 leagues in extent, and overthrew all they met with in their way.

At Mexico the most considerable volcanos are Popochampeche, and the Popoatepec; it was near this last that Cortes passed in his voyage to Mexico ; some of the Spaniards ascended to the top, where they saw the mouth, which was about half a league in circumference. Sulphurous mountains are also met with at Guadaloupe, Tercera, and other islands of the Azores ; and, if we were to consider as volcanos all those mountains which smoke, or emit flames, we might reckon more than sixty; we have only spoken of those formidable volcanos, near which no person dares to inhabit.

These volcanos which are in such great numbers in the Cordeliers, as I have formerly said, cause almost continual earthquakes, which prevent

vent the natives from building with stone above one story high, and to construct the upper stories of their houses with reeds and light wood. In these mountains are also many precipices and large vents, the sides of which are black and burnt, as in the precipice of Mount Ararat, in Armenia, which is called the Abyss; these abysses are the mouths of extinguished volcanos.

There was lately an earthquake at Lima, the effects of which were dreadful. The town of Lima and Port Callao were almost entirely swallowed up; but the evil was still greater at Callao. The sea rose and covered every building in that town, drowned all the inhabitants, and left only one single tower remaining. Of twenty-five ships that were in this port, four were carried a league upon land, and the rest were swallowed up by the sea. At Lima, which was a large town, there remains only twenty-seven houses standing; a great number of persons were buried in the ruins, particularly monks and religious persons, as their buildings were higher and constructed of more solid materials than the other houses. This misfortune happened at night, in October 1746; the shock remained fifteen minutes.

There

There was formerly near the port of Pisca, in Peru, a famous city, situate on the sea shore, which was almost entirely destroyed by an earthquake that happened the 19th of October 1682, for the sea having extended beyond its common bounds, swallowed up this unfortunate place with every person that was in it.

If we consult historians and travellers, we shall find relations of many earthquakes and eruptions of volcanos, whose effects have been as terrible as those we have just mentioned. Pesidonius, whom Strabo quotes in his first book, relates, that a city in Phœnicia, near Sidon, was swallowed up by an earthquake, with the neighbouring territory, and even two thirds of Sidon ; this effect was not so sudden but that many of the inhabitants had time to avoid it by flight. This shock extended throughout all Syria, and as far as the Cyclade islands, and into Eubœa, where the fountains of Arethusa suddenly stopped, and did not re-appear for many days after, and then by many new springs remote from the old ones; that this earthquake did not cease from shaking the island, sometimes in one part and sometimes in another, until the earth opened in the valley of Lepanta, and ejected a great quantity of

lava and other inflamed matters. Pliny, in
his first book, chap. 84, relates, that in the
reign of Tiberius an earthquake happened
which overthrew twelve towns in Asia : and in
his second book he mentions a prodigy caused
by an earthquake. St. Augustin records, that
by a great earthquake there were towns overthrown in Lybia. In the time of Trajan, the
town of Antioch, and a great part of the adjacent country were swallowed up by an earthquake; and in the time of Justinian, in 528,
it was a second time destroyed by the same
cause, with upwards of 40,000 of its inhabitants. Sixty years after, in the time of St.
Gregory, it felt the effects of a third earthquake, when 60,000 of its inhabitants perished.
In the time of Saladin, in 1182, most of the
towns of Syria and Judea were destroyed by
the same calamity. In Calabria and Apulia,
there have been more earthquakes than in any
other part of Europe. In the time of Pope
Pius II. all the churches and palaces of Naples
were overthrown, and above 30,000 of its inhabitants killed; the remainder were obliged to
live in tents till houses were built. In 1629,
there were earthquakes in Apulia, which destroyed 7000 persons, and in 1638, the town

of

of St. Euphemia was swallowed up, and there remains only a stinking lake in its place. Ragusa and Smyrna, at the same time, were also almost destroyed. There was an earthquake in 1692, which extended into England, Holland, Flanders, Germany, and France; it was chiefly felt on the sea coasts and near large rivers; it shook at least 2600 square leagues; it lasted only two minutes, and the motion was more considerable on mountains than in vallies.* On the 10th of July, 1688, there was an earthquake at Smyrna, which began by a motion from west to east; the castle was at first overthrown, its four walls being divided and sunk six feet in the sea; this castle stood upon an isthmus, but is at present a real island, about 100 paces distant from the land. The walls from east to west are fallen down, those from north to south are yet standing; the city, which is ten miles from the castle, was destroyed shortly after; in many places the earth opened, and subterraneous noises were heard; five or six shocks were felt as night came on, the last continued only half a minute; the ships in the roads were shaken; the ground of the town was lowered about two feet; not

U 2

above

* See Ray's Discourses, page 272.

above a quarter of the town withstood the shock, and those principally the houses which stood on rocks; from 15 to 20,000 persons are computed to have been buried under the ruins.* In 1695, an earthquake was felt at Bologna, in Italy, and it was remarked as a particular circumstance, that the water was much troubled a day before.†

At Tercera there happened an earthquake on the 4th of May, 1614, which overthrew in the town of Angra eleven churches and nine chapels, besides private houses; and in the town of Praya it was so terrible, that scarcely an house was left standing. On the 16th of June 1628, there was an earthquake in the island of St. Michael, the effects of which was so great, that in a place where the sea was more than 150 fathoms deep an island was thrown up more than a league and a half long, and upwards of 60 fathoms high. Another happened in 1691, in the island of St. Michael, which began the 6th of July, and lasted till the 12th of the following month: Tercera and Fayal were agitated the next morning with so much violence, that they appeared to move; but

these

* See the Hist. of the Acad. des Sciences, anno 1688.

† Ibid. anno 1696.   ‡ See the Voyages of Mandelso.

these frightful shocks returned there only four times, whereas at St. Michael they did not cease a moment for several days. The islanders quitted their houses, which they saw fall before their eyes, and remained all the time in the fields exposed to the injuries of the weather. The whole town of Villa Pranca was overthrown to its very foundation, and most of the inhabitants buried under its ruins. In many parts the plains rose into hills, and in others, mountains were flattened into vallies. A spring of water issued from the earth, which flowed for four days, and then ceased all on a sudden. The air and sea, still more agitated, resounded with a noise which might have been taken for the roaring of a number of wild animals. Many persons died with the fright; the ships in the harbour suffered dangerous shocks, and those which were at anchor, or under sail at 20 leagues distant from the islands, received great damage. Earthquakes are frequent in the Azores, and about twenty years before a mountain in St. Michael was overturned by one of them.*

In Manilla, in the month of September, 1627, an earthquake levelled one of the two mountains

* Hist. of Voyages.

mountains called Carvallos, in the province of Cagayon; in 1645, one third of the town was destroyed by a like accident, and 300 persons perished. The succeeding year it experienced another; and the ancient Indians say they were more terrible formerly, which was the reason they build their houses only of wood; a custom still continued, and which the Spaniards follow.   .

" The quantity of volcanos in this island confirms that assertion; because at certain times they vomit forth flames, shake the earth, and perform all the effects Pliny attributes to those of Vesuvius; that is, they change the beds of rivers, drive back the adjacent sea, fill with cinders the neighbouring plains, and throw out stones to great distances, with reports louder than those of cannons.

" In 1646, a mountain in the island of Machian split by an earthquake, with a dreadful noise; from this opening issued a number of flames, which destroyed several plantations with the inhabitants and all that was therein. In the year 1685, this prodigious crack was to be seen, and probably is still apparent; it is called the path of Machian, because it descends from

the

* See le Voyage de Gemelli Careri, page 120.

the top to the bottom, like a road hollowed out, but which at a distance appears like a path."*

The history of the French Academy mentions in the following terms, the earthquakes that took place in 1702 and 1703. " The earthquakes began in Italy in October 1702, and continued till July 1703; the country which suffered the most by them, and where they began, is the town of Norcia, with its dependencies under the ecclesiastical government, and the province of Abruzzo, which are situated at the foot of the Apennines on the south side.

" They were often accompanied with terrible noises in the air, which also were heard without any dreadful effects, when the sky was serene. The earthquake which happened on the 2d of February 1703, was the most violent; it was accompanied, at least at Rome, with a great serenity of sky and calmness in the air. It lasted at Rome half a minute, and at Aquila the capital of Abruzzo three hours. It destroyed the whole town of Aquila, buried 5000 persons under the ruins, and made great havock in the environs. The vibration of the earth, according

* See the Hist. of the Conquest of the Malaccas, vol. ii. p. 318,

ing to the observations made by the lamps in the churches, was from south to north.

"It opened two places from whence issued a great quantity of stones, which entirely covered it and rendered it barren; after the stones they threw out water above the height of the trees; this lasted half an hour, and inundated the adjacent fields. The water was whitish, like soap suds, and had not any remarkable taste.

"A mountain near Sigillo, a city twenty-two miles distant from Aquila, had on its summit a very large plain surrounded with rocks like a wall. The earthquake of the 2d of February, changed this plain into a gulph of unequal breadth, whose greatest diameter is twenty-five fathoms and the least twenty; the depth of it has not been discovered, although a line 300 fathoms has been let down in it. At the time this opening was made, flames were seen to issue out, and afterwards a great smoke which lasted three days with some interruptions.

"At Genoa on the 1st and 2d of July 1703, there were two slight earthquakes, the last was felt only by the people on the pier : at the same time the sea in the port sunk six feet, and remained so a quarter of an hour.

"The

" The sulphurous water in the road from Rome to Tivoli it diminished two feet and a half, both in the bason and in the canal. In many places of the plain, called Testine, the springs and rivulets, which formed morasses, are all dried up. The waters of the lake called l'Enfer is also lowered three feet. In place of the ancient springs new ones have appeared at above a league distance, so that possibly they are the same waters which have changeddirection*.

" The same earthquake which, in 1538, formed Monti di Cinere, near Pozzoli, filled lake Lucrin with stones, earth and cinders, so that this lake is now a marshy ground."†

" There are earthquakes. also felt at some distance at sea, says Mr. Shaw; in 1774, being on board the Gazella, an Algerine vessel, mounting 50 guns, three violent shocks were felt one after the other, as if every time a weight of 20 or 30 tons had been thrown on the ballast. This happened on a part of the Mediterranean that was more than 200 fathom deep. He relates also, that others had felt earthquakes much more considerable in

VOL. II.   X   other

---

* Anno 1704, page 10.

† See Ray's Discourses, page 12.

other parts, and one among the rest at 40 leagues west from Lisbon."*

Schouten, speaking of an earthquake in the Malacca islands, says, that the mountains were shaken, and the vessels at anchor in 30 or 40 fathoms water were shook, as if they had struck against rocks or banks. " Experience, continues he, teaches us every day that the same happens in the open sea, where no bottom is to be met with, and that ships are tossed to and fro by earthquakes, even where the sea is tranquil."

Gentil, in his voyage round the world, speaks of earthquakes in the following terms: " I have, says he, made some remarks on these earthquakes ; first, that half an hour before the earth is agitated every animal is struck with fear; horses snort, break their fastenings, and fly from the stable; dogs bark; birds, as if stupified, fly into houses for safety; and rats and mice quit their holes. Secondly, that vessels at anchor are so violently agitated, that every part of them seems as if going to pieces, the cannons force themselves loose, and the masts break in several places. These facts I should scarcely have given credit to if many

unanimous

* See Shaw's Travels.

unanimous testimonies had not convinced me.
I know the bottom of the sea is a continuation
of the land, and that if one is agitated it will
communicate to the other; but I could not
conceive how every part of a vessel, floating in
a fluid, should be affected in the same manner
as if she was on the earth : it appeared to me
that her motion should have been such as she
experiences in a storm; besides, in the circumstance which I speak of, the surface of the sea
was smooth, and there was no wind. Thirdly,
that if the cavern of the earth, where this subterraneous fire is contained, has a direction
from north to south, and if the buildings of an
adjacent town are in a parallel line with it, all
the houses are overthrown, whereas if this vein
or cavern executes its effects by the breadth of
the town, the devastation of the earthquake, is
much less considerable.*

In countries subject to earthquakes, when
a new volcano breaks out earthquakes cease,
and are only felt in the violent eruptions of
the volcano, as is observed in the island of St.
Christopher.†

X 2

The

* See Gentil's Voyages, vol. I. page 172, &c.
† See Abridgement of Phil. Trans. vol. XI. page 302.

The enormous ravages produced by earthquakes have made some naturalists think that
mountains and other inequalities of the surface
of the globe were only the effects of subterraneous fires, and that all the irregularities must
be attributed to the violent shocks which they
have produced. This, for example, is the
opinion of Mr. Ray; he imagines that all
mountains have been formed by earthquakes,
or the explosion of volcanos, as Monti di
Cinere, the new island near Santorini, &c.
but he has not considered that the slight elevations formed by the eruption of a volcano, or by
the action of an earthquake, are not internally
composed of horizontal strata, as all other
mountains are; for by digging in the Monti
di Cinere we meet with calcined stones, cinders, burnt earths, metallic dross, pumice-
stones, &c. all mixed and confounded like a
heap. Besides, if earthquakes and subterraneous fires had produced the great mountains of
the earth, as the Cordeliers, Mount Taurus,
the Alps, &c. the prodigious force necessary to
raise these enormous masses might, at the same
time, have destroyed a great part of the surface
of the globe; and earthquakes, requisite to
produce such effects, must have been of inçon-
ceivable

ceivable violence, since the most famous of which history makes mention have not had sufficient power to form a single mountain; for example, in the time of Valentian I. an earthquake happened, which was felt throughout all the known world;* and yet not a mountain was thrown up by it.

It is nevertheless certain, that although we might be able to find an earthquake sufficiently powerful to throw up the highest mountains, it would not be sufficient to disorder the rest of the globe.

For supposing that the chain of the highest mountains which cross South America from the Magellanic lands to New Grenada, and the Gulph of Darien, had been produced by an earthquake, and then let us see by calculations the effect of this explosion. This chain of mountains is near 1700 leagues in length, and commonly 40 in breadth, comprehending the Sieras, which are not so lofty as the Andes. The surface therefore is 68,000 square leagues; I suppose the thickness of the matter displaced by the earthquake to be about one league, that is, the height of these mountains

taken

* As Ammianus Marcellinus relates, lib. 26. cap. 14.

taken from the top to the caverns, which according to this hypothesis must support them, is one league, then I say, the power of an explosion must have raised a quantity of earth equal to 68,000 cubical leagues to a league in height. Now the action being equal to the reaction, this explosion must have communicated the same motion to the rest of the globe. The whole globe consists of 12,310,523,801 cubical leagues, from which substracting 68,000, there remains 12,310,455,801 cubical leagues, the quantity of which motion will be equal to that of 68,000 cubical leagues raised one league; from whence we perceive that the force which will have been great enough to elevate 68,000 cubical leagues would not have displaced the whole globe a single inch.

There would therefore be no absolute impossibility in the supposition that mountains have been raised by earthquakes, if their internal composition as well as their external form were not evident proofs of their being the work of the sea. Their internal parts are composed of regular and parallel strata, intermingled with shells, and their external consists of a figure whose angles are every where correspondent: is it credible then

that

that this uniform composition and regular form should have been produced by irregular shocks and sudden explosions ?

But as this opinion has prevailed among some philosophers, and as the nature and effects of earthquakes are not well understood, it may possibly be pertinent to hazard a few ideas with a view of explaining those intricate subjects.

The earth has undergone great changes on its surface; we find at considerable depths, holes, caverns, subterraneous rivulets, and void places, which sometimes communicate by chinks, &c. There are two kinds of caverns; the first are those produced by the action of subterraneous fires and volcanos; the action of this fire uplifts, burns, and throws out to a distance the matters that are above, and at the same time divides and deranges those which are on the sides, and thus produces caverns, grottos, and irregular holes, but which however is only effected in the environs of volcanos; and these kinds of caverns are more rare than those produced by water. We have already observed that the different strata which compose the terrestrial globe are all interrupted by perpendicular fissures: the waters which fall on
the

the surface descend through them; collect when stopped by clay, and form springs and rivulets; by their natural propensities they seek out cavities or small vacancies, and always incline to open a passage till they find a vent, carrying along with them sand, gravel, and other matters they can divide and dissolve; by degrees, in the internal part of the earth they form small trenches; and at last issue forth in the form of springs, either at the surface of the earth, or bottom of the sea; the matters which they carry along with them, leave caverns whose extent may be very considerable, the origin of which is quite different from those produced by volcanos or earthquakes.

There are two kinds of earthquakes, the one caused by the action of subterraneous fires, and the explosion of volcanos which are only felt at small distances at the time of eruptions: when the matters which form subterraneous fires ferment, heat, and inflame, the fire makes an effort on every side to get out, and if it does not find a natural vent, it raises the earth above and forces itself a passage by throwing it out; such is the beginning of a volcano whose effects and continuation are in proportion to the quantity of inflammable matters they contain. If

the

the quantity of matters is not considerable, an earthquake may ensue, without a volcano being formed. The air rarefied by the subterraneous fire may also escape through small vents, and in this case there will be only a shock without any eruption or volcano. But when the inflamed matter is in great quantities and confined by solid and compressed bodies, then a commotion and volcano is certain to ensue; but all these commotions form only the first kind of earth-quakes, and can only shake a small space of ground. A violent eruption of Ætna will cause, for example, an earthquake throughout the whole island of Sicily; but it will never extend to the distance of three or four hundred leagues. When any new mouth bursts out in Vesuvius, there are earthquakes at Naples, and in the neighbourhood of the volcano; but these earthquakes never shake the Alps, nor extend into France, or other countries remote from Vesuvius. Therefore earthquakes pro-duced by volcanos, are limited to a small space, are properly but the effects of the re-action of the fire; and they shake the earth, as the explosion of a powder magazine pro-duces a shock perceptible at many leagues distance.

But there is another kind of earthquake very different in its effects, and perhaps equally so in its cause; such are felt at great distances, and shake a long course of ground, without any new volcano, or eruption in the old ones appearing. We have instances of earthquakes being felt at the same time in England, France, Germany, and even in Hungary; these earthquakes always extend more in length than breadth; they shake a zone of ground with greater or less violence in different places, and are almost always accompanied with a rumbling noise like that of a coach rolling over the stones with rapidity.

With respect to the causes of this kind of earthquake, it must be remembered that the explosion of all inflammable matters produces, like gunpowder, a great quantity of air; that this air by the heat is in a state of very great rarefaction, and that by its state of compression in the bowels of the earth, it must produce very violent effects. Let us suppose, that at a depth of one or two hundred fathoms, pyrites and other sulphurous matters are collected in great quantities, and that by the fermentation produced by the filtration of the water, or other causes, they inflame; what must happen? First

these

these matters are not placed in horizontal layers, as are the ancient strata, which have been formed by the sediment of the waters ; on the contrary, they are formed in perpendicular fissures, in caverns, and in other places where the water can penetrate. Inflaming, they produce a quantity of air, the spring of which being compressed in a small space, like that of a cavern, will not only shake the ground directly above, but will seek out for passages by which it may escape. The roads which offer themselves are caverns and trenches, formed by subterraneous rivulets : into these the rarefied air will precipitate with violence, form in them a strong wind, the noise of which will be heard at the surface, accompanied with shocks of the earth, &c. this subterraneous wind, produced by the fire, will extend as far as the subterraneous cavities, and cause an agitation more or less violent as it is distant from the vent, and finds the passages of a larger or lesser extent : this motion being made longitudinal, the shock will be the same, and the earthquake be felt through a long zone of ground. This air will not produce any eruption, or volcano, because it will find sufficient space to expand, or rather because it will have found vents, and issue forth in form

of

of wind and vapour. Even should it not be allowed that there exist internal passages, by which the air and vapours can pass, it may be conceived that in the place where the first explosion is made, the ground being lifted up to a considerable height, that the most adjoining to this spot must divide and split in an horizontal manner by the force of its motion; and by this means passages communicating one with the other may be opened to great distances; and this explanation agrees with every phenomena. It is not at the same moment or hour that an earthquake is felt in two distant places. Neither fire nor eruption attend those earthquakes which are heard at a distance, and the noise always marks the progressive motion of this subterraneous wind. This theory is confirmed by two other facts; it is well known that mines exhale unhealthy air and suffocating vapours, independent of the wind produced by the current of water: it is also known that there are holes, abysses and deep lakes in the earth, which produce winds, as the lake Boleslaw, in Bohemia, which we have already spoken of.

All this being considered, I do not see how it can be imagined that earthquakes produce mountains, since the cause itself of these earthquakes

are

are mineral and sulphurous matters, which are generally found only in perpendicular clefts of mountains and other cavities of the earth; the greatest number of which have been produced by the operation of water; since this matter by inflaming produces only a momentary explosion and a violent wind which follows the subterraneous roads of the water: since the duration of the earthquakes at the surface of the earth is so short that their cause can only be explosion and not a durable fire: and in short, since these earthquakes, which extend to a considerable distance, very far from raising chains of mountains, do not produce the smallest hills throughout their whole extent.

Earthquakes are, in fact, most frequent in places near volcanos, as in Sicily and Naples, but it is known, by observations, that the most violent earthquakes happen in the time of the greatest eruptions of volcanos; that they are very limited, and cannot produce a chain of mountains.

It has been sometimes observed, that the matters thrown out of Mount Ætna, after laying for many years and afterwards moistened with the rain, have rekindled and thrown out

flames

flames with such violent explosions as even to produce a slight shock.

In a furious eruption of Ætna in 1669, which began the 11th of March, the summit of the mountains sunk considerably;* which proves the fire of this volcano comes rather from the top than from the bottom of the mountain. Borelli is of the same opinion, and says, "That the fire of volcanos does not proceed from the centre, nor from the foot of the mountain, but that it issues from the summit, and flames kindle but at a small depth."†

Mount Vesuvius in its eruptions, has thrown out great quantities of boiling water. Mr. Ray, who thinks that the volcanean fire proceeds from a great depth, says, that it is the water of the sea which communicates by subterraneous passages with the foot of the mountain; he gives, as a proof of it, the dryness of the summit of Vesuvius, and the agitation of the sea at the time of these eruptions, which sometimes retreats from the coasts, and leaves the Bay of Naples almost dry. But, if these facts are true, they do not prove, in a solid manner, that the volcanean fire proceeds from a great depth; for the water

which

* See Trans. Phil. Abridged, Vol. II. page 387.
† Borelli, De incendiis Montis Ætnae.

which is thrown out is certainly rain water,
which penetrates through the fissure, and collects in the cavities of the mountains. Rills and
rivulets flow from those containing volcanos as
well as other lofty mountains, and as they are
hollow, and have been more shaken, it is not
astonishing that the water collects in their caverns in their internal part, and that these
waters are thrown out in the time of eruptions
with other matters. With respect to the motion
of the sea, it proceeds solely from the shock
communicated to the waters by the explosion,
which causes them to advance or retreat according to different circumstances.

The matters which volcanos generally throw
out, come forth in the form of a torrent of
melted minerals, which inundates all the environs of those mountains; these rivers of li-
quified matters extend to considerable distances,
and in cooling form horizontal or inclined
strata, which for position are like the strata
formed by the sediment left by the waters : but
it is very easy to distinguish the one from the
other. First, because strata of lava are not
throughout of an equal thickness : secondly,
because they contain only matters which have
evidently been calcined, vitrified, or melted ;
and

and thirdly, because they do not extend to any great distance. As there are a great number of volcanos at Peru, and as the foot of most of the mountains of the Cordeliers is covered with matters thrown out by eruptions, it is not astonishing that marine shells are not met with there, as they must have been calcined and destroyed by the fire; but I am persuaded, if we dig in argilaceous earth, which, according to M. Bourguet, is the common earth of the valley of Quito, shells would be found there, as they are in other places, at least where the ground is not covered, like that at the foot of the mountains, with matters thrown out of a volcano.

It has often been asked, why volcanos are all met with at the top of mountains? I think I have partly given a satisfactory answer to this question in the preceding article, but I have thought it necessary not to finish this without farther explaining what I have said on this subject.

The peaks or points of mountains were formerly covered with sand and earth, which the rain gradually washes along with it into the vallies, and has left only the rocks and stone, which forms the nucleus of the mountain.

This

This being left bare will have been still worn by the injuries of the air, the frost will have loosened the large and small parts, which of course have rolled to the bottom. The rocks, at the base of the summit, being left bare, and no longer supported by the earth which surrounded them, will have given way a little, and by dividing one from the other formed small intervals. This separation of the lower rocks could not be made without communicating a greater motion to the upper. By this means the nucleus of the mountain would be divided into an infinity of perpendicular clefts, from the summit to the base of the lower rocks; the rain will have penetrated into all these clefts, and loosened, in the inside of the mountain, all the mineral parts and other matters that it could carry away or dissolve; they will have formed pyrites and other combustible matters, and when by length of time these matters were accumulated in great quantities, they fermented, and by inflaming produced explosions and other effects of volcanos; perhaps likewise, within the mountains, there were masses of these mineral matters already formed before the rain could penetrate therein; in that case, as soon as holes and clefts were made, which gave passages to the water and air, these matters inflamed and formed a volcano. None of these motions could be made in plains, since all is at rest and nothing can be displaced. It is not therefore surprising that volcanos are found only in high mountains.

When coal-mines are opened, which are generally met with in argile earth, at a great depth, it sometimes happens that the mineral substances have taken fire: there are even mines of coal in Scotland, Flanders, &c. which have burnt for a number of years. The admission of the air suffices to produce this effect; but these fires produce only slight explosions, and do not form volcanos, because all being solid and full in these places, fire cannot be excited like that of volcanos, in which there are cavities and void places where the air penetrates, which must necessarily extend the conflagration and augment the action of the fire, so as to produce the terrible effects we have just described.

ARTICLE

ARTICLE XVII.

OF NEW ISLANDS, CAVERNS, PERPENDICULAR CLEFTS, &c. &c.

NEW islands are formed either suddenly by the action of subterraneous fires, or gently by the deposit of the sediment of waters. Ancient historians and modern travellers relate facts on this subject which put it beyond all kind of doubt. Seneca assures us, that in his time the island Therasia appeared suddenly in the sea, to the astonishment of many mariners who beheld it. Pliny relates, that formerly thirteen islands in the Mediterranean sprung at the same instant out of the sea, and that Rhodes and Delos are the principal of them: it appears, from him, as well as Ammianus Marcellinus, Philo, and others, that these thirteen islands were not produced by an earthquake,

Z 2   nor

nor by any subterraneous explosion, but that they were formerly hid under the water, which lowering left them uncovered. Delos had the name of Pelagia given to it, from having formerly belonged to the sea. Whether the origin of these thirteen islands is to be attributed to the action of subterraneous fires, or to some other cause which might occasion a sinking of the water in the Mediterranean, is uncertain. But Pliny relates, that the island Hiera, near Therasia, had been formed of ferruginous masses, and earth thrown from the bottom of the sea ; and in chapter 89, he speaks of other islands formed in the like manner ; but on this subject we have more clear and certain facts of later date.

On the 23d of May 1707, at the sun's rising, there was seen, at some little distance from the island of Therasia, or Santorini, something like a floating rock in the sea ; some persons, to satisfy their curiosity, went towards it, and found it a shoal which had issued from the bottom of the sea ; it increased under their feet, and they brought with them the pumice-stone and oysters, which the rock still had attached to its surface. There was a slight earthquake at Santorini two days before this

shoal

shoal appeared: it increased considerably till the 14th of June, it was then half a mile round, and from 20 to 30 feet high; the earth was white, and a little argilaceous; after that the sea became more and more troubled; vapours arose which infected the island Santorini; and on the 16th of July several rocks were seen to issue at one time from the bottom of the sea, and unite into one solid body. This was accompanied with a dismal noise, which continued upwards of two months. Flames issued from the new island, which kept increasing in circumference and height, and the violent explosions frequently threw large stones to more than seven miles distance. The island Santorini itself was deemed among the ancients as a modern production, and in 726, 1427, and 1573, it increased in size, and small islands were formed near it.* The same volcano, which in the time of Seneca formed the island of Santorini, in that of Pliny produced Hiera or Volcanella, and in our time the shoal abovementioned.

On the 10th of October 1720, near the island Tercera, a very considerable fire arose out of the sea; some mariners were sent by the

* See the Hist. of the Acad. 1708, page 23, &c.

the order of the governor to take a view of it,
and who having come near it, perceived, on
the 19th of the same month, an island which
appeared only as fire and smoke, with a prodigious quantity of ashes thrown to a distance,
as if caused by the force of a volcano, with a
report like that of thunder. An earthquake
happened at the same time, which was felt in
the circumjacent places, and great quantities of
pumice-stones were observed floating on the
sea around the new island; pumice-stones indeed have sometimes been seen swimming in
the midst of the high seas.*

The historian of the academy, anno 1721,
says on this event, that after an earthquake in
the island of St. Michael, one of the Azores,
there appeared between this island and Tercera
a torrent of fire, which gave birth to two new
shoals; and the next year he gave the following
detail: .

" M. de l'Isle has informed the academy
of many particulars concerning the new island
among the Azores, which he received in a
letter from M. de Montagnac, consul at
Lisbon.

" Being

* See Phil. Trans. Abridg. vol. VI. part ii. page 254.

" Being in a vessel, which was moored the 18th of September 1721, before the fortress of the town of St. Michael, M. de Montagnac learnt the following account from the pilot:

" On the 7th of December 1720, at night, there was a great earthquake in Tercera and St. Michael, which are about 18 leagues apart, and between which a new island sprung up: it was remarked at the same time, that the point of the island of Peak, 30 leagues distant, and which before threw out fire, was sunk and emitted none; but the new island kept throwing out a constant thick smoke, and which I plainly perceived from the vessel I was in. The pilot assured us that he had gone round the island, rowing as near it as he conceived to be safe. On the south side he threw a line of sixty fathoms without finding any bottom; on the west side the water was greatly changed, appearing white, blue and green, and which extended two thirds of a league, where it seemed ready to boil. On the north-west, the part from which the smoke issued, he found, at 15 fathoms, a bottom of thick sand; he threw a stone in the sea, and where it fell the water seemed to boil and bubble with impetuosity: the bottom was so hot that it twice melted

melted some grease fastened at the end of the
sounding line. The pilot observed also on
that side that smoke issued from a small lake
bounded by a sand bank. This island is almost round and high enough to be perceived
at the distance of seven or eight leagues in
clear weather.

" It has since been learnt from a letter of
M. Adrian, French consul in the island of St.
Michael, dated March 1722, that the new
island had considerably diminished, that it was
almost level with the water, and there was
every appearance it would not last long."

It is therefore by these, and a great number
of other facts of a similar nature, very evident
that inflammable matters are enclosed in the
earth under the bottom of the sea, and that they
sometimes cause violent explosions. The places
where this happens might be termed marine
volcanos, and which differ from common volcanos only by the shortness of the duration of
their effects; for the fire having opened itself
a passage, the water must penetrate therein and
extinguish it. The elevation of new islands
must consequently leave a void space which the
water would shortly occupy, and this new earth,
which is only composed of matters thrown out

by

by the marine volcano, must resemble that of
Monti di Cinere and other eminencies which
terrestrial volcanos have formed. Now as the
water rushes in, during the violence of the
explosion, and fills the vacancies that it occasions, that is clearly the reason why these
marine volcanos act less frequently than other
volcanos, although the causes of both are the
same.

These subterraneous, or sub-marine fires
are doubtless the cause of all those ebullitions
of the sea, which sailors have remarked in
various places, and as well as of the water-
spouts we have before mentioned; they likewise produce storms and earthquakes, which
are not less felt on the sea than on the land.
Islands formed by these sub-marine volcanos,
are generally composed of pumice - stone,
and calcined rocks, and produce, like those
of the land, violent earthquakes and commotions.

Fires have been often observed on the surface of the water. Pliny tells us that the lake
Thrasimenia appeared inflamed over all its surface. Agricola relates that when a stone was
thrown into the lake Denstat, in Thuringia,

it appeared, as it descended in the water, like a train of fire.

In short, the quantities of pumice-stones which travellers affirm are met with in many parts of the ocean, and the Mediterranean, prove there are volcanos at the bottom of the sea, similar to those we are acquainted with, and which differ not in the least from them, neither by the matters they cast out, nor by the violence of the explosion, but solely by the rarity and shortness of the duration of their effects. From hence we may fairly infer that the bottom of the sea in every respect resembles the surface of the earth.

We shall find many connections between land and sea volcanos; both are found at the summit of mountains. The islands of Azores and those of the Archipelago are only peaks of mountains, some of which rise above the water, and others are underneath. By the account of the new islands among the Azores we see that the part from whence the smoke issued was only 15 fathoms under water, which, compared with the common depth of the ocean, proves that even this part is the summit of a mountain; as much may be said of the

new

new island near Santorini, which could not be any great depth, since oysters were found attached to the rocks which rose above the water. It appears also that marine-volcanos have, like those of the land, subterraneous communications, since the summit of the volcano of St. George, in the island Peak, sunk at the time the new island among the Azores arose. It must also be observed, that these new islands never appear but near the old ones, and that we have no example of new islands in the high seas; we must therefore look on them as a continuation of the adjacent islands; and when ancient islands have volcanos, it is not astonishing that the ground adjacent should contain matters proper to form them, and which inflame, either by fermentation alone, or by the action of subterraneous winds.

Islands produced by the action of fire and earthquakes are but few, but there are an infinite number produced by the mud, sand, and earth, which the rivers or the sea transport into different places. At the mouth of rivers earth and sand accumulate in such quantities as to form islands of a moderate extent. The sea, retiring from certain coasts, leaves the highest parts of the bottom naked, which

A a 2

forms

forms so many new islands; so likewise the sea, by extending itself on certain shores, covers the lowest parts, and leaves the highest, which appear as so many islands; and thus it is we may account for there being so few islands in the open sea, and so many bordering on the continents.

Water and fire, whose natures appear so different and so contrary, produce many similar effects, independent of the particular productions of these two elements, some of which bear so striking a resemblance as to be mistaken for each other, as glass and crystal, natural and fictitious antimony, &c. There are in nature an infinity of great effects produced by them, which are scarcely to be distinguished. Water, as has been observed, has produced mountains and formed most islands, while others owe their origin to fire. There are likewise caverns, clefts, holes, gulphs, &c. some of which owe their origin to subterraneous fires, and others to waters.

Caverns are met with in mountains, and few or none in plains: there are many in the Archipelago, and in other islands, because they are in general only the tops of mountains: caverns are formed like precipices, by the sinking of

rocks,

rocks, or large abysses, by the action of the fire; for to make a cavern form a precipice or abyss, we need only suppose the tops of adjacent rocks had fallen together and formed an arch, which must often happen when their bottoms are shaken and dislodged by time or earthquakes. Caverns may be produced by the same causes which produce holes, the shaking and sinking of the earth, and which causes are the explosion of volcanos, the action of subterraneous vapours and earthquakes; for they occasion caverns, holes, and hollows of every kind by their shocks and commotion.

St. Patrick's cavern in Ireland is not so considerable as it is famous; it is the same with the Dog's Grotto in Italy; and that which throws out fire, in the mountain of Beniguaxeval in the kingdom of Fez. In the county of Derby, in England, there is a very considerable cavern, much larger than the famous cavern of Beauman, near the Black Forest, in Brunswick. I have been informed by a person as respectable for his merit as his name, Lord Morton, that this large cavern, called the Devil's Hole, at first presents a very considerable opening, larger than any church door; that through this opening a rivulet flows;

that

that in advancing the vault of the cavern becomes so low, that persons who are desirous of
continuing their road are obliged to lie flat in
a boat and be pushed through this narrow passage, where the water almost touches the roof;
but after having passed this part of the vault,
the arch rises to a considerable height, and continues so for some distance, when it sinks again
so low as to touch the water, and where the
cavern ends.   The source of the rivulet which
issues from it sometimes encreases considerably:
it transports and heaps up a great quantity of
sand in one part of the cavern, which is formed
like a kind of alley, whose direction is different
from that of the principal cavern.

In Carniola, near Potpechio, is a very spacious
cavern, in which is a large lake.   Near Adel-
sperg is a cavern, in which we may travel two
German miles, and where very deep precipices
are to be met with.*   There are also large
caverns and beautiful grottos under the mountains of Mendip, in Wales; mines of lead are
found near these caverns, and whole oaks at
fifteen fathoms deep.   In the county of Glou-
cester there is a very large cavern, called Pen
Park-hole, at the bottom of which there is
                                        thirty

* See Act. erud. Lips. anno. 1689, page 558.

thirty fathoms water, and mines of lead are also found.

The Devil's Hole, and other caverns, from whence issue large springs or rivulets, have plainly therefore been formed by the water, and their origin cannot be considered as the effects either of earthquakes or volcanos.

One of the most remarkable and largest caverns known is that of Antiparos, a description of which is given by M. de Tournefort. We enter a rustic cavern about thirty feet broad, divided by some natural pillars; between two of which, on the right, the ground is on a gentle slope, and then becomes more steep to the bottom, about twenty feet; this is the passage to the grotto, or internal cavern, which is very dark, and cannot be entered without stooping and the assistance of torches. We then descend an horrible precipice by the assistance of a rope, fastened at the entrance, into another still more frightful, the borders of which are very slippery, with dark abysses on the left. By the assistance of a ladder we pass a perpendicular rock, and then continue to go through places somewhat less dangerous : but when we think ourselves in a safe path, we are stopped short by a tremendous obstruction, and are obliged

to

to crawl on our hands and knees, or slide on our back, the length of a large rock, and then descend by a ladder. When we are at the bottom of the ladder, we still have to stumble over pieces of rocks for some time, and then we reach the celebrated grotto. It is computed to be three hundred fathoms deep from the surface of the earth, appears to be forty fathoms high by fifty broad. It is filled with large beautiful stalactites of various forms, as well from the roof of the vault as on the bottom.*

In part of Greece called Livadia (the Achaia of the ancients) there is a large cavern in a mountain which was formerly famous for the oracles of Trophonius; it is between the lake Lividia and the adjacent sea; at the nearest part it is about forty miles; and there are forty subterraneous passages across the rock, through which the waters flow.†

In all countries which produce sulphur, volcanos, and earthquakes, there are caverns. The ground of most of the Archipelago islands is cavernous; the islands of the Indian ocean,

principally

---

* See the Voyage de Levant, page 188, and also Remarks in a Journey from Paris to Constantinople, which contains a copious description of this astonishing phenomenon.

† See Gordon's Geography, 1733, page 179.

principally that of the Malacca's, appear to be supported by vaults and cavities. The land Azores, the Canaries, the islands of Cape de Verd, and in general almost every small island, is in many parts hollow and cavernous; because these islands are, as we have observed, only points of mountains where considerable ebullitions are made, either by the action of volcanos, of the water, of frosts, or other injuries of the weather. In the Cordeliers, where there are many volcanos, and where earthquakes are frequent, there are also a great number of caverns.

The famous labyrinth of the island of Candia, is not the work of nature alone; M. de Tournefort assures us that it has evidently been greatly enlarged by men; and most likely this cavern is not the only one which has been augmented by human labour. Every day mines and quarries are digging, and when abandoned for a long time, it is not easy to discover whether they have been the productions of nature, or formed by the hands of men. We know of quarries of considerable extent; for example that of Maestricht, where it is said 50,000 men may conceal themselves, and which is supported by upwards of 1000 pillars, twenty-four feet high, and the earth and rock above is more than twenty-five fathoms thick.*

The salt mines in Poland form still greater excavations than the above. There are generally vast quarries near large towns. But we cannot proceed farther in particulars; besides, the labour of man, however great, will ever hold but a small place in the history of nature.

Volcanos and waters which produce caverns internally, form also external clefts, precipices, and abysses. At Cajeta, in Italy, there is a mountain which had formerly been separated by an earthquake, in a manner so as to appear as if the division was made by the hands of men. We have already spoken of the divisions in the island of Machian, of the abyss of mount Azarat, of the gap in the Cordeliers, and that of Thermopyle, &c. To these may be added, the gap in the mountain of Troglodytes, in Arabia, which nature only sketched out, and which Victor Amadeus caused to be finished. Water as well as subterraneous fires produce considerable sinking of the earth, fall of rocks, and overthrow mountains, of which we can give many examples.

" In the month of June 1714, a part of the mountain

---

* See Abridg. Phil. Trans. vol. XI, page 461.

mountain of Diableret, in Valois, fell suddenly, and some time after, the sky being serene, it appeared to have taken a conical figure. Fifty-three huts belonging to the boors were destroyed, together with several people and a great many cattle, covering a square league with the ruins it occasioned. A profound darkness was caused by the dust; the heaps of stones thrown together were above thirty perches in height, stopped the currents of the water, and formed new and very deep lakes. In all this there was not the least trace of bitumen, sulphur, lime, nor consequently any subterraneous fire, and apparently the base of this great rock was perished and reduced to dust.*"

We have a remarkable example of these sinkings near Folkstone, in the county of Kent; the hills in its environs sunk gradually by an insensible motion, and without any earthquake. These hills internally are rocks and chalk, and by their sinking they have thrown into the sea rocks and earth which were adjacent to it. The relation of this fact may be seen in the Abridgment of the Philosophical Transactions, vol. VI. page 250.

B b 2

In

* Histoire de l'Academie des Sciences, anno 1715, p. 4.

In 1618, the town of Pleurs, in Valtelino, was buried under the rocks, at the bottom of which it was situated. In 1678, there was a great inundation in Gascony, caused by the sinking of some pieces of one of the Pyrennees, which forced the water to spring forth that was contained in the subterraneous caverns of those mountains. In 1680, there happened a still greater in Ireland, by the sinking of a mountain into caverns filled with water. We may easily conceive the cause of these effects. It is well known there are subterraneous waters in an infinity of places; these waters carry off by degrees the sand and earth over which they pass, consequently may in time destroy the bed of earth on which the mountain rests; and this bed of earth being more deficient on one side than on the other, the mountain of course must be overthrown; but if this base is worn every where alike, the mountain will sink and not be overthrown.

Having remarked on the sinkings and other changes on the earth, occasioned by what may be called the accidents of nature, we ought not to pass over the perpendicular clefts found throughout the strata of the earth: these clefts

are

are perceptible not only in rocks and quarries of marble and stone, but also in clays and earths of every kind, which have never been removed. I call them perpendicular clefts, because, like the horizontal strata, they are oblique, by accident only. Woodward and Ray speak of these clefts, but in a confused manner; and they do not term them perpendicular clefts, because they thought they might be indifferently oblique or perpendicular. No author has explained the origin of them, although it is apparent that they have been produced, as we observed in a preceding article, by the dryness of the matters which compose horizontal beds. In whatsoever manner this drying happens, it must have produced perpendicular clefts; for the matters which compose the strata could not have diminished in size without splitting in a perpendicular direction to these strata. I comprehend under this name of perpendicular clefts all natural separations of rocks, as well as those which may have been occasioned by any convulsive accident. When some considerable motion happens to masses of rocks, these clefts are sometimes found obliquely placed, but this is because the mass is of itself oblique, and with a little attention

tention it is always easy to discover that these clefts are in general perpendicular to the horizontal strata, particularly in quarries of marble, lime, stones, and all large chains of rocks.

Mountains internally are principally composed of stone and rocks in parallel beds : between the horizontal beds small strata of a softer matter than stone is found, and the perpendicular clefts are filled with sand, crystals, minerals, metals, &c. these last matters are of a more modern formation than the horizontal beds in which we find sea-shells. The rains have by degrees loosened the sand and the earth on the upper parts of mountains, and have left the stone and rocks entirely naked, in which we readily distinguish the horizontal strata and perpendicular clefts : in plains, on the contrary, the rain-water and flood having brought a considerable quantity of earth, sand, gravel, and other such matters, have formed a bed of tufa, soft and dissoluble stone, sand, gravel, and earth, mixed with vegetables. These beds contain no marine shells, or at least only fragments, which have been detached from mountains, with gravel and earth. We must carefully distinguish these new beds from the old, where almost always a great number of entire

shells

shells are found placed in their natural situation.

If we observe the order and internal disposition of matters in a mountain, composed, for example, of common stones, or calcinable lapidific matters, we generally find a bed of gravel under the vegetable earth, of the nature and colour of the stone which predominates in this ground; and under the gravel we meet with stone. When the mountain is divided by some trench, or deep cut, we easily distinguish all the strata of which it is composed. Each horizontal stratum is separated by a kind of joint, which is likewise horizontal, and their thickness generally increase in proportion as they lower from the summit of the mountain, and are all divided vertically by perpendicular clefts. In common, the first stratum which is met with under the gravel, and even the second, are only thinner than the beds which form the base of the mountain, but are so divided by perpendicular clefts, that pieces of any length are not to be seen: they perfectly resemble the cracks of ground which is very dry, but go not very far, gradually disappearing in proportion as they descend, and towards the bottom there are no great number but where they

they divide the strata in a more regular manner. These beds of stone are often many leagues in extent, without any interruption ; we almost always meet with the same kind of stone in the opposite mountains, whether divided by a small neck or a valley ; and the beds of stone disappear only in places where the mountain sinks and becomes level with some large plain. Sometimes, between the first stratum of vegetable earth and that of gravel, marl is found, which communicates its colour and other qualities to the other two : then the perpendicular clefts of the quarries which are beneath are filled with this marl, where it acquires an hardness in appearance equal to that of stone, but by exposing it to the air it crumbles, softens and becomes ductile.

In most quarries the beds of stone formed on the summit of a mountain are soft, and those near the base are hard ; the first is commonly white, of so fine a grain as scarcely to be perceived ; it becomes more grained and harder in proportion as it descends, and the lowest stone is not only harder than that of the upper, but it is also closer, more compact and heavier ; its grain is fine and glossy, and often brittle, and breaks as clear as flint.

The

The interior part of a mountain is therefore composed of different beds of stone, the upper of which are of soft stone and the lower of hard, and much broader at the bottom than at the top; which indeed almost necessarily follows, for, as they become so much the harder as they descend, it may be fairly supposed that the currents and other motions of the water which have hollowed the vallies and given a shape to the turnings of a mountain, will have laterally worked on the matters of which the mountain is composed, and have worn them away in proportion as they were hard or soft. Now the upper strata being the softest, it will naturally have suffered the greatest diminution. This is one of the causes to which the inclination of mountains may be attributed, and this inclination will be still less steep in proportion as the earth and gravel have been washed away by the rain; and for these reasons it is, that hills and mountains composed of calcinable matters, have an inclination much less than those composed of live rock and flint in large masses; the last in general are of considerable heights and nearly perpendicular, because, in these masses of vitrifiable matters, the upper beds, as well as the

lower, are of great hardness, and have alike re-
sisted the action of the waters.

When on the top of a hill, whose summit is
flat, and of a pretty large extent, we meet with
hard stone directly under the stratum of vegetable earth, we must remark, that what appears
to be the summit, is not so in fact, but only the
continuation of some higher hill, whose upper
strata are soft stone and the lower hard; and it is
the prolongation of these last strata that we
meet with again at the top of the first hill.

On the summit of mountains which are not
surmounted by any considerable height it is generally only soft stone, and we must dig very
deep to meet with hard. Banks of marble are
never found but between these beds of hard
stone, which are diversely coloured by the metallic earths which the rain introduces into the
strata by filtration, and possibly in every country where there is stone, marble would be found
if dug for to a sufficient depth; *Quoto enim loco
non suum marmor invenitur?* says Pliny. In
fact it is a much more common stone than it is
thought to be, and differs from other stones
only by the fineness of its grain, which renders
it more compact and susceptible of a brilliant
polish;

polish; and from which quality it took its denomination from the ancients.

The perpendicular fissures and joints of quarries are often filled and incrusted with concretions, which are sometimes as transparent as crystal, of a regular figure, sometimes opaque: the water flows through the perpendicular clefts, and penetrates even the compact texture of the stone; the stones which are porous, imbibe so great a quantity of water, that the frost splits and divides them. The rain by filtrating through the beds of marle, stone, and marble, load themselves with every matter they can take up or dissolve. These waters at first run along the perpendicular clefts, afterwards penetrate the beds of stone, and deposit between the horizontal joints, as well as in the perpendicular clefts, the matters they have brought with them, and form these different congelations according to the nature of the matters they have deposited; for example, when the water filters through marle, chalk, or soft stone, the matters which they deposit are a very pure and fine marle, which generally enters in the perpendicular cleft of the rocks under the form of a porous, soft substance, commonly very white and light,

C c 2

which

which naturalists have called *Lac lunac*, or *Medulla Saxi.*

When these streams of water, loaded with lapidific matter, flow through the horizontal joints of soft stone or chalk, this matter attaches itself to the surface of the blocks of stone, and forms white, scaly, light, and spongy crust; which some authors have named *Mineral Agaric*, from its resemblance to Vegetable Agaric : but if the strata are of common hard stone, proper to make good lime, the filter being then more close, the water will issue from it loaded with lapidific matter, more pure and homogeneous, and whose molecules uniting more intimately, will form nearly concretions of the hardness of stone, with a little transparency, and we shall find on the surfaces of the blocks in these quarries, stony incrustations variously disposed, which entirely fill up the horizontal joints.

In grottos and cavities of rocks, which may be looked upon as the basons of perpendicular clefts, the diverted direction of the streams of water, give different forms to the concretion which result therefrom.   They in general have the appearance of a cone attached to the top of the vault, although they may more properly be

con-

considered as hollow and white cylinders, formed by a concentrical surface; these congelations sometimes descend, by drops, to the bottom, and form pillars, and a thousand other figures, as uncouth and ridiculous as the names which naturalists have been pleased to give them, such as, *Stalactites, Stelegmites, Osleocollae,* &c.

When these concretic juices issue immediately from marble and hard stone, the lapidific matter conveyed by the water being rather dissolved than loosened, the small constituent parts take a regular figure, and form columns, terminated by triangular points, which are transparent and consist of oblique strata; this is called Spar, or Spall. It is generally transparent and colourless, but when the stone or marble, from whence it issues, contains metallic parts, this spar is as hard as stone; it dissolves, like stone, by acid spirits, and calcines with the same heat; therefore we cannot doubt that it is real stone, and perfectly homogeneous. It might even be said that it is a pure and elementary stone, under its proper and specific form.

Most naturalists nevertheless look on this matter as a direct substance, existing independent of stone; it is the lapidific or crystalline juice which, according to them, not only binds

the

the parts of common stone, but even those of flint. This juice, say they, constantly augments the density of stones by reiterated filtrations, and at length converts them into real flint. When this juice is fixed in spar, it continues to receive still more pure juices, which increase its density and hardness, so that this matter successively becomes glass, then crystal, and at last a perfect diamond.

But if this is true, why, in whole provinces, does this crystalline juice form only stone, and in others nothing but flint? Will they say, that the two soils are not of a like age, and that this juice has not had time to circulate and complete the end of its natural action? This is not probable. Besides, from whence does this juice proceed? If it produces stone and flints, what is it that produces this juice? It is apparent that it has no existence independent of these matters, which of themselves can give to the water that penetrates them a petrifying quality, always relative to their native and specific character; insomuch that when it filtrates through stones it forms spar, and when it issues from flints, crystal: and there are as many different kinds of this juice, as matters from which they proceed. Experience perfectly agrees with

this

this idea. The waters which filtrate through stone quarries, generally form soft and calcinable matters like the stones themselves; on the contrary, those which spring from rock and flint form hard and vitrifiable congelations, which have all the other properties of flint, as the first have all those of stone; so the waters which have penetrated the beds of mineral and metallic substances produce pyrites, marcasites, and grains.

We have observed, that we might divide all matters into two great classes, vitrifiable and calcinable; clay and flint, marle and stone, may be looked upon as the two extremes of each of these classes, the intervals of which are filled with an almost infinite variety of the mixt matters that have always one or other of these substances for their basis.

The substances of the first class can never acquire the nature and properties of the other. Stone will always be as remote from the nature of flint, as potters earth is from marle; no known agent will ever be capable of making them quit the combinations peculiar to their nature: the country which produces stone and marble will remain to do so as certainly as those wherein there is only flint and granate will never have either stone or marble.

If

If we observe the order and distribution of matters in a hill composed of vitrifiable matters, we shall commonly find, under the first bed of vegetable earth, a bed of clay, a vitrifiable matter, analogous to flint, and which, as I have observed, is only a decomposed vitrifiable sand : this bed of argilaceous earth or sand answers to a bed of gravel met with in hills composed of calcinable matters : beneath which we meet with some beds of free-stone scarcely ever more than six inches thick, and divided into small pieces by perpendicular clefts. Under these beds are many others of the same matters, and also beds of vitrifiable sand, the free-stone becomes harder and its blocks encrease in size in proportion as we descend ; underneath these we find a very hard matter which I have called live rock, or flint in large masses, which is so hard as to resist the file, graver, and acid spirits, more than vitrifiable sand, and even powdered glass, on which aqua-fortis seems to have some effect. If struck by another hard body it emits sparks, and exhales a very penetrating smell of sulphur. This massy flint, as I have termed it, is generally found with beds of clay, earth, coals, and vitrifiable sand, answers to the strata of hard stone

and

and marbles, which serve as a base to hills composed of calcinable matters.

Water, by flowing through perpendicular
clefts, and by penetrating the strata of these
vitrifiable sands, clays, and earths, becomes im-
pregnated with the fine and most homogeneous
parts of these matters, and forms many different
concretions, such as talcs, amianthus's, and various other substances produced by distillations
through vitrifiable matters.

Flint, notwithstanding its hardness and density, has, like common marble and hard stone,
its exudations, from whence stalactites of different kinds result, whose varieties of transparency, colours and configuration, are according
to the nature of the flint which produces them,
and the different metallic or heterogeneous
matters which it contains. Rock crystal, all
precious stones, white or coloured, and even
diamonds, may be regarded as stalactites of
this kind. Flints in small pieces, whose strata
are generally concentric, are also stalactites, or
parasitical stones ; from flints of large dimensions, and most fine opaque stones, are only species of flint. Matters of a vitrifiable kind, as
we have observed, do not produce so great a

variety of concretions as those of the calcinable class; and these concretions, produced by flints, are almost all hard and precious stones; whereas those of the calcareous are only soft matters of no value.

Perpendicular clefts are found in rocks of flint, as well as in those of marble and hard stone; they are sometimes even larger there, which proves that matter is still dryer than stone: hills, whether of calcinable or vitrifiable matters, are supported by clay or vitrifiable sand; these are the common and general matters of which the globe is composed, and which I look on as the lightest parts, or the scoria of vitrified matter, with which it is internally filled; thus all mountains or plains have argilaceous earth or sand for their common foundation. For example, we see that in the pits at Amsterdam and Marly la Ville, vitrifiable sand was below every other stratum.

In most naked rocks it is observable that the sides of the perpendicular clefts, whether broad or narrow, correspond as exactly as those of a piece of slit wood. In the large quarries in Arabia, which are almost composed of granate, these perpendicular separations are very frequent; and although some are twenty or thirty

yards

yards wide, yet the ridges exactly correspond
and leave a deep cavity between them.* It is
very common to find in perpendicular clefts
shells broken in half, and each piece remaining
fastened to the stone on the opposite side; which
proves these shells were placed in the solid stratum, and before the cleft was made.†

In some matters the perpendicular clefts are
very wide, as in the quarries quoted by Shaw,
which perhaps is the reason that they are not
so frequently met with. In the quarries of
flint and granate, the stone may be cut out in
very large pieces without the smallest incon-
veniency, as the obelisks and pillars seen at
Rome, which are upwards of sixty, eighty, an
hundred, or one hundred and fifty feet long.
It appears that these large pillars were raised
from the quarry, and that they are to be had of
any required thickness, as well as some species
of free-stone. There are other matters where
these perpendicular strata are very narrow; as
in clay, marl, and chalk, and they are wider,
in marble and most hard stones. Some are
imperceptible from being filled with a matter
nearly similar to that of the stone itself, which

D d 2 nevertheless

* See Shaw's Travels, vol. II. p. 83.
† See Woodward, page 198.

nevertheless breaks off the continuity of the
stone, and are what the workmen call hairs.   I
have often remarked that in marble and stone
these hairs cross the blocks entirely, and differ
from particular clefts only because their separation is not complete; these kind of clefts are
filled with a transparent matter, which is a
true spar.   There are a great number of considerable clefts in the quarries of free-stone;
this proceeds from these rocks often resting
on less solid bases than marble or calcinable
stones, which generally rest on clay.   There
are many places where free-stone is not to
be met with in large masses; and in most
quarries where it is good it lies in the form of
cubes and parallel pipedes placed on each
other in a very irregular manner, as in the hills
of Fontainbleau, which at a distance appear
to be the ruins of ancient buildings.   This irregular disposition proceeds from the base of
these hills being composed of sand, which per-
mits the rocks to sink one on the other, particularly in places that formerly have been
worked, which has occasioned a great number
of clefts and intervals between the blocks; and
we may observe, in every country where sand
and free-stone abound, that there are many

pieces

pieces of rock and large stones in the middle
of plains and vallies; whereas in a country
consisting chiefly of marble and hard stone,
these scattered pieces, which have rolled from
the hills and mountains, are very scarce, which
proceeds only from the different solidity of the
base on which these stones rest, and from the
extent of the banks of marble and calcinable
stone, which is more considerable than that of
free-stone.

ARTICLE XVIII.

OF THE EFFECTS OF RAIN—OF MARSHES, SUBTERRANEOUS WOOD, AND WATER.

WE have already observed that rains, and
the currents of water they produce,
continually detach from the heights of mountains sand, earth, gravel, &c. which they

carry

carry into plains, from whence the rivers convey a part of them into the sea. Plains therefore are successively filled, and by degrees raised higher, while mountains daily diminish. Joseph Blancanus relates various facts on this subject, which were of public notoriety in his time, and which prove that mountains have been considerably lowered. In the county of Derby, in England, the steeple of the village Craich was not visible in 1572 from a certain mountain, on account of the height of another which intervened; in eighty or an hundred years after, not only this steeple but every part of the church became visible from that very spot. Dr. Plot gives a similar example of a mountain between Sibbertoft and Ashby, in Northamptonshire. The rain waters not only carry with them the lightest parts of the mountains, as earth, gravel, and small stones, but even undermine and roll down large rocks, which considerably diminish the height of them. The mountains of Wales are very steep and high, and the fragments of these rocks are to be seen in large pieces at their feet, which as well as all fragments of rocks met with in vallies are the works of frosts and water. It is not mountains of sand and earth alone

alone which the rain causes to sink, for they
attack the hardest rocks, and carry with them
large fragments into the vallies. In a valley
in Nant-phrancon, in 1685, a part of a large
rock, which rested on a narrow base, having
been undermined by the waters, fell and broke
in many pieces, the largest of which, in descending, tore up a considerable trench in the
plain, and crossed a small river on the other
side of which it stopped. It is to similar accidents we must attribute the origin of all the
large stones found adjacent to the mountains.
We must recollect, as before observed, that
these large stones, scattered abroad, are more
common in countries whose mountains are
composed of sand and free-stone, than in those
where their composition is marble and clay,
because sand is a less solid foundation than
clay.

To give an idea of the quantity of earth
which the rain detaches from mountains and
carries into the vallies, we shall quote a circumstance related by Dr. Plot; he says, in his
Natural History of Staffordshire, that 18 feet
deep in the earth a great number of pieces of
money had been found, coined in the reign
of Edward IV. two hundred years before his
                                        time,

time, from which he concludes that the ground which is marshy has increased above a foot in eleven years, or an inch and a twelfth every year. A similar observation occurs with respect to some trees buried seventeen feet deep from the surface under which medals of Julius Cæsar were found ; so the earth, brought from the top of mountains by the waters, considerably increases the elevation of the ground of plains.

This gravel, sand, and earth which the waters from mountains convey into plains form strata, which must not be confounded with the ancient and original strata of the globe. In the former class must be placed those of soft stone, gravel, and sand, the grains of which are washed and rounded ; to these may be added, the strata of stones which are formed by a kind of incrustation ; neither of which owe their origin to the motion or sediments of the sea. In these strata of soft and imperfect stones are found an infinity of vegetables, leaves, land and river shells, and small bones of terrestrial animals, but never sea shells, or other marine productions ; which evidently proves, together with their want of solidity, that these strata are formed on the

surface

surface of the dry land; and that they are more
modern than those of marble and other stones
which contain shells, and were originally
formed by the sea. All these modern stones
appear to be hard and solid when they are first
hewn out, but when exposed to the weather,
the air and rain presently dissolve them; their
substance is so different from true stone, that
when reduced into minute parts, to make sand
of them, they are converted into a kind of earth
or clay. Stalactites, and other stony concretions, which Tournefort took for vegetated
marble, are not real stones, no more than those
formed by the incrustations. We have already
shewn that tufa is not of ancient formation, and
must not be ranked in the class of stones.
Tufa is an imperfect matter, differing from
stone or earth, but which derives its origin
from both by the means of rain water, as incrustations derive theirs from the deposit of the
water of certain springs; therefore the strata
of these matters are not ancient, nor been
formed like the rest, by the sediments of the
sea. The strata of turf are also modern, and
have been produced by the successive assemblage of leaves and other perishable vegetables,
and which are only preserved by a bitumous

earth. Among these modern strata we never meet with any marine production; but, on the contrary, many vegetables, bones of land animals, and land and river shells, as may be seen in the meadows, near Ashby, in the county of Northampton, where a great number of snail shells, plants, herbs, and many river shells are found all in good preservation, some feet deep in the earth, but not a single marine shell among them.*

These new strata have been formed by the water which runs on the surface of the earth, often changing situation and dispersing on every side. Part of these waters penetrate internally and flow across the clefts of rocks and stones; and the reason we meet with no water in high lands, no more than on the tops of hills, is, because all elevations are generally composed of stone and rocks, therefore to find water we must dig through the rock till we come to clay, or firm earth, on which these rocks stand, and we shall not meet with any water until the stone is pierced to the bottom: therefore, when the thickness of the rock, which must be pierced, is very considerable, as in lofty mountains, where they are often up-

wards

* See Philosophical Trans. Abridg. XI. page 271.

wards of 1000 feet in height, it is impossible to
dig to their base, and of course to have any
water. There are even large parts of land
where there is not any water, as· in Arabia
Petrea, which is a desert where no rain ever
falls, where the scorching sand covers the whole
surface of the earth, where there is scarcely
any vegetable soil, where the few plants found
are sickly, and where springs and wells are so
very scarce that only five are reckoned between
Cairo and Mount Sinai, and the water of them
is salt and bitter.

When the waters on the surface cannot find
vent to flow they form marshes and fens. The
most famous marshes in Europe are those of
Muscovy, at the source of the Tanais; and
those of Savolaxia and Enasak, in Finland;
there are also some in Holland, Westphalia,
and other low countries: in Asia are the marshes
of the Euphrates, of Tartary, and of the Palus
Meotis; nevertheless there are fewer of them
in Asia and Africa than in Europe; but America may be said to be but one continued marsh
throughout all its plains, which is a greater proof
of the modern date of the country, and of the
small number of inhabitants than of their want
of industry.

E e 2

There

There are very great bogs in England, especially near the sea in Lincolnshire, which has lost much ground on one side and gained it on the other. In the ancient ground a great number of trees are found buried below the new ground, which has been deposited there by the water. The same also are met with in Scotland, particularly at the mouth of the river Ness. Near Bruges, in Flanders, in digging to the depth of 40 or 50 feet, a great quantity of trees were found, as close to each other as in a forest : the trunks, branches, and leaves, were so well preserved that the different kinds were easily distinguished. About 500 years since, the land where these trees were found was covered by the sea, and before that time there is no trace or tradition that it ever existed; nevertheless it must have been so, when these trees stood and vegetated ; therefore this ground, which formerly was covered with wood, has been overwhelmed by the sea, the waters of which has, by degrees, deposited there between 40 and 50 feet of earth upon the former surface, and then retired. A number of subterraneous trees have been also found at Youle, in Yorkshire, 12 miles below the town, near the river Humber ; there are some

large

large enough for building ; and it is said, perhaps improperly, that this wood is as durable
as oak. The people cut them into long thin
slips, and sell them in the neighbouring towns,
where they are used for lighting of pipes. All
these trees appear broken, and the trunks are
separated from the roots as if they had suffered
the violence of a hurricane, or an inundation.
This wood greatly resembles willow, it has the
same smell when burnt, and makes charcoal
exactly like it.* In the Isle of Man there is
a marsh six miles long by three broad, it is
called Curragh ; subterraneous trees, like willows, are found there, and although they are
18 or 20 feet high, they are, nevertheless, firm
on their roots.† Trees are met with in almost
every morass, bog, and marsh, in Somerset,
Chester, Lancaster, and Stafford. There are
some places where trees are found under the
earth, which have been cut, sawed, squared,
and worked by the labour of man ; and even
wedges and saws have likewise been found
by them. Between Birmingham and Bromley,
in the county of Lincoln, there are lofty hills
of fine light sand, which the rain and wind

sweep

* See Philosophical Transactions, No. 228.
† See Ray's Discourses, page 232.

sweep away, leaving uncovered the roots of large willow trees, on which the impression of the axe is exceedingly plain. These hills, without doubt, have been formed like downs, by the accumulation of sand, which the waters of the sea has brought there and deposited at different periods. A great number of these subterraneous trees are also found in the marshy lands of Holland, Friesland, and near Groningen, from whence the turfs which they burn are dug.

In the earth are found trees of almost every kind, as willows, oaks, firs, aspins, beach, yew, ash, hawthorn, &c. In the fens of Lincoln, along the river Ouse, and in Hatfield-Chace, in the county of York, these trees are as straight as we see them in a forest. The oaks are very hard and used in buildings; they are said to last a long time, but which I must doubt, as all trees that are dug out of the earth, at least all those which I have seen, whether oak or others, lose, in drying, all the solidity which they appeared to have at first. The ash is tender, and soon crumbles to dust. There are many trees which have clearly been shaped and sawed by men, and the hatchets, sometimes found near them, resemble, in form, the knives

anciently

anciently used in sacrifices.   Besides trees, nuts, acorns, &c. are met with in great quantities, in many other fenny parts of England and Ireland, as well as the morasses of France, Sweden, Savoy, and Italy.*

In the city of Modena, and four miles round, whatever part of the earth is dug, to the depth of sixty-three feet, and then bored five more with an auger, the water springs out with such great force, that the well is filled instantly; and this water continues always the same, neither diminishing nor increasing by rain nor draught. What is more remarkable in this ground, when we reach the depth of fourteen feet, we find the ruins of an ancient town, as paved streets, houses, different pieces of mosaic work, &c.   After this is a very solid ground, which appears to have never been stirred; yet below it we find a moist earth mixed with vegetables; and at twenty-six feet entire trees, as filberds with nuts thereon, and a great quantity of branches and leaves.   At twenty-eight feet is a stratum of chalk mixed with shells, and this bed is eleven feet in thickness; after this we again meet with vegetables; and so on alternatively

* See Transactions Philosophical Abridg. Vol. IV. page 218, &c.

tively to the depth of sixty-three feet, when there is a bed of sand mixed with gravel and shells, like those formed on the coasts of the Italian sea ; these successive beds are always met with in the same order, wheresoever it has been dug, and very often the auger meets with large trunks of trees, which the workmen bore through with much labour. Bones of animals, coals, flint, and pieces of iron are also found. Ramazzini, who relates these circumstances, thinks that the gulph of Venice formerly extended beyond Modena, and, that by the sediments of rivers in the course of time, assisted perhaps by the inundations of the sea, this ground has been formed.

I shall no longer dwell on the varieties in the formation of modern strata, it suffices to have shewn that they have been produced by no other causes than the running and stagnate waters, which are upon the surface of the earth, and that they are neither so hard nor solid as the ancient strata which are formed under the waters of the sea.

ARTICLE

ARTICLE XIX.

OF THE CHANGES OF LAND INTO SEA AND SEA INTO LAND.

BY what has been said in the Articles I, VII, VIII, and IX, it appears that great and general changes have happened to the terrestrial globe; and it is as certain, from what we have related in other articles, that the surface of the earth has undergone particular alterations. Although the order, or succession, of these particular alterations is not perfectly known, yet we are acquainted with the principal causes; we can even distinguish their different effects; and if we could collect all the facts, which Natural and Civil History furnishes on the subject of the revolutions which have happened to the surface of the earth, we do not doubt but that the Theory of the Earth which we have laid down would receive additional support.

One of the principal causes of these alterations is the motion of the sea; a motion it has endured from the earliest ages; for since the sun, moon, earth, waters, air, &c. have existed from the time of the creation, the effects of the tides, the motion of the sea from east to west, as well as that of the winds and currents, must have been felt for the same space; and if even we should suppose the axis of the globe had formerly another inclination, and that the continents, as well as the sea, had another disposition, it does not destroy the motion of flux and reflux, nor alter the cause and effects of the winds: it is sufficient that the immense quantity of waters, which fill the vast space of the sea, is found in some part on the globe of the earth, for wherever they had been collected they would have still been subject to the same motions, and produced similar effects.

When it was once supposed that our continent was formerly the bottom of the sea, there was soon no doubt remaining thereon. The devastations of the sea, which are every where to be met with; the horizontal situation of the

strata

strata of the earth; and the correspondence of
hills and mountains, appear as so many convincing proofs; for by examining the plains,
vallies, and hills, we clearly perceive that the
surface of the earth has been formed by the waters. It is equally evident, when we look into
the interior parts of the earth, that those stones
which contain sea-shells, have been formed by
the sediments of the waters, since the shells are
found filled with the same matter as that which
surrounds them; and lastly, by reflecting on the
corresponding angles of opposite hills, we cannot doubt that their directions are the works
of the currents of the sea. It is true, that since
the earth has been left uncovered, the original
form of the surface has been constantly changing; the mountains have diminished in height;
the plains have been elevated; the angles of
hills become more obtuse; many matters washed away by floods, or rivers, have taken a
round shape; beds of gravel, soft stone, &c.
have been formed; but the essential matter is
still remaining, the ancient form is still apparent, and I am persuaded that all the world may
be convinced by their own inspection of what
has been advanced on this subject; and whoever attends to the observations and proofs I

 have

have given, will not doubt, the earth was formerly covered by the waters of the sea, and that it is the currents of the sea which have given to the surface of the earth, the form we at present perceive.

The principal motion of the sea is, as we have already observed, from east to west. It also appears that the sea has gained above 500 leagues of ground on the eastern coasts of both the old and new continents; for the proofs of which we refer to those given in Article XI. and shall only add thereto, that all straits which join two seas, are directed from east to west; the straits of Magellan, Frobisher, of Hudson, of Ceylon, and those of the seas of Corea and Kamtschatka have all this direction, and appear to have been formed by the currents of the waters, which being impelled from east to west, opened these passages in the same direction, and in which they preserve a more considerable motion than in any other; for in these straits there are high and violent tides, whereas in those situated on the western coasts, like that of Gibraltar, Sund, &c. the motion of the tides is almost insensible.

The inequalities of the bottom of the sea change the direction of the water's motion;

they

they have been successively produced by the sediments of the water, and by matters transported by the tides or other motions; for we do not consider the motion of the tides as the sole cause of those inequalities, but only as the principal and first, because it is the most constant and acts without interruption; the action of the winds is another cause; the action of which beginning at the surface, extends to considerable depths, as is plain from the matters that are loosened and thrown up by a storm from the bottom of the sea, and which never happens but in tempestuous weather.

We have already mentioned that between the tropics, and even some degrees beyond them, an east wind continually blows; this wind, which contributes to the general motion of the sea from east to west, is as ancient as the flux and reflux, since it depends on the rarefaction of the air, produced by the heat of the sun. Here then are two united causes of motion, the greatest of which is near the equator. The first, the tides which are more sensibly felt in southern latitudes: and the second, the east wind which blows continually in the same climates. These two causes have concurred, ever since the formation of the globe, to produce a motion in the

waters

waters from east to west, and to agitate them more in that part of the globe than in all the rest. It is for this reason that the greatest inequalities of the surface of the globe are found between the tropics. The part of Africa, comprehended between these two circles, is only a group of mountains whose different chains extend for the most part from east to west, as is evident from the direction of the great rivers of this part of the world; it is the same with those parts of Asia and America which are comprised between the tropics.

From the combination of the general motion of the sea from east to west, with the flux and reflux of the currents, and the winds, an infinite number of different effects has resulted, both on the bottom of the sea, and on the coasts. Varenius says, it is very probable that the gulphs and straits have been formed by the reiterated efforts of the ocean against the land; that the Mediterranean sea, the gulphs of Arabia, Bengal, and Cambay, have been formed by the eruption of the waters, as well as the straits between Sicily and Italy, between Ceylon and India, between Greece and Euboea, and that it is the same with respect to the straits of the Manillas, Magellan, &c. that one proof of

these

these eruptions, and that the sea has forsaken different lands is, that but few islands are to be met with in the great seas, and never a great number of islands close to each other; that in the immense space occupied by the Pacific sea, not above two or three small islands are to be found towards the middle of it; that in the vast Atlantic ocean, between Africa and the Brazils, we only find the small islands of St. Helena and Ascension; but that all islands are near the great continents, as those of the Archipelago, near the continents of Europe and Asia, the Canaries, near Africa, all the islands of the Indian sea, near the eastern coast of Asia; the Antille islands, close to that of America, and that only the Azores lie at any great distance in the sea between Europe and America.

The inhabitants of Ceylon say, that their island was separated from the peninsula of India by an eruption of the ocean; and this popular tradition is very probable. It is also imagined the island of Sumatra has been separated from the continent, and the great number of shoals and sand banks are a strong proof of it. The Malabars assert, that the Maldivian islands formed a part of the continent of India, and in general it may be reasonably supposed that all the

eastern

eastern islands have been divided from the continents by eruptions of the ocean.*

There is an appearance that formerly the island of Great Britain was part of the continent, and that England was joined to France; the similarity of the stones on the two coasts, and the narrowness of this strait seem plainly to indicate it. By supposing, says Dr. Wallis, " that England formerly communicated with France, by an isthmus between Dover and Calais, it must follow that the sea would be carried against both sides of it with great violence by the tides twice in every twenty-four hours, the German ocean, which is between England and Holland, striking of it on the eastern side, and that of France on the west, would be sufficient in time to wear away so narrow a neck of land, as we have supposed. The tides acting with great violence, not only against this isthmus but also against the coasts of France and England, must have washed away a great quantity of sand, earth, and clay, from every part against which the sea was forced: but, being stopt in its course, it would not deposite, as might be supposed, their sediments against this isthmus, but transported them into the great plain that now

forms

* See Varenius Geography, page 203, 217, and 220.

forms Romney Marsh, which is eight miles long by four broad; for whosoever has seen this plain, cannot doubt but that it was formerly covered with the sea, as it would be still overflowed by spring tides if it was not for the Dikes of Dimchurch.

The German sea must have acted in the same manner against this isthmus, and the coasts of England and Flanders would convey its sediments into Holland and Zealand, the ground of which, though formerly covered with water, is now forty feet above. On the coast of England, the German sea must have filled up that large valley, where the river Stour actually flows for more than 20 miles, beginning at Sandwich, passing Canterbury, Chatham, Chilham as far as Ashford. At this place the ground is much higher than it was formerly, since at Chatham the bones of an hippopotamus were found seventeen feet deep in the earth, together with anchors and marine shells.

It is very probable the sea may form new land, by bringing and depositing, at particular places, sand, earth, mud, &c. for in the island of Orkney, which is adjacent to Romney Marsh, there was a tract of low land continually in danger of being inundated by the river Rother ; but in less than 60 years this ground has been considerably elevated by quantities of earth and mud being brought thither every tide, and the channel through which it enters, in less than fifty years has deepened so much as to admit of the reception of large vessels, whereas at that time it was a ford over which people might pass.

In this manner, the sand bank was formed which extends obliquely from the coast of Norfolk to that of Zealand. This bank forms that part where the tides of the German and French sea meet, since the isthmus has been broken, and where the earth and sand are deposited which are washed away from the coasts; nor is it by any means improbable but that in the course of time this bank may become an isthmus.*

There is a great appearance, says Ray, that the island of Great Britain was formerly joined to France, and formed part of that continent : but it is not known whether its separation was caused by an earthquake, an eruption of the ocean, or by the labour of man ; but that this island

* See Abridgment of Philosophical Transactions, vol. 11, page 227.

island formed part of the continent is evident, from the rocks and coasts of both being of the same nature, composed of the same matters, and exactly of the same height; the length of the rocks, along these coasts, are also nearly the same, about six miles on either side. The little breadth of the channel, which in this part is not more than twenty-four English miles, and its shallowness, comparatively with the neighbouring sea, is another reason to suppose that England has been divided from France by accident. We may add to these proofs, that there were formerly wolves and bears in this island; it is not to be presumed that they could swim over, nor that men transported such destructive animals; for in general we find the noxious animals of the continent in the adjacent islands, and never in those which are separated from them by a great distance; as the Spaniards remarked when they landed in America.*

In the reign of Henry I. King of England, a great inundation happened by an eruption of the sea in part of Flanders. In 1446 by a like eruption 10,000 persons were drowned in the territory of Dordrecht, and more than

G g 2

100,000

* See Ray's Discourses, page 208.

100,000 round Dullart, Friezeland, and in Zealand. In these last two provinces upwards of 300 villages were overflowed; the tops of their towers and steeples are still to be seen rising out of the water.

From the coasts of France, England, Holland and Germany, the sea has retreated in many parts. Hubert Thomas relates, in his description of Liege, that the sea formerly surrounded the walls of the city of Tongres, which is now more than 35 leagues distant from it; this he proves by many eligible reasons, and, among others, he says, that in his time the iron rings, to which the ships were moored, were to be seen remaining in the walls. We may likewise look on as lands deserted by the sea, the fens of Lincoln in England, Provence in France, and which has also very considerably retreated from the mouth of the Rhone since the year 1665. In Italy a considerable tract of land has been gained at the mouth of the Arno; and Ravenna, formerly a sea-port, is no longer a maritime town. Holland appears to be an entire new country, where the surface of the earth is almost on a level with the sea, although the land is considerably elevated by the daily deposit of mud

and

and earth from the Rhine, Maese, &c. for it was formerly computed that the ground of Holland was, in many places, 50 feet lower than the bottom of the sea.

It is asserted, that in the year 860, a furious tempest drove on the coast so great a quantity of sand that it shut up the mouth of the Rhine, near the Cat, and that this river inundated the whole country, tore up trees and houses, and, at last, emptied itself into the channel of the Maese. In 1421 another inundation separated the town of Dordrecht from the main land, submerged 72 villages, many castles, and drowned 100,000 souls, beside a great number of cattle. The dyke of Yssel was broken in 1638 by the ice brought down by the Rhine, which, having shut up the passage of the water, made an opening of some fathoms, and a great part of the province was over-flowed before the breach could be repaired. In 1682 there was a similar inundation in the province of Zealand, which destroyed upwards of 30 villages, and drowned a considerable number of people and cattle, from their being surprised by the waters in the night. It was a fortunate circumstance for Holland that a

south

south wind opposed the inroad of the sea, for it was so greatly swelled that the water was 18 feet higher than the highest ground of the province.[*]

At Hithe, in the county of Kent, the harbour has filled up in defiance of every expence and precaution that was made to prevent it. A surprising number of sea-shells, &c. are met with for several miles round, which were formerly heaped together, and which are now covered by earth, and are beautiful meadows. On the other side the sea has gained in several places, as for instance, the Goodwin Sands, which was an estate belonging to an Earl of that name, but at present is no more than sand covered by the waters of the sea : thus the sea in many places gains on the land and loses in others, according to the different situation of the coasts, and other circumstances.[†]

On Mount Stella, in Portugal, is a lake in which the wrecks of ships have been found, notwithstanding this mountain is more than 12 leagues from the sea.[‡] Sabinius, in his Commentaries

---

[*] See the Historical Voyages of Europe, vol. v. page 70.

[†] See Abridg. Philosophical Trans. vol. IV. p. 234.

[‡] See Gordon's Geography, page 149.

mentaries on Ovid's Metamorphoses, says, that in the year 1460 a ship, with its anchors, was found in a mine of the Alps.

It is not in Europe alone we meet with these vicissitudes of land into sea and sea into land ; other parts of the world might furnish more remarkable, and in a greater number, if investigated with precision.

Calecut was formerly a famous city and the capital of a kingdom of that name; at present it is only a trifling town, meanly built, and but thinly inhabited : the sea, which for a century has gained greatly on this coast, has overflowed the greatest part of the old city, with a beautiful fortress of stone which was therein. Vessels at present moor on their ruins, and the port is filled with a great number of shoals, and on which ships are frequently wrecked.*

The province of Jucatan, a peninsula in the gulph of Mexico, was formerly a part of the sea. This neck of ground extends 100 leagues in length, and is not more than 25 leagues at its greatest breadth. The air is perfectly hot and moist. Although there are neither rivulets nor rivers throughout so long a space, the water is every where so nigh the surface as to furnish

plenty ;

* See Letters Edifiantes Recueil 11. page 187.

plenty; and, by opening the earth, so great a number of shells are found as to leave no doubt that this great extent may be regarded as a place which formerly was part of the sea.

The inhabitants of Malabar pretend that formerly the Maldivian islands were attached to the Indian continent, and that the violence of the sea has divided them from it. The number of these islands is so great, and some of the channels, which separate them, are so narrow, that the boltsprits of vessels which pass them tear off the leaves of the trees on each side, and in some places an active man, by holding by the branch of a tree, may leap into another island.*

The cocoa-trees, which are at the bottom of the sea, is a proof that the Maldivians were formerly part of the continent : cocoa-nuts are often detached from them and thrown on the shore by a storm.

It is imagined that the island of Ceylon was formerly united to the continent, and that the currents, which are extremely rapid in many parts of India, have divided that as well as Rammanakoil, and many other islands.† However,

ever,

* See the Dutch Travels to the East-Indies, page 274.

† See the Dutch Travels to the East-Indies, vol. ii. p. 486.

ever, it is certain that the island of Ceylon has lost 30 or 40 leagues of ground towards the north-west side, which the sea has gained.

It appears that the sea has recently forsaken a great part of the projecting lands and islands of America. We have just observed, that the ground of Jucatan is filled with shells. It is the same with the low lands of Martinico and the other Antille islands. The inhabitants have termed the earth below the surface *lime*, because they make their lime with these shells, considerable banks of which are found immediately under the vegetable earth. In the new voyages to the islands of America it is said, " lime, which is found in the land of Guadaloupe, when the earth is turned up, is of the same kind as that drawn out of the sea, the reason of which is difficult to be assigned. Might it not be possible, that all the extent of ground, which composes this island, was, in former times, only a high ground filled with lime-plants, which having grown and filled the void spaces that were occupied by the water, have raised up the ground, obliged the water to retire, and leave all the superficies dry? This conjecture, as extraordinary as at first it may appear, has, nevertheless, nothing impossible in it; and if the people who reside there were to dig in different parts of the earth they would discover what the real soil is, and by that means destroy or strengthen my conjecture."

There are some lands which are sometimes covered with water and sometimes uncovered, as many islands in Norway, Scotland, Maldivias, the gulph of Cambaya, &c. The Baltic has, by little and little, gained a great part of Pomerania, and covered and destroyed the famous port of Vineta. So likewise the sea of Norway has projected into the continent, and formed many small islands. The German sea has projected into Holland near Catt, insomuch that the ruins of an ancient citadel of the Romans, which was formerly on the coast, are now very far in the sea. The marshy grounds in the Isle of Ely, in England, and those in Provence, in France, are, on the contrary, as we have observed, land which the sea has abandoned. Downs have been formed by the sea-winds, which have thrown and accumulated earth, sand, shells, &c. on the shore. For example, on the western coast of France, Spain, and Africa, durable and violent westerly winds reign,

which

which impel the waters towards the shore with great impetuosity, and on which coasts downs are very frequent. In the like manner the easterly winds, when they remain any long time, so strongly drive the waters from the coasts of Syria and Phœnicia that the chain of rocks, which are covered with water during the westerly winds, are left quite dry. Thus downs are never composed of stone, or marble, like mountains formed in the bottom of the sea, because they have not been long enough under the water. In our discourse on minerals we shall shew that the sea possesses the power of petrifaction, and that the stones formed in the earth are quite different from those formed in the sea.

When I had just finished my Theory of the Earth, which I composed in 1744, I received from Mons. Barrere, his dissertation on the origin of figured stones, and I was pleased to find myself of the same opinion with this able naturalist, on the subject of the formation of downs, and the time the water remained on the earth which we inhabit; he recounts many alterations which have happened to the sea coasts : " *Aiguis-mortes*, which is now more than a league and a half from the sea, was

a port

a port in the time of St. Louis : Psalmodi was an island in 815, and at present it is inland two leagues from the sea. It is the same with respect to Maguelone. The greatest part of the vineyards of Agde, was forty years ago covered by the sea : and in Spain the sea has considerably retreated within a short space of time from Blancs, Badalona, the mouth of the river Vobregat, Cape Tortosa, along the coasts of Valentia, &c.

" The sea may form hills and mountains in many different manners; first, by the transportations of earth, sand, and shells, from one place to another; secondly, by depositing sediments, consisting of small particles detached from the coasts and bottom, and which it might have transported from a considerable distance; and lastly, by sand, mud, and other articles, which the sea winds often drive against coasts, downs and hills may be produced, which the water forsaking, by degrees, become parts of the continent." The downs of Flanders and Holland are of this kind, being only hills composed of sand and shells, which the sea winds have driven towards the land. Mons. Barrere quotes another example which merits a place in this work. " The

sea,

sea, by its motion, detaches from its bottom an infinity of plants, shells, slime, and sand, which the waves and winds continually drive towards the shore. Now, all these different operations must continually form new strata, elevate the beds of earth, gradually raising downs and hills, retrenching the bounds of the ocean, and by that means extending the lands on the continents."

"It is visible that new strata have been successively formed by the same reiterated motion of the waters from the deposition of sediments and other constant causes from time immemorial; of which I find strong proofs in the different beds of fossils, shells, and other marine productions found in Roussillon near the village of Naffiac, about seven or eight leagues from the sea; these beds of shells which are inclined from the west to the east, and in different angles, are separated from each other by banks of sand and earth, are sometimes from one and a half to two or three feet in thickness. They appear as if sprinkled with salt in dry weather, and form together hillocks from twenty-five to thirty fathoms in height: now a long chain of hills of such an height can only be formed gradually, and at different successions of time. Such

Such might be the effect of an universal deluge, which must have disturbed all nature; but which could not have given a regular form to these different beds of fossil shells, but would have jumbled them together without any order or regularity."

On this subject I am perfectly of the same opinion as M. Barrere, excepting as to the formation of mountains, which I cannot agree ought to be entirely attributed to the causes which occasion the ocean to gain upon the land on some parts, and lose it upon others. As I am, on the contrary, of opinion, I could produce many convincing arguments to prove that most of the eminencies seen on the surface of the earth have been actually formed in the sea itself. First, because they have a corre- spondence of saillant and returning angles, which necessarily implies the cause we have assigned, that is, the motion of the currents. Secondly, because downs and hills, which are formed by the materials that the sea brings on its shores, are not composed of marble and hard stone, like common hills; the shells also in the former are generally only fossils, whereas in the latter, the petrifaction is compleat; be- sides the beds of earth are not so horizontal

in

in downs as in the hills composed of marble and hard stone, but are more or less inclined, as in the hills of Naffiac, whereas in the hills and mountains, formed under the water by the sediment of the sea, the strata are always parallel, and very often horizontal, and the shells and other marble are entirely petrified. I have no doubt of proving that marble and other calcinable matters, which are almost all composed of madrepores, astroites, and shells, have acquired their hardness and perfection at the bottom of the sea; on the contrary, gravel, soft stones, incrustations, stalactites, &c. which are also calcinable and found in the earth, and formed since our continent has been discovered, cannot acquire this degree of hardness and petrifaction which marble or hard stones have.

In the history of the French Academy for 1708, may be seen the observations of Saulmon, on the subject of the galets found in many places. These galets are round and flat flints very smooth, and which are cast on the shores by the sea. At Bayeux, and at Prutel, which are a league from the sea, we find them in digging wells or pits. The mountains of Bonneuil, Broie, and Quesny, which are eighteen leagues from the sea, are all covered with galets; they are also found in the valley of Clermont in Beauvois. M. Saulmon likewise relates, that a hole, 16 feet deep, was bored horizontally into the beach of Tresport, which is soft earth, and that it entirely disappeared in 30 years: so that if the sea always encroaches alike, it would gain half a league in 12,000 years.

The motions of the sea are therefore the principal causes of the alterations which have happened, and which daily happen on the surface of the globe. But there are many other causes, which, though less considerable, contribute to those changes. Running waters, rivers, streams, the melting of snow, torrents, frosts, &c. have occasioned many changes; the rains have diminished the height of mountains; rivers and rivulets have raised plains, and stopped up the sea at their mouths; the melting of snow, and torrents, have dug hollows in vallies; and the frosts have split rocks and separated them from their former stations. We might quote an infinity of examples on the alterations these causes have occasioned. Varenius says, that rivers convey into the sea great quantities of earth, which they deposit at a greater or less distance from the coasts, according

cording to the rapidity of their currents ; these earths fall to the bottom of the sea, and, at first, form those small banks which daily encrease, become shoals, and, at last, form islands, which are fertile and inhabitable. This is the manner in which the islands of the Nile are formed, as well as those of St. Laurence, the Isle of Landa, situate on the coast of Africa, near the mouth of the river Coanza, the island of Norway, &c.* To these may be added the island of Trong Ming, at China, which has been gradually formed by the earth that the river Nankin has brought and deposited it at its mouth. This island is more than 20 leagues long by five or six broad.†

The Po, Trento, Athesis, and other rivers of Italy, bring with them great quantities of earths into the lakes of Venice, especially during the time of inundations, which, in course of time, must fill them up. In many places they are now dry at low water, and, excepting the canals, which are kept up at a great expence, have no depth of water.

At the mouths of the Nile, the Ganges, the Indus, the Plata, the Nankin, and of many

* See Varenni Geograph. page 214.
† See Letters Edifiantes, Recueil xi. page 234.

other rivers, the earth and sand deposited form considerable banks. Loubere, in his Voyage to Siam, says, that the banks of sand and earth daily increase at the mouths of the great rivers of Asia, insomuch that the navigation of them becomes every day more difficult, and will one day be impassable. The same remark may be made of the large rivers of Europe, and particularly of the Wolga, which has more than 70 mouths in the Caspian sea, and of the Danube, which has seven in the Black sea, &c.

As it seldom rains in Egypt the regular inundations of the Nile proceed from the torrents which fall therein from Ethiopa. These annually bring with them great quantities of mud, which they not only deposit on the land of Egypt but even throw to a considerable distance in the sea, and thus lay the foundation of a new land, which, in the course of time, arises therefrom; for, by sounding with the lead, we find, at more than 20 leagues distance from the coast, the mud of the Nile at the bottom of the sea, and which is every year increasing. Lower Egypt, where * Dela at present stands, was formerly a gulph of the sea.

* See Diodorus de Suc, lib. 3. Aristotle, lib. 1. of Meteors, h. xiv. Herodotus, f. 4, 5, &c.

sea. Homer tells us that the island of Pharos was 24 hours voyage from Egypt, and at present it is almost contiguous to it. The soil of Egypt has not the same depth of good ground throughout its extent, it lessens as we approach the sea. Near the borders of the Nile there is sometimes near thirty feet depth of good earth, whereas at the extremity of the inundation there is scarcely more than seven inches.* The town of Damietta, at present more than 10 miles from the sea, in 1243 was a seaport. The town of Fooah, which, 300 years ago, was situate at the mouth of the Canopic, a branch of the Nile, is now more than seven leagues from it. Within 40 years the sea has retreated half a league from before Rosetta and Idern.

The great rivers of America, and even those which have been but lately discovered, have suffered great alterations at their mouths. Charlevoix, speaking of the river Mississipi, says, that at its mouth, below New Orleans, the country forms a point of land which does not appear to be very ancient, for by digging but a little into the earth water is met with; besides, the quantity of small islands which

I i 2

have

* See Shaw's Travels, vol. II. page 185, and 186.

have recently been formed at all the mouths of this river, leaves no doubt of this neck of land being formed after the same manner. It appears certain, says he, that when M. de la Salle went down the Mississipi, to the sea, the mouth of this river was not as it is at this present time.

" The nearer we approach towards the sea, adds he, the more it becomes perceptible, the bar has scarcely any water in most of the small outlets which the river has opened, and which have multiplied so greatly from the trees that are carried along with the currents, one of which stopt in a part where it is shallow, will entangle hundreds. I have seen, continues he, 200 leagues from New Orleans, collections of trees, one of which would have filled all the timber-yards of Paris. Nothing can set them free; the mud which the river brings down serves to cement, and, by degrees, covers them. Each inundation leaves a new stratum, and, after 10 years, shrubs and vegetables grow thereon: after this manner most points and islands are formed, which so often change the course of rivers."*

Nevertheless

* See Charlevoix Travels, vol. II. page 440.

Nevertheless all the changes which rivers cause are very slow, and become not consider-able till after a long series of years : but quick and sudden changes have happened by in-undations and earthquakes. The ancient Egyptian priests, 600 years before the birth of Christ, asserted, according to the Timaeus of Plato, that there was a great island near Hercules Pillars, called *Atlantns*, which was larger than Lybia and Asia taken together ; and that this island was buried under the waters of the ocean after a great earthquake. " Tra-ditur Atheniensis civitas restitisse olim innu-meris hostium copiis quæ, ex Atlantico mari profectæ, propè cunctam Europam Asiamque obsederunt ; tunc enim fretum illud navigabile habens in ore et quasi vestibulo ejus insulam quam Herculis columnas cognominant ; fer-turque insula illa Lybiâ simul et Asiâ Major fuisse, per quam ad alias proximas insulas patebat aditus, atque ex insulis ad omnem continentem è conspectu jacentem vero mari vicinam : sed intrà os ipsum portes augusto sinu traditur, pelagus illud verum mare, terra quoque illa verè erat continens, &c. Post . hæc ingenti terræ motu jugique diei unius et

noctis

noctis illuvione factum est, ut terra dehiscens omnis illos bellicosos absorberet, et Atlantis insula sub vasto gurgite mergeretur." *Plato in Timaeo.* This ancient tradition is not abso-lutely contrary to all probability. The earths which were absorbed by the waters are per-haps those which join Ireland to the Azores, and those to the continent of America; for in Ireland there are the same fossils, shells, and marine productions as in America, some of which are different from any found in other parts of Europe.

Eusebius relates two testimonies on the sub-ject of deluges : one of which is Melo, who says that the plains of Syria had formerly been laid under water ; the other is Abydenus, who says, that in the time of King Sisithrus there was a great deluge, which had been predicted by Saturnus, Plutarch *De Solestia Animalium.* Ovid, and other mythologists, speak of the deluge of Deucalion, which, according to them, was in Thessaly, about 700 years from the universal deluge. It is also asserted that there had been one more ancient in Attica, in the time of Ogiges, about 230 years before that of, Deucalion.

In

In the year 1095 there was a deluge in Syria, which drowned a number of people.* In 1164 there was so considerable a one in Friezeland, that all maritime coasts were covered, and several thousands of the inhabitants drowned.† In 1218 there was another inundation which destroyed near an hundred thousand people. There are a multitude of other examples of great inundations, like that of 1604 in England, and many more.

A third cause of the change on the surface of the globe, are impetuous winds. They not only form downs and hills on the sea shores, but they often stop and choak up rivers, and change their directions; they tear up cultivated land, destroy trees, overthrow edifices, and cover entire countries with sand. We have an example of these inundations of sand on the coasts of Britany in France: the history of the Royal Academy at Paris, anno 1722, makes mention of it in the following terms.

" In the environs of St. Paul de Leon, in Lower Britany, there is a quarter near the sea, which before the year 1666, was inhabited; but is so no longer, by reason of a sand which

covers

* See Alsted. Chron. chap. 25.
† See Krank, Lib. 5, cap. 4.

covers it to the height of more than twenty feet, and which gains ground every year. Reckoning from that time it has proceeded upwards of six leagues into the country, and is now not more than about half a league from St. Paul, so that according to all appearance that town must soon be deserted. The tops of some steeples and chimnies are still seen peeping out of this sea of sand; the inhabitants of the interred villages have always had sufficient time to quit their houses in safety.

" An east or north wind increases this calamity, by raising up a sand of a very fine nature, which sweeps it away in such great quantities, and with such velocity, that M. Deslandes, to whom the academy are indebted for this observation, when walking in that country during an east wind, was obliged, from time to time, to wipe it off his hat and cloaths, they were so loaded with sand, and felt so heavy. Besides, when this wind is violent, it throws this sand over a small arm of the sea into Roscof, a small port much frequented by foreign vessels; the sand collects in their streets to the height of two feet, and the inhabitants are obliged to have it carted away. There are

many

many ferruginous particles in this sand, which are easily discovered by a magnet.

" The coast which furnishes this sand extends from St. Paul as far as Plouefoat, somewhat more than four leagues. The disposition of the place is such that only the east or the north-east wind can convey the sand over the lands. It is easy to be conceived how the sand, conveyed and accumulated by the wind in one part, can again be taken up by the same wind and carried farther, and that the sand can thus advance into and cover the country while the mine which furnishes it continues unexhausted; for without this the sand, by advancing, would always diminish in height, and would cease its destructive ravages. Now it is but too possible that the sea throws up or deposits new sand in the place from whence the wind raises it up, and therefore the dreadful effects may long continue.

" The disaster is but of modern date, possibly the shoal which furnishes it has not yet a sufficient quantity to lift itself above the surface of the sea, or perhaps the sea has but just left it uncovered. There has been some alteration on the coast, and the sea at present

 reaches,

reaches, at high water, half a league beyond certain rocks that formerly it never passed.

" This unhappy province justifies what the ancient and modern travellers relate concerning the tempests of sand in the deser's of Arabia, in which cities and armies have been enveloped and destroyed."

Mr. Shaw tells us that the ports of Laodicea, Jebila, Tortosa, Rowada, Tripoli, Tyre, Acra, and Jaffa, are all filled up with sand brought thither by the great waves which beat on that side of the Mediterranean when the west wind blows impetuously.*

It is useless to give a greater number of examples of the alterations that have happened on the surface of the globe. Fire, air, and water, produce continual changes, which become very considerable by time. It is not from general causes alone, whose effects are periodical and regular, that the sea successively takes the place of the earth, and forsakes its own dominions. There are a number of particular causes which contribute to these mutations, such as earthquakes, inundations, sinking of mountains, &c. Thus the most solid thing,

at

* See Shaw's Travels, vol. II.

at least to our conception, like the rest of nature, undergoes continual and perpetual vicissitudes.

CONCLUSION

OF THE

THEORY OF THE EARTH.

BY the proofs we have given in Articles VII. and VIII. it appears certain that the whole of the present dry land was formerly covered by the sea. It appears also as certain, from Article XII. that the flux and reflux, and other motions of the ocean, continually detach, from the side and the bottom of the sea, shells

and

and matters of every kind, some part of which are deposited in other places in form of sediments, and which are the origin of the parallel and horizontal strata every where to be met with. We have proved in Article ix. that the inequalities of the globe have been caused by the motion of the sea, and that mountains have been produced by the successive masses and heapings of the sediments we have just described. It is evident by Article xiii. that the currents, which at first followed the direction of these inequalities, afterwards gave to them all the figure which they at present preserve; that is, that alternate correspondence of the saliant angles always opposed to the returning angles. It appears likewise by Articles viii. and xviii. that the greatest part of the matters which the sea has detached from its sides and bottom were, when deposited as sediments, in form of a fine impalpable powder, which perfectly filled the cavities of the shells, whether it was of the same nature or only analogous to that with which they were composed. It is certain, from Article xvii. that the horizontal strata which have been produced by the accumulation of sediments, and which at first were

in

in a soft state, acquired hardness in proportion as they became dry, and that this drying has produced perpendicular clefts, which cross the horizontal strata.

It is impossible to doubt, after perusing the facts in the Articles X. XI. XIV. XV. XVI. XVII. XVIII. and XIX. that an infinite number of revolutions, particular changes and alterations, have happened on the surface of the globe, as well from the natural motion of the waters of the sea as by the effects of rain, frost, running waters, winds, subterraneous fires, earthquakes, inundations, &c. and that consequently the sea has alternately changed places with the earth, especially in the earliest times after the creation, when the terrestrial matters were much softer than they are at present. It must nevertheless be acknowledged, that we can but very imperfectly judge of the succession of natural revolutions; that we can still less judge of the cause of accidents, changes, and alterations; that the defect of historical monuments deprives us of the knowledge of particular facts, and experience and time is deficient to us. We do not pay any consideration that, though the time of our existence is very limited, nature

proceeds

proceeds in her regular course. We would condense into our momentary existence the transactions of ages past and to come, without reflecting that this instant of time, nay even human life itself, is only a single fact in the history of the acts of the Almighty.

HISTORY

HISTORY OF ANIMALS.

CHAPTER I.

A COMPARISON BETWEEN ANIMALS, VEGETABLES, AND OTHER PRODUCTIONS OF NATURE.

AMIDST the infinite number of objects that offer themselves to our view, and with which the surface of the earth is every where covered, Animals hold the first rank both on account of their formation, and their evident superiority over vegetables and other matters. Animals, by their senses, form, motion, and many other properties, have a more intimate connection with those things which surround them than vegetables; and the latter, by their figure, growth, and variety of component parts, have also a nearer relation with external objects,

objects, than either minerals or stones, which have not any kind of life or motion. By this number of properties it is, that the animal claims pre-eminence over the vegetable, and the vegetable over the mineral. Man, to consider him by his material form alone, is only superior to the brute creation by possessing some few peculiar properties, such as those given to him by his tongue and hands; and although the works of the Creator are in themselves equally perfect, the animal, according to our mode of perception, is the most complete, and man the most perfect animal.

What variety of springs, what forces, and what mechanical motions are enclosed in this small part of matter which composes the body of an animal? What properties, what harmony, and what correspondence between the various parts? How many combinations, arrangements, causes, effects, and principles, conspire to complete one end, and which we know only to be results so very difficult to comprehend, that they only cease from being marvellous by the long custom of not reflecting on them?

Nevertheless, however admirable this work appears, it is not the individual that is the most
wonderful;

wonderful; but it is in the succession, reproduction, and duration of species, that nature
becomes inconceivable. This faculty of reproduction, which resides alone in animals and
vegetables ; this kind of unity always subsisting,
and seemingly eternal; this procreative power,
which perpetually exercises itself without being
destroyed, is a mystery, the depth of which we
are not enabled to fathom.

Inanimate bodies, even the stones and dirt
under our feet, have some properties ; their existence alone supposes a great number ; and the
least organic matter has an infinity of relations
with the other parts of the universe. We shall
not say, with some philosophers, that matter,
under whatever form it may be, is sensible of
its existence and relative faculties. This is a
metaphysical question, and of which we do not
here propose to treat, it will be sufficient to observe, that not having a perfect knowledge of
our own relation with external objects, we cannot doubt that inanimate matters are still more
ignorant; besides, as our sensations do not in the
least resemble the objects which cause them,
we must conclude, by analogy, that inanimate
matter has neither sentiment, sensation, nor a
consciousness of its existence; to attribute any

of these faculties to it, would be giving it the power of thought, action, and perception, nearly in the same manner as we think, act, and feel, which is as much repugnant to reason as it is to religion.

Inanimate bodies being formed of earth and dust, we have, of course, some properties in common with them, but they are merely relative to what arises from general matter, such as extent, impenetrability, weight, &c. but as these properties, purely material, make no impression of themselves, as they exist entirely independent, and do not at all affect us, we cannot consider them as a part of our being; it is therefore the organization, the soul, and the life, which constitute our existence. Matter, considered in this light, is less the principal than the accessor. It is a foreign expansion, the union of which is unknown, and the presence hurtful to us; and thought, which is the constituent principle of our being, is very probably entirely independent.

We exist, therefore, without knowing how, and we think without knowing why; but whatever is the manner of our being or thinking, whether our sensations are true or false, the result of them are not less certain. This

order

order of ideas, this train of thoughts, which internally exist from ourselves, although very different from the objects that cause them, give rise to the most real affections, and occasion relations with external objects, which we may consider as real affinities, since they are invariable, and always the same. The human species, therefore, may be said to hold the first rank in the order of nature, the brute creation the second, vegetables the third, and minerals the last ; for although we cannot clearly distinguish between our animal and spiritual qualities, and although the brute creation are endowed with the same senses, possess the same principles of life and motion, and perform a number of actions like man, yet they have not the relation with external objects in the same extensive manner we have, and consequently the resemblance must fail in various respects. The distance is greater between man and vegetables, and still more so from minerals, as vegetables possess a degree of animation, while minerals are destitute of every principle that tends to organization.

To compose, therefore, the history of an animal, we must first nicely inspect into the general order of his particular relations, and

 afterwards

afterwards distinguish those he has in common with vegetables and minerals. An animal has nothing in common with a mineral, excepting general properties of matter; his nature and œconomy are totally different: the mineral is a mere senseless and inactive matter, without organization, faculties, or power of re-production; a dead mass, fit only to be trod under foot by man and animals; even the most precious metals are thus considered by the philosopher, as they possess but an arbitrary value, subordinate to the will, and dependent on the convention of men.

In an animal all the powers of nature are united; the properties by which it is animated are peculiar to it; by its senses it can will, act, determine, and communicate with the most distant objects: its body is a centre, to which every thing is connected; a point where the whole universe is reflected; a world in miniature. These are the properties which peculiarly belong to it; those which it possesses in common with vegetables are the faculties of growth, expansion, re-production, and increase.

The most apparent difference between animals and vegetables seems to be the faculty of moving from place to place, which animals

are

are endowed with and vegetables not. It is true we are not acquainted with any vegetable that has a single progressive motion ; and there are many kinds of animals, as oysters, &c. to which this motion seems to have been denied ; the distinction, therefore, is neither general nor necessary.

A more essential difference might be drawn from the faculty of sensation ; but sensation includes such a variety of ideas, that we ought not to mention the word without giving some explication ; for if by sensation we understand only a motion, occasioned by a check or resistance, we shall find the *sensitive*-plant is also possessed of it ; if, on the contrary, we would have it signify to apprehend and compare ideas, we are not certain that brute animals possess it ; if it is allowed to dogs, elephants, &c. whose actions seem to result from the same causes as those of men, it must be denied to an infinite number of others, especially to those which seem to be motionless. If we could give to oysters, for example, the same faculty of sensation as to dogs, though in an inferior degree, why should we not allow it to vegetables in a still lesser degree ? This difference

between

between animals and vegetables is not, therefore, general, nor well decided.

A third difference seems to arise from their
method of feeding. Animals, by the means
of certain external organs, seize those things
which are agreeable to them : they seek their
pasture and chuse their food. Plants are reduced to the necessity of receiving such nutriment as the earth furnishes : they have no di-
versity in the manner of procuring it; no choice
in the kind, but the humidity of the earth is
their only aliment; nevertheless, if we attend
to the organization and action of roots and
leaves, we shall presently discover that there
are in those parts external organs, which vegetables make use of to obtain their food; that the
root avoids and turns from an obstacle, or vein
of bad earth, to seek for one that is better; that
they divide their fibres, and even go so far as to
change their form to procure nutriment for the
plant. The difference between animals and
vegetables cannot, therefore, be established on
the manner in which they receive their nutriment.

This investigation induces us to conclude
that there is no absolute essential and general
difference

difference between animals and vegetables, but that nature descends by degrees imperceptibly from an animal which is the most perfect, to that which is the least, and from the latter to the vegetable. The water polypus may therefore be considered as the line where the animal creation ends and that of plants begin.

If, after having examined the distinctions, we search after the resemblances between animals and vegetables, we shall find the power of re-production is general, and very essential to both; a faculty which would almost lead us to suppose that animals and vegetables are nearly of the same order of beings.

A second resemblance may be drawn from the expansion of their parts, a property which is common to both; for vegetables grow as well as animals, and if the manner in which they expand is different, it is not totally nor essentially so, since there are very considerable parts in animals, as the bones, the hair, the nails, the horns, &c. whose expansion is a perfect and real vegetation; and the fœtus, at its first formation, may be said rather to vegetate than live.

A third resemblance arises from there being some animals which propagate like plants, and

by

by the same method. The multiplication of the vine-fretter, which is made without copulation, is like that of plants by seeds; and that of polypuses, by cutting them, resembles the multiplication of trees by slips.

We can then assert with greater foundation, that animals and vegetables are beings of the same order, and that nature passes from one to the other by insensible links; since the properties wherein they resemble each other are general and essential, and those on which they differ confined and particular.

If we compare animals and vegetables by other lights, for example, by number, situation, size, form, &c. we shall draw fresh inductions from them.

The number of the animal species is much greater than that of plants. In the class of insects alone there are a greater number of species than there are kinds of plants on the surface of the earth. Animals likewise much less resemble each other than plants; and it is this resemblance among the latter which makes the difficulty of knowing and discerning them, and has given rise to so many botanical systems; and it is for this reason that more labour has been bestowed on that than on zoology.

Besides

Besides, there is another advantage of knowing the species of animals, and distinguishing
them one from another, which is by regarding
those as one and the same species, who, by means
of copulation, produce and perpetuate beings
like themselves; and as a different species, those
from a connection between whom nothing is
produced, or whose product are unlike their
parents. Thus a fox will be a different species from a dog, if nothing results from a
copulation of a male and female of these two
animals, and when even there should result a
bipartite animal, or a kind of mule, which
cannot generate, that will be sufficient to
establish the fox and dog of two different species. There is not the same advantage to be
had in plants, for although some have pretended to discover sexes, and although divisions
of breeds have been established by the parts
of fecundation; yet, as these distinctions
neither are so certain, nor so apparent as
in animals, and the production of plants is
made in many modes, that the sex has no part
in, and where the parts of fecundation are
not necessary, this idea cannot be made use
of with any success; it is only on a misappre-
hended analogy that this sexual method has

been pretended to distinguish all the different species of plants.

Notwithstanding the number of animals is greater than that of plants, yet that is not the case with respect to the number of individuals in each species. In animals as well as in plants, the number of individuals is much greater in the small species than in the large. Flies are, perhaps, a million times more numerous than elephants; so likewise there are more kinds of plants than trees; but, if we compare the quantity of individuals in each species, we shall find that the plant is more abundant than the animal; for example, quadrupeds bring forth but a small number of young, and at considerable distances of time: trees, on the contrary, produce every year, a great quantity. It may be said that this comparison is not exact, and to render it so, we should compare the quantity of seeds produced by a tree, with a quantity of germs contained in the semen of an animal, and then, perhaps, we should find, that animals are still more abundant in their seed than vegetables. But it should be considered that it is possible by collecting and sowing all the seeds of an elm, for instance, that we might have 100,000 young

ones

ones from the product of a single year; and that should we supply a horse with as many mares as he could cover in one year, there would be a great difference between the production of the animal and that of the vegetable. I shall not examine into the quantity of germs; first, because we are not acquainted with it in the animal creation: and secondly, because possibly there is the same number of seminal shoots in the vegetable: for the seed of a vegetable is not a germ, being as perfect a production as the fœtus of an animal, and to which, like that, a greater expansion is only wanting.

To my comparison may likewise be opposed the prodigious multiplication of certain kinds of insects: as the bee in particular, one of which will produce thirty or forty thousand. But it must be observed, that I speak in general of animals compared with vegetables; and besides, this example of bees, which perhaps is the greatest multiplication among animals, does not constitute a proof against what we have observed; for of thirty or forty thousand flies produced by the female bee, there is but few females; fifteen hundred, or two thousand males, and all the rest moles, or rather

neutral

neutral flies, without sex, and incapable of procreating.

It must be owned, that in insects, fish, and shell-fish, there are species which seem to be very abundant; oysters, herrings, fleas, beetles, &c. are perhaps in as great numbers as mosses and the most common plants; but on the whole, the greatest number of the animal species is less abundant than the vegetable; and by comparing different kinds of plants with each other, there is not found such great differences in the number, as in the animal species; some of which bring forth a prodigious number, and others only a few; whereas the number of productions in plants is always very great throughout.

By what we have observed, it appears that the smallest and basest species seem to be the most prolific: the most minute are the most plentiful as well in animals as in plants, and in proportion as the animals are more perfect, they appear to decrease in number of individuals. Can it be thought, that certain forms of the body, as those of quadrupeds and birds, requisite for the perfection of sensation, would cost nature more organic particles than the production of less important animals?

Let

Let us now pass to the comparison of animals and vegetables, with respect to situation, form, and size. The earth is the only place wherein vegetables can subsist. The greatest number grow above the surface, and are attached to the soil by roots. Some, as truffles, are entirely covered with earth, and a few grow under the water, but all require the surface of the earth to exist upon. Animals, on the contrary, are more generally dispersed; some dwell on the surface, and others in the bowels of the earth; some live at the bottom, and others swim in the waters of the ocean: some exist in the air, others dwell in the internal parts of plants, on the bodies of men and other animals, liquors, and even stones are not without them.

By the use of the microscope, a great number of new species of animals have been discovered: but singular as it may appear, we have not found more than one or two new species of plants by the help of this instrument. The small moss is, perhaps, the only microscopical plant spoken of; and we might, therefore, imagine that nature refused to produce very small plants, while she formed animalcules with profusion; but we might deceive our-

selves

selves by adopting this opinion without examination, and our error might arise from plants, in fact, resembling each other more than animals; so that this moldiness, which we only take for a very minute moss, may possibly be a kind of forest or garden, filled with abundance of various plants, although we are unable to mark the difference.

By comparing the size of animals and plants there will be found a great inequality, for the distance is much greater between the size of a whale and one of these microscope animals, than between the highest oak and the moss we are now speaking of. Although bulk be only a relative attribute, it may, nevertheless, be useful to inspect into the extreme boundaries nature has allotted to her productions. In bigness animals and plants seem to have a near equality; a large whale and a large tree forms a volume not very different; whereas, among the small it has been asserted there are animals so very minute that a million of them united together, would not equal, in size, the smallest moss-plant ever seen.

The most general and most sensible difference between animals and vegetables is that of figure, for the form of animals, although infinitely

finitely varied, has not any resemblance to
that of plants; and although the polypus will,
like plants, reproduce by cutting, and may be
regarded as the link between the animal and
vegetable kingdoms, not only by the mode of
their reproduction but also by their external
form, nevertheless the figure of the animal is .
so different from the external form of a plant
that it is difficult to be deceived therein. Some
animals form things resembling plants or
flowers, but plants never produce any thing
like an animal; and those admirable insects
which produce and form the coral, would not
have been taken for flowers if coral had not
been regarded as a plant. Thus the errors
wherein we might fall, by comparing plants
with animals, will never have any influence
but on a few objects which compose the link
between both, and the more observations we
shall make the more we shall be convinced
that the Creator has not placed a fixed line between animals and vegetables; that these two
species of organized beings have many more
common properties than real differences; that
the production of an animal does not require
of nature more, and possibly, less exertion
than that of a vegetable; that in general the
production

production of organized beings does not require exertion, and that, in short, the living animated nature, instead of composing a metaphysical degree of beings, is a physical property, common to all matter.

CHAPTER II.

OR * REPRODUCTION IN GENERAL.

WE shall now make a more minute inspection into this common property of animal and vegetable nature; this power of producing its resemblance; this chain of successive individuals, which constitutes the real existence of the species ; and without attaching ourselves

---

* This word is used by the author in an enlarged sense of propagation, for as generation applies to animated beings, so by this he includes the vegetable as well as animal system.

ourselves to the generation of man, or to that
of any particular kind of animal, let us inspect
the phenomenas of reproduction in general, let
us collect facts, and enumerate the different methods nature makes use of to renew organized
beings. The first, and as we think the most
simple method, is, to collect in one body an
infinite number of resembling organic bodies,
and so to compose its substance, that there is
not a part of it which does not contain a germ
of the same species, and which consequently
of itself might become a whole, resembling that
of which it constitutes a part. This prepara-
tion seems to suppose a prodigious waste, and to
carry with it profusion; yet it is a very common munificence of nature, and which mani-
fests itself even in the most common and inferior
kinds, such as worms, polypuses, elms, willows,
gooseberry-trees, and many other plants and insects, each part of which contains a whole, and
by the single effect of expansion alone may become a plant, or an insect. By considering
organized beings in this point of view, an
individual is a whole, uniformly organized in
all its parts; a compound of an infinity of
resembling figures and similar parts, an assem-

blage of germs, or small individuals of the same kind, which can expand in the same mode according to circumstances, and form new bodies, composed like those from whence they proceed.

By examining this idea thoroughly, we shall discover a connection between animals, vegetables, and minerals, which we could not expect. Saits, and some other minerals, are composed of parts resembling each other, and to all that composes them; a grain of salt is a cube, composed of an infinity of smaller cubes, which we may easily perceive by a microscope; these are also composed of other cubes still smaller, as may be perceived with a better microscope; and we cannot doubt, but that the primitive and constituting particles of this salt are likewise cubes so exceedingly minute as to escape our sight, and our imagination. Animals and plants which can multiply by all their parts, are organized bodies, of which the primitive and constituting parts are also organic and similar, of which we discern the aggregate quantity, but cannot perceive the primitive parts only by reason and analogy.

This

This leads us to believe that there is an infinity of organic particles actually existing and living in nature, the substance of which is the same with that of organized bodies. As we have just observed, in a structure of a similar kind, though of inanimate matter, that it was composed of an infinity of particles which have a perfect semblance to the whole body, and as there must perhaps be millions of small cubes of accumulated salts to form a sensible individual grain of sea-salt, so likewise millions of organic particles, like the whole, are required to form one out of that multiplicity of germs contained in an elm, or a polypus; and as we must separate, bruise, and dissolve a cube of sea-salt to perceive, by means of crystallization, the small cubes of which it is composed; we must likewise separate the parts of an elm or polypus to discover, by means of vegetation and expansion, the small elms or polypuses contained in those parts.

The difficulty of giving way to this idea arises from a prejudice strongly established, that there is no method of judging of the complex, except by the simple, and that, to conceive the organic constitution of a body we must reduce it to its simple and unorga-

N n 2

nized

nized parts, and that it is more easy to conceive how a cube is composed of other cubes than how one polypus is composed of others; but if we attentively examine what is meant by simple and complex, we shall then find that in this, as in every thing else, the plan of nature is quite different from the very rough draught of it formed by our ideas.

Our senses, as is well known, do not furnish us with exact representations of external objects, insomuch that if we are desirous of estimating, judging, comparing, measuring, &c. we are obliged to have recourse to foreign assistance, to rules, principles, instruments, &c. All these helps are the works of human knowledge, and partake more or less of the abstraction of our ideas; this abstraction, therefore, is what is called the simple, and the difficulty of reducing them to this abstraction, the complex. Extent, for example, being a general and abstracted property from nature, is not very complex; nevertheless, to form a judgment of it, we have supposed extents without depth, without breadth, and even points without any extent at all. All these abstractions have been invented for the support of our judgment, and the few definitions made use of in geometry

have

have occasioned a variety of prejudices and false conclusions. All that can be reduced by these definitions are termed *simple*, and all that cannot be readily reduced are called *complex*; from hence a triangle, a square, a circle, a cube, &c. are simple subjects, as well as all curves, whose geometrical laws we are acquainted with; but all that we cannot reduce by these abstracted figures and laws are complex. We do not consider that these geometrical figures exist only in our imagination; that they are not to be found in nature, or, at least, if they are discoverable there, it is because she exhibits every possible form, and that it is more difficult and rare to find simple figures of an equilateral pyramid, or an exact cube in nature, than compounded forms of a plant or an animal. In every thing, therefore, we take the abstract for the simple, and the real for the complex. In Nature, on the contrary, the abstract has no existence, every thing is compounded; we shall never, of course, penetrate into the intimate structure of bodies: we cannot, therefore, pronounce on what is complex in a greater or lesser degree, excepting by the greater or lesser each subject has to ourselves and to the rest of the universe;

from

from which reason it is we judge that the animal is more compounded than the vegetable, and the vegetable more than the mineral. This notion is just with relation to us, but we know not, in reality, whether the animal, vegetable, or mineral, is the most simple or complex; and we are ignorant whether a globule, or a cube, is more indebted for an exertion of nature, than a seed or an organic particle. If we would form conjectures on this subject, we might suppose that the most common and numerous things are the most simple; but then animals would be the most simple, since the number of their kind far exceeds that of plants or minerals.

But without taking up more time on this discussion, it is sufficient to have shewn that the opinions we commonly have of the simple and complex are ideas of abstraction, that they cannot be applied to the compound productions of nature, and that when we attempt to reduce every being to elements of a regular figure, or to prismatic, cubical, or globular particles, we substitute our own imaginations in the place of realities; that the forms of the constituting particles of different bodies are absolutely unknown to us, and that, consequently,

quently, we can suppose, that an organized body is composed of organic particles, as well as that a cube is composed of other cubes.

We have no other rule to judge by than experience. We perceive that a cube of sea-salt is composed of other cubes, and that an elm consists of other smaller elms, because, by taking an end of a branch, or root, or a piece of the wood separated from the trunk, or a seed, they will alike produce a new tree. It is the same with respect to polypuses, and some other kinds of animals, which we can multiply by cutting off, and separating any of the different parts ; * and since our rule for judging in both is the same, why should we judge differently of them ?

It therefore appears very probable, by the above reasons, that there really exists in nature a number of small organized beings, alike, in every respect, to the large organized bodies seen in the world ; that these small organized beings are composed of living organic particles, which are common to animals and vegetables, and are their primitive and incompatible particles ; that the assemblage of these particles form an animal

or

* See Supplement to this Work, containing History of Birds, Fish, Insects, &c. vol. v. p. 377.

or plant, and consequently that reproduction, or generation, is only a change of form made by the addition of these resembling parts alone, and that death or dissolution is nothing more than a separation of the same particles. Of the truth of this we apprehend there will not remain a doubt, after reading the proofs we shall give in the following chapters. Besides, if we reflect on the manner in which trees grow, and consider how so considerable a volume can arise from so small an origin, we shall be convinced that it proceeds from the simple addition of small resembling organized particles. A grain produces a young tree, which it contained in miniature. At the summit of this small tree a bud is formed, which contains the young tree for the succeeding year, and this bud is an organic part, resembling the young tree of the first year's growth. A similar bud appears the second year, containing a tree for the third; and thus, successively, as long as the tree continues growing, at the extremity of each branch new buds will form, containing young trees like that of the first year. Thus it is evident, that trees are composed of small organized bodies, similar to themselves, and that the whole individual is formed by the union of small resembling individuals.

But

But, it may be asked, were not all these organized bodies contained in the seed, and may not the order of their expansion be traced from that source, for the bud which first appeared was evidently surmounted by another similar bud, which was not expanded till the second year, and soon to the third; and consequently the seed may be said really to contain all the buds, or young trees that would be produced for a hundred years, or till the dissolution of the tree itself? This seed it is also plain not only contained all the small organized bodies which one day must constitute the individual tree, but also every seed, every individual, and every succession of seeds and individuals, to the total destruction of the species.

This is the principal difficulty, and we shall examine it with the strictest attention. It is certain that the seed produces by the single expansion of the bud, or germ, it contains, a young tree the first year, and that this tree existed in miniature in that bud, but it is not equally certain that the bud of the second year, and those of the succeeding, were all contained in the first seed, no more than that every organized body and seed, which must succeed to the end of the world, or to the destruction of the species, were so. This opinion supposes a progress to infinity, and forms, of each individual, a source of eternal generations. The first seed, in that case, must have contained every plant of its kind which have existed or ever will exist; and the first man must actually and individually have contained in his loins every man which has or will appear on the face of the earth. Each seed, and each animal, agreeable to this opinion, must have possessed within an infinite posterity. But the more we suffer ourselves to wander into these kind of reasonings, the more we lose the sight of truth in the labyrinth of infinity; and instead of clearing up and solving the question, we confuse and involve it in more obscurity; it is placing the object out of sight, and afterwards saying it is impossible to see it. .

Let us investigate a little these ideas of infinite progression and expansion. From whence do they arise? What do they represent? The ideas of infinity can only spring from an idea of that which is limited, for it is in that manner we have an idea of an infinity of succession, a geometrical infinity : each individual is an unit, many individuals compose a finite number, and the whole species is the infinite multitude. Thus in the same manner as a geometrical infinity may be demonstrated not to exist, so we may be

assured

assured that an infinite progression or expansion does not exist; that it is only an abstract idea, a retrenchment of the idea of finity, of which we take away the limits that necessarily terminate all size; and that, of course, we must reject from philosophy every opinion which leads to an idea of the actual existence of geometrical or arithmetical infinity.

The partizans, therefore, of this opinion must acknowledge, that their infinity of succession and multiplication is, in fact, only an indeterminate or indefinite number; a number greater than any we can have an idea of, but which is not infinite. This being granted, they will tell us, that the first seed of an elm, for example, which does not weigh a grain, really contains all the organic particles necessary for the formation of this, and every other tree of the same kind which ever shall appear. But what do they explain to us by this answer? Is it not cutting the knot instead of untying it, and eluding the question when it should be resolved.

When we ask how beings are multiplied? and it is answered that this multiplication was compleatly made in the first body, is it not acknowledging that they are ignorant how it is

made,

made, and renouncing the will of conceiving it? The question is asked, how one body produces its like? and it is answered, that the whole was created at once. Can we receive this as a solution? for whether one or a million of generations have passed the like difficulty remains, and so far from explaining the supposition of an indefinite number of germs, increases the obscurity, and renders it incomprehensible.

I own, that in this circumstance, it is easier to start objections than to establish probabilities, and that the question of reproduction is of such subtle nature, as possibly never to be fully resolved; but then we should search whether it is totally inscrutable, and by that examination, we shall discover all that is possible to be known of the subject; or at least, why we must remain ignorant of it.

. There are two kinds of questions, some belonging to the first causes, the others have only particular effects; for example, if it is asked, why matter is impenetrable? it must either remain unanswered, or be replied to by saying, matter is impenetrable, because it is impenetrable. . It will be the same with respect to all the general qualities of matter, whether rela-

. tive

tive to gravity, extension, motion or rest; no other reply can be given, and we shall not be surprised that such is the case, if we attentively consider, that in order to give a reason for a thing, we must have a different subject from which we may deduce a comparison, and therefore if the reason of a general cause is asked, that is, of a quality which belongs to all in general, and of which we have no subject to which it does not belong, we are consequently unable to reason upon it; from thence it is demonstrable, it would be useless to make such enquiries, since we should go against the supposition that quality is general and universal.

If, on the contrary, the reason of a particular effect depends immediately on one of the general causes above mentioned, and whether it partakes of the general effect immediately, or by a chain of other effects, the question will be equally solved, provided we distinctly perceive the dependence these effects have on each other, and the connections there are between them.

But if the particular effect, of which we enquire the reason, does not appear to depend on

these

these general effects, nor to have any analogy with other known effects, then this effect, being the only one of its kind, and having nothing in common with other effects, at least known to us, the question is insolvable : because, not having, in this point, any known subject which has any connection with that we would explain, there is nothing from whence we can draw the reason sought after. When the reason of a general cause is demanded, it is unanswerable, because it exists in every object; and, on the other hand, the reason of a singular or isolated effect is not found, because not any thing known has the same qualities. We cannot explain the reason of a general effect, without discovering one more general; whereas the reason of an isolated effect may be explained by the discovery of some other relative effect, which although we are ignorant of at present, chance or experience may bring to light.

Besides these, there is another kind of question, which may be called, the question of fact. For example. Why do trees, dogs, &c. exist? All these fact questions are totally insoluble, for those who answer them by final causes do not consider that they take the effect for the cause ;

the

the connection particular objects have with us having no influence on their origin. Moral affinity can never become a physical reason.

We must carefully distinguish these questions where the *why* is used, from those where the *how* is employed, and more so from those where the *how many* is mentioned. *Why* is always relative to the cause of the effect, or to the effect itself. *How* is relative to the mode from which the effect springs, and the *how many* has relation only to the proportionate quantity of the effect.

All these distinctions being explained, let us proceed to examine the question concerning the reproduction of bodies. If it is asked, why animals and vegetables reproduce? we shall clearly discover, that this being a question of fact, it is insolvable, and useless to endeavour at the solution of it. But if it is asked, *how* animals and vegetables reproduce; we reply by relating the history of the generation of every species of animal, and of the reproduction of each distinct vegetable; but, after having run over all the methods of an animal engendering its resemblance, accompanied even with the most exact observations, we shall find it has only taught us facts without indicating

causes;

causes; and that the apparent methods which Nature makes use of for reproduction, do not appear to have any connection with the effects resulting therefrom; we shall be still obliged to ask, what is the secret mode by which she enables different bodies to propagate their own species?

This question is very different from the first and second; it gives liberty of enquiry and admits the employment of imagination, and therefore is not insolvable, for it does not immediately belong to a general cause; nor is it entirely a question of fact, for provided we can conceive a mode of reproduction dependent upon, or not repugnant to, original causes, we shall have gained a satisfactory answer; and the more it shall have a connection with other effects of nature, the better foundation will it be raised upon.

By the question itself it is, therefore, permitted to form hypotheses, and to select that which shall appear to have the greatest analogy with the other phenomena of nature. But we must exclude from the number all those which supposes the thing already done; for example, such as suppose that all the germs of the same species were contained in the first

seed,

seed, or that every reproduction is a new creation, and immediate effect of the Almighty's will; because these hypotheses are questions of fact, and on which it is impossible to reason. We must also reject every hypothesis which might have final causes for its object; such as, we might say, that reproduction is made in order for the living to supply the place of the dead, that the earth may be always covered with vegetables, and peopled with animals; that man may find plenty for his subsistence, &c. because these hypotheses, instead of explaining the effects by physical causes, are founded only on arbitrary connections and moral agreements. At the same time we must not rely on these absolute axioms and physical problems, which so many people have improperly made use of, as principles; for example, there is no fecundation made apart from the body, *nulla fœcondatio extra corpus*; every living thing is produced from an egg; all generation supposes sexes, &c. We must not take these maxims in an absolute sense, but consider them only as signifying things generally performed in one particular mode rather than in any other.

Let us, therefore, search after an hypothesis which has not any of those defects, and by which we cannot fall into any of these inconveniences; if, then, we do not succeed in the explanation of the mechanical power Nature makes use of to effect the reproduction of beings, we shall, at least, arrive at something more probable than what has hitherto been advanced.

As we can make moulds, by which we can give to the external parts of bodies whatever figure we please, let us suppose Nature can form the same, by which she not only bestows on bodies the external figure but also the internal. Would not this be one mode by which reproduction may be performed?

Let us, then, consider on what foundation this supposition is raised: let us examine if it contains any thing contradictory, and afterwards we shall discover what consequences may be derived from it. Though our senses are only judges of the external parts of bodies, we perfectly comprehend external affection and different figures. We can also imitate Nature, by representing external figures by different modes, as by painting, sculpture, and moulds;

moulds; but although our senses are only
judges of external qualities, we know there are
internal qualities, some of which are general,
as gravity. This quality, or power, does not
act relatively to surfaces, but proportionably to
the masses, or quantities of matter; there is,
therefore, very active qualities in Nature,
which even penetrate bodies to the most internal parts; but we shall never gain a perfect
idea of these qualities, because, not being
external, they cannot fall within the compass
of our senses; but we can compare their effects,
and deduce analogies therefrom, to answer for
the effect of similar qualities.

If our eyes, instead of representing to us
the surface of objects only, were so formed as
to shew us the internal parts alone, we should
then have clear ideas of the latter, without the
smallest knowledge of the former. In this
supposition the internal moulds, which I have
supposed to be made use of by Nature, might
be as easily seen and conceived as the moulds
for external figures. In that case we should
have modes of imitating the internal parts of
bodies as we now have for the external. These
internal moulds, although we cannot acquire,

P p 2

Nature

Nature may be possessed of, as she is of the qualities of gravity, which penetrate to the internal particles of matter. The supposition of these moulds being formed on good analogies it only remains for us to examine if it includes any contradiction.

It may be argued that the expression of *an internal mould* includes two contradictory ideas; that the idea of a mould can only be related to the surface, and that the internal, according to this, must have a connection with the whole mass, and, therefore, it might as well be called a massive surface as an internal mould.

I admit, that when we are about to represent ideas which have not hitherto been expressed, we are obliged to make use of terms which seem contradictory; for this reason philosophers have often employed foreign terms on such occasions, instead of applying those in common use, and which have a received signification; but this artifice is useless, since we can shew the opposition is only in the words, and that there is nothing contradictory in the idea. Now I affirm that a simple idea cannot contain a contradiction, that is, when we can form an idea of a thing; if this idea is simple

it

it cannot be compounded; it cannot include any other idea, and, consequently, it will contain nothing opposite nor contrary.

Simple ideas are not only the primary apprehensions which strike us by the senses, but also the primary comparisons which form from those apprehensions; for the first apprehension, itself is always a comparison. The idea of the size of an object, or of its remoteness, necessarily includes a comparison with bulk or distance in general; therefore, when an idea only includes comparison it must be regarded as simple, and from that circumstance, as containing nothing contradictory. Such is the idea of the internal mould. There is a quality in Nature, called *gravity*, which penetrates the internal parts of bodies. I take the idea of internal mould relatively to this quality, and, therefore, including only comparison, it bears not any contradiction.

Let us now see the consequences that may be deduced from this supposition; let us also search after facts corresponding therewith, as it will become so much the more probable, as the number of analogies shall be greater. Let us begin by unfolding this idea of internal moulds, and by explaining in what manner we understand

understand it, we shall be brought to conceive the modes of reproduction.

Nature, in general, seems to have a greater tendency to life than death, and to organize bodies as much as possible; the multiplication of germs, which may be infinitely encreased, is a proof of it; and we may assert with safety, that if all matter is not organized, it is because organized beings destroy each other; or we can augment as much as we please the quantity of living and vegetating beings, but we cannot augment the quantity of stones or other inanimate matters. This seems to indicate that the most common work of Nature is the production of the organic part, and in which her power knows no bounds.

To render this intelligible, let us make a calculation of what a single germ might produce. The seed of an elm, which does not weigh the hundredth part of an ounce, at the end of 100 years will produce a tree whose volume will be 60 cubic feet. At the tenth year this tree will have produced 1000 seeds, which being all sown, at the end of 100 years would each have also a volume equal to 60 cubic feet. Thus in 110 years there is produced more than 60,000 cubic feet of orga-

nized

nized matter; 10 years more there will be 10,000,000 of fathoms, without including the 10,000 encreased every year, which would make 100,000 more; and ten years after there will be three times that number; thus in 130 years a single shoot will produce a volume of organized matter, which would fill up a space of 1000 cubic leagues; 10 years after it would comprehend a 1,000,000, and in 10 years more 1,000,000 times 1,000,000 cubic leagues; so that in 150 years the whole terrestrial globe might be entirely converted into one single kind of organized matter. In this production of organized body Nature would know no bounds, if it were not for the resistance of matters which are not susceptible of organization, and this proves that she does not incline to form inanimate but organized beings, and that in this she never stops but when irresistible inconveniences are opposed thereto. What we have already said on the seed of an elm may be said of any other; and it would be easy to demonstrate, that if we were to hatch every egg produced by hens for the space of 30 years, there would be a sufficient number of fowls to cover the whole surface of the earth.

These

These kind of calculations demonstrate that organic formation is the most common work of Nature, and, apparently, that which costs her the least labour. But I will go farther; the general division which we ought to make of matter seems to me to be in *living* and *dead matter*, instead of organized and brute; the brute is only that matter produced by the death of animals or vegetables; I could prove it by that enormous quantity of shells, and other cast-off matters of living animals, which compose the principal part of stones, marble, chalk, marle, earth, turf, and other substances, which we call brute matter, and which are only the ruins of dead animals or vegetables; but a reflection, which seems to me well founded, will, perhaps, make it better understood.

Having meditated on the activity of Nature to produce organized bodies, and seen that her power, in this respect, is not limited; having proved that infinity of organic living particles, which constitute life, must exist; having shewn that the living body costs the least trouble to Nature, I now search after the principal causes of death and destruction, and I find that bodies in general, which have the

power

power of converting matter into their proper substance, and to assimilate the parts of other bodies, are the greatest destroyers. Fire, for example, turns into its own substance almost every species of matter, and is the greatest means of destruction known to us. Animals seem to participate of the qualities of flame; their internal heat is a kind of fire; therefore, after fire, animals are the greatest destroyers, and they assimilate and convert into their own substance every matter which may serve them for food: but although these two causes of destruction are very considerable, and their effects perpetually incline to the annihilation of organized beings, the cause of reproduction is infinitely more powerful and active; she seems to borrow, even from destruction itself, means to multiply, since assimilation, which is one cause of death, is at the same time a necessary means of producing life.

To destroy an organized being is, as we have observed, only to separate the organic particles of which it is composed; these particles remain separated till they are re-united by some active power. But what is this active power?—It is the power which animals and vegetables have to assimilate the matter that serves them for food ; and is not this the same, or at least has it not great connection with that which is the cause of reproduction ?

CHAPTER III.

OF NUTRITION AND GROWTH.

THE body of an animal is a kind of internal mould, in which the nutritive matter assimilates itself with the whole in such a manner that, without changing the order and proportion of the parts, each receives an augmentation, and it is this augmentation of bulk which some have called *expansion*, because they imagined every difficulty would be removed by the supposition that the animal was completely formed in the embryo, and that it would be

easy

easy to conceive that its parts would expand, or unfold in proportion as it would increase by the addition of accessory matter.

But if we would have a clear idea of this augmentation and expansion, how can it be done otherwise than by considering the animal body, and each of its parts, as so many internal moulds which receive the accessory matter in the order that results from the position of all their parts? This expansion cannot be made by the addition to the surfaces alone, but, on the contrary, by an intimate susception which penetrates the mass, and thus increases the size of the parts, without changing the form, from whence it is necessary that the matter which serves for this expansion should penetrate the internal part in all its dimensions; it is also as necessary that this penetration be made in a certain order and proportion, so that no one point can receive more than another, without which some parts would expand quicker than others, and the form be entirely changed. Now what can precribe this rule to accessory matter, and constrain it to arrive perpetually and proportionally to every point of the internal parts, except we conceive an internal mould?

It

It therefore appears certain that the body of an animal or vegetable is an internal mould of a constant form, but where their masses may augment proportionably, by the extension of this mould in all its external and internal dimensions. That this extension also is made by the intus-susception of any accessory or foreign matter which penetrates the internal part, and becomes similar to the form and identical substance with the matter of the moulds themselves.

But of what nature is this matter which the animal or vegetable assimilates with its own substance? what can be the nature of that power which gives it the activity and necessary motion to penetrate the internal mould? and if such a power does exist, must it not be similar to that by which the internal mould itself would be produced?

These three questions include all that can be desired on this subject, and seem to depend on each other so much, that I am persuaded the reproduction of an animal or vegetable cannot be explained in a satisfactory manner, if a clear idea of the mode of the operation of nutrition is not obtained; we must, therefore, examine these three questions separately, in order

order to compare the consequences resulting therefrom.

The first, which relates to the nutritive nature of this matter, is in part resolved by the reasons we have already given, and will be fully demonstrated in the succeeding chapter. We will shew that there exists an infinity of living organic particles in Nature; that their production is of little expence to Nature, since their existence is constant and invariable, and that the causes of death only separate without destroying them. Therefore the matter which the animal or vegetable assimilates is an organic matter of the same nature as the animal or vegetable itself, and which consequently can augment the size without changing the form or quality of the matter of the mould, since it is in fact of the same form and quality as that which it is constituted with. Thus, in the quantity of aliments which the animal takes to support life, and to keep its organs in play, and in the sap, which the vegetable takes up by its roots and leaves, there is a great part thrown off by transpiration, secretion, and other excretory modes, and only a small portion retained for the nourishment of the parts and their expansion. It is

very

very probable, that in the body of an animal
or vegetable there is formed a separation of the
brute particles of the aliments and the organic ;
that the first are carried off by the causes just
mentioned ; that only organic particles remain,
and that the distribution of them is made by
means of some active power which conducts
them to every part in an exact proportion,
insomuch that neither receive more or less than
is needful for its equal nutrition, growth, or
expansion.

The second question, What can be the active
power which causes this organic matter to penetrate and incorporate itself with this internal
mould? By the preceding chapter it appears,
that there exists in Nature powers relative to
the internal part of matter, and which have no
relation with its external qualities. These
powers, as already observed, will never come
under our cognizance, because their action is
made on the internal part of the body, whereas
our senses cannot reach beyond what is external ; it is therefore evident, that we shall never
have a clear idea of the penetrating powers, nor
of the manner by which they act ; but it is not
less certain that they exist, than that by their
means most effects of Nature are produced ;

we

we must attribute to them the effects of nutrition and expansion, which cannot be effected by any other means than the penetration of the most intimate recesses of the original mould : in the same mode as gravity penetrates all parts of matter, so the power which impels or attracts the organic particles of food, penetrates into the internal parts of organized bodies, and as those bodies have a certain form, which we call the internal mould, the organic particles, impelled by the action of the penetrating force, cannot enter therein but in a certain order relative to this form, which consequently it cannot change, but only augment its dimensions, and thus produce the growth of organized bodies ; and if in the organized body, expanded by this means, there are some particles whose external and internal forms are like that of the whole body, from those reproduction will proceed.

The third question, Is it not by a similar power the internal mould itself is reproduced? It appears, that it is not only a similar but the same power which causes expansion and reproduction, for in an organized body which expands, if there is some particle like the whole, it is sufficient for that particle to become one

day

day an organized body itself, perfectly similar to that of which it made a part. This particle will not at first present a figure striking enough for us to compare with the whole body; but when separated from that body, and receiving proper nourishment, it will begin to expand, and in a short time present a similar being, both externally and internally, as the body from which it had been separated: thus a willow or polypus, which contain more organic particles similar to the whole than most other substances, if cut into ever such a number of pieces, from each piece will spring a body similar to that from whence it was divided.

Now in a body, every particle of which is like itself, the organization is the most simple, as we have observed in the first chapter; for it is only the repetition of the same form, and a composition of similar figures, all organized alike. It is for this reason that the most simple bodies, or the most imperfect kinds, are reproduced with the greatest ease, and in the greatest plenty; whereas, if an organized body contains only some few particles like itself, then, as such alone can arrive to the second expansion, consequently the reproduction will be more difficult, and not so abundant in number; the

organization

organization of these bodies will also be more
compounded, because the more the organized
parts differ from the whole, the more the organization of this body will be perfect, and the
more difficult the production will be.

Nourishment, expansion, and propagation,
then, are the effects of one and the same cause..
The organized body is nourished by the particles
of aliments analagous to it; it expands by the
intimate susception of organical parts which
agree with it, and it propagates because it contains some original particles which resemble itself. It only remains to examine, whether these
similar organic particles come into the organized body by nutriment, or whether they were
there before, and have an independent existence.
If we suppose the latter, we shall fall in with
the doctrine of the infinity of parts, or similar
germs contained one in the other; the insuffi-
ciency and absurdity of which hypothesis we
have already shewn; we must therefore conclude that similar parts are extracted from the
food; and after what has been said, we hope to
explain the manner in which the organic molecules are formed, and how the minute particles
unite.

There is, as we have said, a separation of the parts in the nutriment; the organic from those analogous to the animal or vegetable, by transpiration and other excretory modes; the organical remain and serve for the expansion and nutriment of the body. But these organic parts must be of various kinds, and as each part of the body receives only those similar to itself, and that in due proportion, it is very natural to imagine, that the superfluity of this organic matter will be sent back from every part of the body into one or more places, where all these organical molecules uniting, form small organized bodies like the first, and to which nothing is wanting but the mode of expansion for them to become individuals of the same species; for every part of the body sending back organized parts, like those of which they themselves are composed, it is necessary, that from the union of all these parts, there should result organized bodies like the first. This being admitted, may we not conclude this is the reason why, during the time of expansion and growth, organized bodies cannot produce, because the parts which expand absorb the whole of the organic molecules which belong to them, and

not

not having any superfluous parts, consequently
are incapable of reproduction.

This explanation of nutrition and reproduction will not probably be received by those
who admit but of a certain number of mechanical principles, and reject all which do
not depend on them; and as what has been
said of nutrition and expansion comes under
the latter description, they will possibly treat
it as unworthy dependance. But I am quite of
a different opinion from these philosophers;
for it appears to me that, by admitting only
a certain number of mechanical principles,
they do not see how greatly they contract the
bounds of philosophy, and that for one phenomenon that can be explained by a system so
confined, a thousand would be found exceeding
its limits.

The idea of explaining every phenomenon
in nature by mechanical principles was certainly a great and beautiful exertion, and which
Descartes first attempted. But this idea is only a
project, and if properly founded, have we the
means of performing it? These mechanical
principles are the extent of matter, its impenetrability, its motion, its external figure, its

R r 2　　　　　　divisibility,

divisibility, and the communication of move-
ment by impulsion, by elasticity, &c. The
particular ideas of each of these qualities we
have acquired by our senses, and regard them as
principles, because they are general and belong
to all matter. But are we certain these qualities are the only ones which matter possesses,
or rather, must we not think these qualities,
which we take for principles, are only modes
of perception; and that if our senses were
differently formed, we should discover in matter, qualities different from those which we
have enumerated? To admit only those qualities to matter which are known to us, seems
to be a vain and unfounded pretension. Matter may have many general qualities which we
shall ever be ignorant of; she may also have
others that human assiduity may discover, in
the same manner as has recently been done
with respect to gravity, which alike exists in
all matter. The cause of impulsion, and such
other mechanical principles, will always be
as impossible to find out as that of attraction,
or such other general quality. From hence is
it not very reasonable to say, that mechanical
principles are nothing but general effects,
which

which experience has pointed out to us in matter, and that every time a new general effect is discovered, either by reflection, comparison, measure, or experience, a new mechanical principle will be gained, which may be used with as much certainty and advantage as any we are now acquainted with?

The defect of Aristotle's philosophy was making use of particular effects as common causes; and that of Descartes in making use of only a few general effects as causes, and excluding all the rest. The philosophy which appears to me would be the least deficient, is that where general effects are only made use of for causes, and seeking to augment the number of them, by endeavouring to generalize particular effects.

In my explanation of expansion and reproduction, I admit the received mechanical principles, the penetrating force of weight, and, by analogy, I have strove to point out that there are other penetrating powers existing in organized bodies, which experience has confirmed. I have proved by facts, that matter inclines to organization, and that there exists an infinite number of organic particles. I

have

have therefore only generalized some observations, without having advanced any thing
contrary to mechanical principles, when that
term is used as it ought to be understood, as
denoting the general effects of Nature.

CHAPTER IV.

OF THE GENERATION OF ANIMALS.

AS human and animal organization is the most perfect and compounded, their propagation is also the most difficult and least abundant; I here except those animals which, like the fresh-water polypus or worms, are reproduced from their divided parts, as trees are by slips, or plants by their divided roots or suckers; also those which may be found to multiply without copulation; it appears to me that the nature of those have been sufficiently explained in the preceding chapter; and from which, in every kind where an individual pro-

duces

duces its resemblance, it is easy to deduce the explanation of the reproduction from expansion and nutrition.

But how shall we apply this mode of reasoning to the generation of man and animals distinguished by sexes, and where the concurrence of two individuals is required? We understand, by what has just been advanced, how each individual can produce its like; but we do not conceive how a male and a female produces a third.

Before I answer this question, I cannot avoid observing, that all those who have written upon this subject have confined their systems to the generation of man and animals, without paying any attention to other kinds of generation which Nature presents us with, and reproduction in general; and as the generation of man and animals is the most complicated of all kinds, their researches have been attended with great disadvantages, not only by attacking the most difficult point, but also by having no subject of comparison, from which they could draw a solution of the question. To this it is that I principally attribute the little success of their labours; but by the road I have taken we may arrive at the explanation of the phe-

nomena

nomena of every kind of generation in a satisfactory manner.

The generation of man will serve us for an
example. I take him in his infancy, and I
conceive that the expansion and growth of the
different parts of his body being made by the
intimate penetration of organic molecules
analogous to each of its parts, all these organic
molecules are absorbed in his earliest years, and
serve only for the expansion and augmentation
of his various members, consequently there
is little or no superfluity until the expansion
is entirely completed; and this is the reason
why children are incapable of propagation;
but when the body has attained the greatest
part of its growth, it begins to have no longer
need of so great a quantity of organic particles,
and the superfluity, therefore, is sent back from
each part of the body into the destined reservoirs for its reception. These reservoirs are
the testicles and seminal vessels, and it is at this
period that the expansion of the body is
nearly completed, when the commencement
of puberty is dated, and every circumstance
indicates the superabundance of nutriment;
the voice alters and takes a deeper tone; the

beard begins to appear, and other parts of the body are covered with hair; those parts which are appointed for generation take a quick growth; the seminal liquor fills the prepared reservoirs, and when the plentitude is too great, even without any provocation, and during the time of sleep, it emits from the body. In the female this superabundance is more strongly marked, it discovers itself by periodical evacuation, which begin and end with the faculty of propagating, by the quick growth of the breasts, and by an attraction in the sexual parts, as shall be explained.

I think, therefore, that the organical molecules, sent from every part of the body into the testicles and seminal vessels of the male, and into the ovarium of the female, forms there the seminal liquor, which is, as has been observed, in both sexes, a kind of extract of every part of the body. These organical molecules, instead of uniting and forming an individual, like the one in which they are contained, can only unite when the seminal liquors of the two sexes are mixed; and when there is more organical molecules of the male than of the female, in such mixture the produce will be a male, a male; and, on the contrary, when there is more of the female then a female will be the result.

I do not mean to say that the organic molecules of either could unite to form small organized bodies of themselves, but that it is necessary a mixture of the seminal fluid of both sexes should take place, and that it is only those formed in that mixture which can expand and become individuals. These small moving bodies, called *spermatic animals*, are seen, by a microscope, in the seminal liquor of every male, and are, probably, small organized bodies, proceeding from the individual which contains them, but which cannot expand or produce any thing of themselves. We shall evince that there are the same in the seminal liquor of the female, and shall indicate the place where this liquor is to be found.

It is very possible that organical molecules are, at first, only a kind of fœtus of a small organized body, in which there are only essential parts. We shall not enter into a detail of proofs, in this respect, but content ourselves with remarking, that the pretended spermatic animals, which we have been speaking of, might possibly be but imperfectly organized,

or

or that these pretended animals are only living organic particles, common both to animals and vegetables, or, at most, only the first union of those particles.

But let us return to our principal object. How can we conceive, it may be asked, that the superfluous particles can be sent back from every part of the body, and afterwards unite when the seminal liquor of the two sexes are mixed? Besides, is it certain that this mixture is made? Has it not been pretended that the female did not furnish any fluid of this kind? Is it certain that the liquor of the male enters the matrix, &c.

To the first question I answer, if what I have said on the subject of the penetration of the internal mould by organic molecules, in nutrition or expansion, be well understood, it will easily be conceived that these molecules, not being able any longer to penetrate those parts they did before, they will be necessitated to take a different road, and consequently arrive at some part, as the testicles or seminal vessels; for to explain the animal economy, and the different movements of the human body, solely by mechanical principles, is the same as if a man would give an account of a picture by

shutting

shutting his eyes and feeling on it; for it is
evident that neither the circulation of the
blood, nor the motion of the muscles, nor the
animal functions, can be explained by impulsion, nor other common laws of mechanics:
it is as evident that nutrition, expansion, and
reproduction, is made by other laws, why
therefore not admit of acting and penetrating
powers on the masses of bodies, since we have
examples of it in gravity, in magnetical attractions, and in chemical affinities? And as we
are now convinced by facts, and the multitude
of constant and uniform observations, that
there exists in nature powers which do not
act by the mode of impulsion, why should we
not make use of those powers as mechanical
principles? Why should we exclude them from
the explanations of effects, which we are convinced they produce? Why should we be confined to employ only the power of impulsion?
Is not this like judging of a picture by the
touch, and explaining the phenomena of the
mass by those of the surface, and the penetrating power by superficial action? Is not this
making use of one sense instead of another;
and, on the whole, is it not confining the faculty of reasoning on a small number of mechanical

chanical principles, totally inadequate to follow
the various productions of nature.

But those penetrating powers being once
admitted, is it not natural to suppose that the
most analogous particles will unite and bind
themselves intimately together; that each part
of the body will appropriate the most agreeable
to itself, and that from the superfluity of all
these particles there will be formed a seminal
fluid, which will contain all the organic molecules necessary to form a small organized body,
perfectly like that from which this fluid is extracted? A power like that which was necessary to make them penetrate into each part,
and produce expansion, may be sufficient to
collect them in an organized form, like that of
the body in which they originated.

I conceive, that in the aliments we take
there is a great quantity of organical molecules, which needs no serious proof, since we
live on animals and vegetables, which are organized substances. In the stomach and intes-
tines a separation is made of the gross parts,
which are thrown off by the excretories. The
chyle, which is the purest part of the aliment,
enters into the lacteal vessels, and from thence
is transported into every part of the body.

By

By the motion of the circulation it purifies
itself from all inorganical molecules, which are
thrown off by secretion and transpiration; but
the organic particles remain, because they are
analogous to the blood, and that from thence
there is a power of affinity which retains them
afterwards; for as the whole mass of blood
passes many times through the body, I apprehend, that in this continual circulation every
particular part of the body attracts the particles
most analogous to it, without interrupting the
course of the others. In this manner every
part is expanded and nourished, not, as it is
commonly said, by a simple addition of the
parts, and a superficial increase, but by an intimate penetration of substance, produced by a
power which acts on every point of the mass;
and when the parts of the body are at a certain
growth, and almost filled with these analogous
particles, as their substance is become more
solid, I conceive they then lose the faculty of
attracting or receiving those particles, but as
the circulation will continue to carry them to
every part of the body, which not being any
longer able to admit them as before, must necessarily be deposited in some particular part,
as in the testicles or seminal vessels. This

fluid

fluid extract of the male, when mixed with that of the female, the similar particles, possessing a penetrating force, unite and form a small organized body like one of the two sexes, and no more than expansion is wanting to render it a similar individual, and which it afterwards receives in the womb of the female.

The second question, Whether the female has really a seminal liquor similar to the male? demands some discussion. I shall first observe, as a certain matter, that if such a fluid exists, the manner in which the emission of the female is made is not so apparent as by the male, being in general retained within the body.* The ancients so little doubted of the female having a seminal liquor, that it was by the different mode of its emission that they distinguished the male from the female. But physicians, who have endeavoured to explain generation by the egg, or by spermatic animalcules, insinuate that females have no particular fluid, that we have been deceived by taking the mucus for the seminal, and that the supposition of the ancients upon this subject was destitute of all foundation.

* Quod intra se semen jacit fæmina vocatur : quod in hac jacit, mas, Aristotle, art. 18 de Animalibus.

foundation. Nevertheless this fluid does exist, and it has only been doubted by those who chose to give way to systems, and from the difficulty of discovering the parts which serve for its reservoirs. The fluid which issues from the glands at the neck of the womb, and at the orifice of the urethra, has no apparent reservoir, and as it flows outwardly it cannot be thought to be the prolific liquor, since it cannot concur in the formation of the fœtus which is performed within the matrix. The prolific fluid of the female must have a reservoir in another part. It flows even in great plenty, although such a quantity is not necessary, no more than in the male, for the production of the embryo. It is sufficient for propagation if ever so little of the male fluid enters the matrix, so it meets with the smallest drop of that of the female; therefore the observations of some anatomists, who have pretended that the seminal liquor of the male does not enter the womb, makes nothing against what we have advanced, especially as other anatomists, who rely on observations, have pretended the contrary. But the subject will be better discussed in the subsequent pages.

 T t Having

Having thus given answers to possible objections, let us now look into the reasons
which may serve as proofs to our explanation.
The first is derived from the analogy there is
between expansion and reproduction ; expansion cannot be explained in a satisfactory
manner, without employing those penetrating
powers, and those affinities or attractions we
have already made use of to explain the formation of small organized beings, resembling
the great ones which contain them.   A second
analogy is, that nutrition and reproduction are
both not only produced by the same efficient,
but also by the same material cause, the organic particles of the nutriment.   And a proof
that it is the superfluity of those particles which
serves for reproduction, is the body not being
in a condition to propagate before they have
done growing; and we daily see in dogs, and
other animals, who more exactly follow the
laws of nature than we, that they nearly attain
their full growth before they attempt to copu-
late, and by which we may know whether a
dog will increase any more or not ; for we may
be assured he will not after being in a condition
to engender.

It

It is another proof that the superfluous nutriment forms the seminal liquor, that eunuchs, and all mutilated animals, grow larger or thicker than those who have not that deficiency. The superabundance of nutriment not being able to evacuate, for the defect of proper organs, alters the habit of the body; the thighs and haunches of eunuchs grow very large: the reason is evident; after their body has attained the common size, if the superfluous organic molecules found an issue, as in other men, this growth would no longer increase; but as there are no longer organs for the emission of the seminal fluid, which is no more than the superfluous matter which served for growth remains, it endeavours to expand the parts beyond their usual dimensions. Now it is known, that the growth of the bones is made by the extremities, which are soft and spongy, and when they have once acquired solidity, they are no longer capable of extension; and for this reason, the superfluous organic particles can only expand the spongy extremities of bones, which causes the thighs, knees, &c. of eunuchs to thicken so considerably.

But what more strongly proves the truth of our explanation, is the resemblance of chil-

dren

dren to their parents. A son, in general, more resembles his father than his mother, and the daughter more her mother than her father; because a man has a greater resemblance to a man than to a woman, and a woman resembles more a woman than a man, in respect to the whole habitude of the body; but for the features and particular habits, children sometimes resemble the father, sometimes the mother, and sometimes both. They will have, for example, the father's eyes, and the mouth of the mother, or the complexion of the latter, and the size of the former; which is impossible to be conceived, unless it is admitted that both parents have contributed to the formation of the child, and that consequently there was a mixture of the two seminal fluids.

I acknowledge that resemblances raised many difficulties in my own mind; before I had maturely examined the question of generation, I was prepossessed with ideas of a mixed system, by which it appeared that I could explain in a probable manner every phenomena, excepting resemblances, and these I thought I had found very specious reasons to doubt, and which deceived me a long time, until having minutely observed, with all the exactness I was

capable

capable of, a great number of families, and especially the most numerous, I have not been able to resist the multiplicity of proofs; it is only after being fully convinced in this respect, that I · have began to think differently, and to credit what I now believe to be the fact.

Besides, although I had found the mode to avoid those arguments that would be made on the subject of mulattos, mongrels, and mules, I could not be prevented from observing that every explanation, where a reason could be given for the phenomena, cannot be satisfactory; and I am now perfectly convinced that the objections which might be used with respect to them, as well as particular parental resemblances, instead of opposing would confirm my explanation.

I now proceed to draw some consequences. In youth the seminal fluid is less abundant, although more stimulating; its quantity encreases to a certain age, because in proportion as we approach that age, the parts of the body become more solid, admit less nutriment, send back a greater quantity to the common reservoirs, and consequently produce a greater abundance of seminal fluid. When the ex-

ternal

ternal organs have not been used, persons of a middling age, and even old men, more easily engender than young ones. This is evident in the vegetable system, the older a tree is, the more fruit or seed it produces.

Young people who emit, or force irritation, draw a greater quantity of seminal fluid towards the organs of generation than would naturally arrive there, the consequence is, they cease from growing, become thin, and fall at length into consumptions, and that because they lose by premature, and too often reiterated evacuations, the necessary substance for the growth and nutrition of every part of the body.

Those whose bodies are thin without emaciation, or fleshy without being fat, are the most vigorous; as soon as the superabundant nutriment has begun to form fat, it is always at the expence of the seminal fluid, and other faculties of generation. When also, not only the growth of every part of the body is entirely completed, but the bones are grown solid, the cartilages begin to ossify, the membranes have received all the solidity possible, the fibres are become hard and rough, and at length every part of the body can no longer scarcely admit of nutriment, the fat
considerably

considerably increases, and the quantity of seminal fluid diminishes, because the superfluous
particles, stopped in every part of the body, and
the fibres, having no longer any suppleness or
elasticity, cannot return it into the reservoirs of
generation.

The seminal liquor not only becomes more
abundant till a certain age, but it also becomes
thicker, and contains a greater quantity of
matter under the same bulk. A person, very
observant in this point, assured me that the seminal fluid is as heavy again as the blood, and
consequently specifically heavier than any other
fluid of the body.

When a man is in good health the evacuation
of this fluid produces an appetite, and he soon
feels the necessity of repairing, by a new nutriment, the loss of the old; from whence it may be
concluded, that the most efficacious check to
every kind of luxury is abstinence and fasting.

A number of other things remain to be said
on this subject, but which I have treated of in
the History of Man; however, before I entirely close, I shall make some few observations. The greatest part of animals do not
seek for copulation until they are nearly arrived
at their full growth; those which have only a

particular

particular season in the year have only seminal liquor at that time. A very capable observer of Nature * not only saw this liquor forming in the roe of a Calmar, but even observed the spermatic animals and the roe itself, which have no existence till the month of October, the time when the Calmar spawns on the coast of Portugal, where Mr. Needham made these observations. As soon as the season is over neither seminal liquor nor spermatic animals are longer seen in the milt, which then dries up and becomes imperceptible till the season returns in the succeeding year, when the superfluous nutriment renews the milt, and fills it as before. In the history of the stag we have an opportunity of remarking on the different effects of rutting; the most general is, the increased size of the animal; and in those kinds of animals whose rutting or spawning is only made at great intervals, the extenuation of the body is proportionably great.

As women are smaller and weaker than men, of a more delicate temperament, and eat much less, it is natural to imagine that their superfluous organic particles are not so plentiful;

* Mr. Needham's New Microscopical Discoveries, London, 1745.

ful; from hence their seminal liquor will be weaker, and less in quantity, than that of men. Since, likewise, the seminal liquor of females contains fewer organic particles than that of males, must there not result a greater number of males than females from the mixture of these two liquors? This is really the case, for which it has hitherto been thought impossible to find a reason. About a sixteenth more male children are born than females; and we find that the same cause produces the same effect in all kinds of animals on which we have been able to make this observation.

CHAPTER V.

EXPOSITION OF THE SYSTEMS IN GENERATION.

PLATO * not only explains the generation of man, animals, plants, and elements, but even that of heaven and the gods, by reflected representations and images extracted from the

* See the Timæus.

Divine Creator, which, by an harmonic motion, are ranged according to the properties of numbers in the most perfect order. The universe, according to him, is a copy of the Deity : time, space, motion, and matter, are images of his attributes; and secondary and particular causes are results of numerical and harmonical qualities of those representations. The world is the most perfect being, and to have a complete perfection it was necessary that it contained every other animal, every possible representation, and every imaginable form, of the creative faculty. The essence of all generation consists in the unity and harmony of the number Three, or of the triangle, viz. that *which* generates, that *in which* generation is performed, and that *which is* engendered. The succession of individuals in the species is only a fugitive image of the immutable eternity of this triangular harmony, the universal prototype of every existence and every generation; for this reason two individuals are required to produce a third, and it is this which constitutes the essential order of father, mother, and child.

This philosopher is a painter only of ideas; disengaged from matter he elevates into the

regions

regions of abstraction, and, losing sight of sensible objects, perceives and contemplates the intellectual alone. One cause, one end, and one sole mode, form the whole of his perceptions. God is the cause, perfection the end, and harmonic representations the modes. What can be a more sublime idea! This plan of philosophy is replete with simplicity, and the views truly noble! but how void and destitute for speculation? We are not purely spiritual beings, nor have we the power to give a real existence to our ideas. Confined to matter, our rather dependent on what causes our sensations, the real substance can never be produced by the abstracted. I answer Plato in his own language, " The Creator realizes every thing he conceives; his perceptions engender existence: the created being, on the contrary, conceives nothing by retrenching them but from reality, and the production of his ideas do not amount to any thing."

Let us then content ourselves with a more humble and more material philosophy; and by keeping within the sphere Nature has allotted us, let us examine the rash steps and the rapid flight of those who attempt to soar beyond it. All this Pythagorean philosophy, which is

purely

purely intellectual, turns entirely on two principles, one of which is false and the other pre-
carious : those are, the real power of abstraction, and the actual existence of final causes.
To take numbers for real beings ; to say that
unity is a general individual, which not only
represents every individual, but even communicates existence to them ; to pretend that
unity has the actual power to engender another
unity nearly similar to itself, and constituting
two individuals, two sides of a triangle, which
can have no bound or perfection without a third
side, or by a third individual, which they necessarily engender. To regard numbers, geometrical lines, and metaphysical abstractions,
as efficient and real physical causes, on which
the formation of the elements, the generation
of animals and plants, and all the phenomena
of Nature depend, seems to me to be the most
absurd abuse of reason, and the greatest obstacle
that can be put against the advancement of
our knowledge. Besides, what can be more
false than such suppositions ? Admitting, with
Plato and Malebranche, that matter does not
exist, that external objects are only ideal images
of the creative faculty, and that we perceive
every thing in the Deity, must it be concluded

from

from thence that our ideas should be of the same order as those of the Creator, or that they can produce existences? Are not we dependent on our sensations? Whether the objects that cause them are real or not; whether this cause of our sensations exists outwardly or inwardly; whether it be the Creator or matter we perceive, what does it signify to us? Are we less certain of being always affected in the same manner by the same causes? Have not our sensations an invariable order of existence, and a necessary relation between them and the objects? This, therefore, is what must constitute the principles of our philosophy; and what has no relation with it is vain, useless, and false in the application. Can a triangular harmony form the substance of the elements? Is fire, as Plato affirms, an acute triangle, and light and heat properties of this triangle? Air and water, are they rectangular and equilateral triangles? Is the form of the terrestrial element a square, because, being the least perfect of all the four elements, it recedes as much as possible from a triangle without losing its essence? Do the male and female embrace only to complete the triangle of generation? These platonic ideas have two very different

aspects

aspects. In speculation they seem to flow from noble and sublime principles, but in application nothing but false and puerile consequences can be drawn from them.

Is it difficult to discover that our ideas proceed only from our senses? that the things we look on as real and existing are those of which our senses have always rendered us the same testimony? that those which we conceive to have certain existence are those which ever present themselves in the same order? that consequently our ideas, very far from being the causes of things, are only effects, and so far from resembling particular things, become less similar to the objects as they are more general; that at length our mental abstractions are only negative beings, which do not exist even intellectually but by the retrenchment which we make of sensible qualities to real beings.

From hence is it not plain that abstractions can never become principles, neither of existence nor real knowledge? on the contrary, our knowledge can only proceed from the results of properly comparing our sensations. These results are what is termed *experience*, the sole source of all real science. The adoption of every other principle is an abuse, and

every

every edifice built on abstracted ideas is a temple
founded on error.

Error bears a much more extended signification in philosophy than in morality : in morals
a thing may be false, only because it is misre-
presented. Metaphysical falsehood consists
not in misrepresentation alone, but in cre-
diting that which has no existence, and even
in not being of any mode whatever. It is
in this kind of error, of the first order, that
the Platonists, the Sceptics, and the Egotists
have fallen into, their false suppositions have
obscured the natural light of truth, clouded
reason, and retarded the advancement of philosophy.

The second principle made use of by Plato,
and by most of the speculative philosophers, is a
final cause. Nevertheless, to reduce this principle to its just value, a single moment of reflection is only requisite. To say there is light
because we have eyes, and sounds because we
have ears, or to say that we have ears and eyes
because there is light and sound, is it not exactly the same thing ? shall we ever discover any
thing by this mode of explanation ? Is it not
evident that final causes are only arbitrary relations and moral abstractions, which should im-

pose

pose on us still less than metaphysical abstractions, because their origin is less noble and a
more false supposition ; and although Leibnitz
has endeavoured to raise this principle to the
highest degree by the name of *sufficient reason,*
and Plato has represented it by the most flatter-
ing portrait, under the title of *perfection,* yet it
cannot prevent our seeing it as trifling and pre-
carious. Are we better acquainted with the
effects of Nature, from being told that nothing
is made without a reason, or that all is made in
view of perfection? What is this sufficient reason? what is this perfection? are they not
moral beings created by intellects purely human? are they not arbitrary relations which we
have generalized? on what are they founded? on
moral affinities which, far from producing any
physical or real existence, only alter the reality
and confound the objects of our sensations, perceptions and knowledge, with those of our sentiments, our passions and our wills.

I could adduce many arguments on this subject, but I do not pretend to make a treatise on
philosophy, and shall return to physics, from
which the ideas of Plato on universal generation
made me digress. Aristotle, who was as great
a philosopher as Plato and a much better physician,

sician, instead of losing himself in the region of hypotheses, relied, on the contrary, on collected facts, and speaks in a more intelligible language.

Matter, which is only a capacity of receiving forms, takes in generation a form like that of the individual which furnishes it ; and with respect to the generation of animals that have sexes, he thinks that the male alone furnishes the prolific principle, and that the female affords nothing that can be looked upon as such.* For though he says elsewhere, speaking of animals in general, that the female emits a seminal fluid within herself, yet he does not regard that as a prolific principle : nevertheless, according to him, the menstrual blood serves for the formation, growth, and nutriment of the fœtus, but the efficient principles exist only in the seminal fluid of the male, which does not act like matter, but as the cause. Averrhois, Avicenna, and other philosophers, who followed the sentiments of Aristotle, have sought for reasons to prove that females have no prolific fluid ; they urge, that as females have a menstrual fluid that was necessary and sufficient for gene-

 ration,

---

* See Aristotle, de gen. lib. i. cap. 20 and lib. xi. cap. 4.

ration, it does not appear natural to suppose they possess any other ; particularly because it begins to appear, like the seminal fluid in the males, at the age of puberty ; besides, continue they, if females have really a seminal and pro-lific fluid, why do they not produce without the approach of the male, since they contain the prolific principle as well as the matter necessary for the nutriment and growth of the embryo ? This last reason seems to be the only one which merits any attention. The menstrual blood seems to be necessary for the support, nutri-ment, and growth of the fœtus, but it can have no part in the first formation, which is made by the mixture of two fluids alike prolific. Fe-males therefore may have, as well as the males, a prolific fluid for the formation of the embryo, besides the menstrual blood for its nutriment and expansion; and certainly a female being possessed of a prolific fluid, extracted from all parts of her body, as well as the necessary means of nourishment and expansion, it is no impossible imagination that she would produce females without any communication with the male: It must be allowed, that this metaphy-sical reasoning which the Aristotelians adopt to prove that females have no prolific fluid, may

become

become the most considerable objection that can be made against all systems of generation, and particularly against our explanation.

Let us suppose, it may be said, as you have attempted to prove, that the superfluous organic molecules are sent back into the testicles and seminal vessels of the male, why, by the power of your supposed attracting forces, do they not form small organized beings, perfectly resembling the male ? and for the same reason similar beings in the female ? If you answer, that there is an appearance that the liquor of the male contains only males, and that of the female only females, but that all these perish for want of the necessary means for expansion, and that there are only those formed by the mixture of both which can expand and come into the world; may we not be asked why this mode of generation, which is the most complicated, difficult, and least abundant, is that which Nature prefers in so striking a manner, that almost all animals multiply by this mode of communication of the male with the female ?

I shall content myself at present with answering, that the fact is such as we have represented it ; the objection becomes a fact question ;

to which, as we have observed, there is no other solution to be given than that of the fact itself. It may be insisted, it is the most complicated mode of production; yet this mode, which appears the most complicated to us, is certainly the most simple for nature, because, as we have remarked, what happens the most often, however difficult it may appear to our ideas, must in reality be the most simple; which does not prevent us from conceiving it to be complex, as we judge of it according to that knowledge which our senses and reflections can give us thereon.

The assertion of the Aristotelians, that females have no prolific fluid, must fall to the ground, if we pay attention to the resemblance of children to their mothers, of mules to the female that produces them, of mongrels and mulattos, all of which resemble more the mother than the father. If, besides these, we consider the organs of females are, like those of the males, formed so as to prepare and receive the seminal fluid, we shall be readily persuaded that such a fluid must exist, whether it resides in the spermatic vessels, the testicles, or in the matrix: or whether it issues, when provoked, by the passages of de Graaf, situated

tuated at the neck, and near the external orifice of the urethra.

But it is right here to examine the ideas of Aristotle more generally on the subject of generation, because this great philosopher has written the most on the subject, and treated it the most generally. He distinguishes animals into three classes; first, those which have blood, and, excepting some few, multiply by copulation; the second, those which have no blood, but, being at the same time both male and female, produce of themselves, and without copulation; and thirdly, those bred by putrefaction, which do not owe their origin to parents of any kind. I shall first remark, that this division must not be admitted of; for though in fact all kinds of animals which have blood are composed of males and females, it is not equally true, that animals who have no blood are for the most part male and female in one; for we are only acquainted with the snail and worm on earth which are in this state; nor can we ascertain whether all shell-fish, and other animals which have no blood, be hermaphrodites. With respect to those animals which he says proceed from putrefaction, as he has not enumerated them, many exceptions

tions occur; for most of the kinds which the ancients thought engendered by putrefaction have been discovered by the moderns to be the produce of eggs.

After this he makes a second division of animals; those which have the faculty of moving themselves progressively, as walking, flying, swimming, and those which have no such faculty. All animals which can move, and have blood, have sexes; but those which, like oysters, are adherent, or who scarcely move at all, have no sex, and are, in this respect like plants, distinguished only, as he says, into males and females by difference of size. It is not yet ascertained whether shellfish have sexes or not; there are in the oyster-kind fruitful individuals, and others which are not so; those which are fruitful are distinguished by a delicate border which surrounds the body of the oyster, and they are called males.*

But to proceed, the male, according to Aristotle, includes the principle of generative motion, and the female contains the material parts of generation. The organs which serve

for

* See the observation of M. Deslands, in the Tracte de la raine, Paris, 1747.

for this purpose are different in the different
kind of animals ; the principal are the testicles
in the males, and the matrix in the females.
Quadrupeds, birds, and cetaceous animals,
have testicles ; fish and serpents are deprived of
them ; but they have both proper conduits to
receive and prepare the seed These essential
parts are always double, both in the male and
female, and serve in males to stop the motion
of the blood, which forms the seed. This he
proves by the example of birds, whose testicles
swell in the season of their amours, and diminish so greatly when this season is over that
they are scarcely perceptible.

All quadrupeds, as horses, oxen, &c. which
are clothed with hair, and cetaceous fishes, as
dolphins and whales, are viviparous ; but car-
tilaginous animals, and vipers, are not truly viviparous, because they produce an egg within
themselves before the live animal appears.
Oviparous animals are of two kinds, those
which produce perfect eggs, as birds, lizards,
turtles, &c. and those which produce imperfect
eggs, as fishes, whose eggs augment and come
to perfection after they have been laid in the
water by the female ; and in all kinds of oviparous animals, excepting birds, the females

are

are generally larger than the males, as fishes,
lizards, &c.

After having mentioned these general varieties in animals, Aristotle begins with examining the opinion of the. ancient philosophers, that the seed, as well of the male as of
the female, proceeded from all parts of the
body; he declares against this opinion, because, he says, although children often resemble their fathers and mothers, they also
sometimes resemble their grandfathers; and,
besides, they resemble their parents by the voice,
hair, nails, carriage, and manner of walking.   Now the seed, he continues, cannot proceed from the hair, voice, nails, or any external quality, like that of walking; therefore
children do not resemble their parents because
the seed comes from every part of the body,
but for some other reason.   It appears to me
unnecessary here to point out the weakness of
these arguments; I shall only observe that it
appears to me this great man expressly sought
after methods to separate himself from the
sentiments of those philosophers who preceded
him; and I am persuaded, that whoever reads
his treatise on generation with attention, will
discover that a strong design of giving a new
                                        system,

system, different from that of the ancients, obliged him always to give the preference to the least probable reasons, and to elude, as much as he could, the force of proofs, when they were contrary to his general principles of philosophy.

According to Aristotle the seminal liquor is secreted from the blood; and the menstrua, in females, is a similar secretion, and the only one which serves for the purpose of generation. Females, he says, have no other prolific liquor; there is, therefore, no mixture of that of the male with that of the female. He pretends to prove this from some women conceiving without receiving the least pleasure, and because few women emit this liquor externally during copulation; that in general those who are brown, and have a masculine appearance, do not emit at all, yet engender equally with those who are more fair in complexion and feminine in appearance, and whose emissions are considerable. Thus he concludes woman furnishes nothing but the menstrual. This blood is the matter of generation; and the seminal fluid of the male does not contribute as matter but as form; it is the efficient cause, the principle of motion; it is to generation what the sculptor is to a block of marble: the liquor of the male is the sculptor, the menstrual blood the marble, and the fœtus the image.

The menstrual blood receives from the male seed a kind of soul, which gives life and motion. This soul is neither material nor immaterial, because it can neither act upon matter nor enter in generation as matter, the menstrual blood being all that is necessary for that purpose. It is, says our philosopher, a spirit, whose substance is like that of the starry region. The heart is the first work of this soul; it contains in itself the principle of its own growth; and it has the power to arrange the other members. The menstrual blood contains every other principle of all the parts of the fœtus: the soul, or spirit, of the male seed, makes the heart begin to act, and that communicates the power of bringing the other viscera to action; and thus, successively, is every part of the animal unfolded and brought into motion. All this appeared very clear to our philosopher; there only remained to him one doubt, which was, whether the heart was realized before the blood; and in fact he had reason for this doubt; for, although he had

adopted

adopted the opinion of the heart existing first, Harvey has since pretended, by reasons of the same kind as those used by Aristotle, that it was not the heart but the blood which is first realized.

This is the system that great philosopher has given us of generation, and I shall leave it to the opinion of the reader whether that of the ancients, which he rejects, can be more obscure or more absurd than his; nevertheless, his system has been followed by most of the learned. Harvey has not only adopted the ideas of Aristotle, but has added new ones of the same kind. As this system of generation is of the same kind as the rest of Aristotle's philosophy, where form and matter are the grand principles; where the vegetative and sensitive are the active beings in Nature; and where final causes are real objects; I am not surprised that it has been received by scholastic authors; but it is astonishing that so able a physician and observer of Nature as Harvey was, should be carried away with the stream, while every physician followed the opinion of Hippocrates and Galen; which we shall explain in order. We must not, however, imbibe a disadvantageous idea of Aristotle from the

above

above exposition of his System of Generation. It would be like judging of Descartes by his Treatise on Man. The explanations which these two philosophers give of the formation of the fœtus should not be considered as complete systems on the subject of generation; they are rather general consequences drawn from their philosophical principles.

END OF THE SECOND VOLUME.